She was familiar with temptation and resistance, but surrender?

That was a new possibility for Kat. She was afraid if she spent too long in John Severne's company her limits might be tested. He was a daemon, but he had taken the guise of a very attractive man. She was drawn to the burn beneath his control. She was drawn to what he might hide beneath the hardness he cultivated for the world. His penchant for sugary kisses and his reaction to her cello music gave her a glimpse at what vulnerabilities he might hide.

He wasn't a forthright man. He was a daemon.

His every move seemed to scream those truths to her even though his words and demeanor were enigmatic.

D1412955

BRIMSTONE SEDUCTION

BARBARA J. HANCOCK

First Published in Great Britain 2016
By Mills & Boon, an imprint of HarperCollins*Publishers*
1 London Bridge Street, London, SE1 9GF

© 2016 Barbara J. Hancock

ISBN: 978-0-263-92187-8

89-1016

Barbara J. Hancock lives in the foothills of the Blue Ridge Mountains where her daily walk takes her to the edge of the wilderness and back again. When Barbara isn't writing modern gothic romance that embraces the shadows with a unique blend of heat and heart, she can be found wrangling twin boys and spoiling her pets.

For Lucienne Diver. . .a hell of an agent and the ultimate finishing kick when the race has been long.

Chapter 1

She was used to being followed. Sometimes she lost him. Sometimes she didn't. It was those times she feared. Father Reynard wasn't her enemy, but as she cut down the familiar side street that formed an alley between the auditorium and her apartment, she knew what he was to her was more complicated and more frightening than if he was something she could fight.

The Savannah, Georgia, air was muggy in July, and her efforts to evade Reynard had left her damp with a sheen that was more humidity kissing her skin than sweat. But she didn't pause to set down her cello case so she could mop her forehead with a lace hanky like a flustered Southern belle. Instead, tendrils of her thick chestnut hair curled around her face as strands loosened from the diamanté clips the salon had used when she'd been cool and collected and air-conditioned that morning, preparing for the afternoon's performance.

She heard his footfalls behind her. She knew his step.

Others from his Order often hunted as well, but Reynard considered her his own.

Her faltering steps had brought the sound of his relentless pursuit closer. A desperate instinct to run, to hide, rose up in her chest, squeezing her lungs so that she breathed more quickly than her current exertions required. It was fear, plain and simple and stark.

Because there was no escape.

The soft blanket of gloaming draped the city in a muted haze. The muggy haze had dimmed to purple with the setting of the Georgia sun. In the distance, she could hear the traffic and the hum of people on the sidewalks of the historic district preparing for ghost tours and streetlight-lit carriage rides. But here, on the leftover cobblestones of a distant time, she was alone…except for Father Reynard.

His whistle began as it always did, with a lilting trio of notes that led into song. She recognized it as a Verdi piece she'd played that afternoon. Gooseflesh rose on her arms in spite of the oppressive heat from the summer day trapped in the narrow alley. The whistle meant he had her. It meant there must be a daemon nearby that she'd been drawn to. Her affinity had reliably led Father Reynard right where he most wanted to be. Again.

She did stop then.

Not giving up. Never that. She only paused to brace herself for what might be an ugly, dark and dangerous evening more from the violent monk who dogged her steps than the daemons he hunted. Although there was danger there, too. Certainly.

She was trapped in the middle of a war that would never have a winning side.

Katherine saw the daemon then. A woman. The glow of the horizon narrowly visible at the end of the alley cast her stiff form in stark relief. She stood poised for a fight. Her arms akimbo. Her knees slightly bent. It was going to be one of those times when the daemon didn't go quietly. This was no hopeless soul longing to be sent back home. Katherine could see determination tense every muscle in the figure she faced.

"A female. Good job, Katarina. It's so important to banish these before they breed," Father Reynard said as he came up behind her. She kept her focus on the daemon, but she was totally aware of Reynard's movements. The same way she would be if she were a hiker who was suddenly forced to skirt a mountain ledge over a steep precipice. Her footing was just as precarious. One wrong move with the deadly daemon hunter and she might be dead herself. She could feel the suck of gravity as if she was on the ledge, inches from death. *His* steps were slow and steady. Not rushed. He was confident. His voice was already smug with success. She was the one who was in danger. She was the one who might slip and fall.

Kat cringed at the utter contempt Reynard had for the daemon as a living, breathing creature, whether it was human or not. And at his total disregard for her and her disgust for his bloodthirsty quest.

Kat fisted her hands, but the woman leaped before she could decide how best to give her a chance to flee. The alley was too wide, an access point for delivery trucks to service the buildings on either side. She dropped her cello case and jumped but had no chance to keep the hunter and his prey apart. Not when the prey was determined to get around her. Kat was pushed to the side. She slammed against solid brick, and all the air left her lungs in a painful rush.

The daemon attacked Reynard with a fury Kat had never seen.

He was the one with the drawn blade, but Kat was as much a weapon as the bloodstained blade in Reynard's hand. She didn't deserve to be bypassed. The daemon should have attacked her first.

The sight of the deadly knife always repelled her. But it was Kat's ability that had led Reynard and his weapon here. Like deadly magnets with a pull she couldn't resist, daemons called and called to Katherine.

She was inexorably drawn to daemons, and Father Reynard followed with crimson death across all their throats.

"Stop," Kat choked out as her own throat empathetically tightened—to the daemon or to Reynard or to the family gift she hadn't asked to receive.

It was too late. Grizzled and gray, Reynard had fifty years of experience in killing. An extension of his wiry, muscled arm, the long knife gleamed red in the last hurrah of sunset on the horizon. Then it dripped a much darker stain from the daemon's blood. Kat shuddered and backed away.

It was always the same.

The body went up in flames, consumed from the inside out, eyes and mouth and the gaping wound across the daemon's throat gone to glowing with an impossible heat of coals in a fiery furnace. It was the freed Brimstone that did it, an otherworldly fuel that flowed through a daemon's veins. Reynard said it was a little bit of the hell dimension they took with them wherever they roamed.

Kat always forced herself to watch until there were only curls of smoke where a daemon had been, but this time there was a sound discernible beneath Reynard's triumphant chants.

To the left, behind a Dumpster, there was a shuffle of rubbish and gravel. There was also a sob. A small face peeked from around the refuse container. As the embers died, Kat could see chubby wet cheeks and eyes widened in shock and fear.

By then, the sun was gone and the sky was dark. It was only the glow of the daemon's banishment that lit the scene. The light flickered and faded, but the daemon's last dying illumination caused an eerie spotlight on the cowering child.

This time, she wasn't too slow to react. While Reynard was occupied with ritual, in those few seconds it took for him to finish with one daemon and turn his attention when he realized there was another, Kat was the one who leaped. She wouldn't let the mother's last light aid Reynard in his hunt.

The child tried to get away. After all, Kat was part of his mother's murder. Or so it seemed. So it felt. Regardless of what Reynard said about the daemons rematerializing in their own hellish dimension.

Kat was faster than the child. He was young. No more than five. And the mother's desperation had transferred itself to Kat's arms and legs. In those moments, Katherine D'Arcy was fit, fast and nobody's bloodhound. Not anymore.

She grabbed the reluctant boy. He balked, planting his small feet on the pavement as if he planned to remain a statue in the alley, a fierce little memorial to his mother forever. He wouldn't run with her. She had to pick him up. She tucked his squirming limbs against her side and bolted, deciding to base jump instead of fearing the fall. She'd never openly defied Reynard. Her grandmother's fear had been passed to her mother. Her mother's had been passed to her and her sister, their legacy darkened by his long shadow. His surprise at Kat's action gave her precious seconds to get away with the child.

But even if she was faster than the small boy, Reynard was faster than her.

She'd long since realized his obsession drove him to superhuman lengths. His madness gave him strength beyond that of a mortal man.

Her only hope was to get back to the crowded street with the boy, where a blade across his throat would be too bold a move even for Father Reynard. The trench coat he wore like a monk's robes flapped as he ran, great dark wings on either side of his lean body.

He seemed supernaturally unstoppable. As if he would never need rest. Her back. Her arms. Her shoulders. They all screamed under the squirming boy's weight. Far too mortal in comparison to Reynard. She didn't look back again.

"Hold still. Hang on. We've got to get you away from him," she said into the boy's towheaded curls.

The strands smelled like baby shampoo against her face. The simplicity of that impacted her even harder than the sneakers kicking her side. The daemon woman who had attacked Reynard to defend her child had also lovingly washed his hair like any human mother would. Kat couldn't let Reynard kill him. She couldn't let the boy die because of her gift.

She heard booted footfalls catching up behind them as she flew from alley to street to sidewalk, trying to get back to the main thoroughfare where people would be.

If the boy had been a few pounds lighter or a few years younger or less panicked in his struggle against her, she might have made it.

"Katarina!" Reynard boomed close behind her. His pet name for her grated on her nerves as always. Now it was a proclamation of her guilt. She had betrayed him.

Resignation softened the muscles in her legs as adrenaline deserted her. She would never beat him in a foot race, even if she wasn't carrying the child. Her only hope was to reason with a madman. No hope at all. Fortunately, the lack of hope made her more determined to try. Though she stopped to turn and face him and his blade with a pounding heart and ice in her veins, she couldn't help noting his giddiness was gone. He was raw anger personified now. The guise of his righteous joy had burned away as surely as the daemon's human form.

The boy had stopped his efforts to wiggle out of her arms. Perhaps between the man who had cut his mother's throat and the woman who held him, he chose her.

Being the lesser of two evils didn't seem a triumph at all.

"I won't let you kill him, Father," she said.

She held the boy close. She wrapped him tighter in her arms. She could feel the frantic beat of his heart against her chest, an echo to the thud of her own. She placed a hand on the back of his shampoo-scented head and pressed him even closer.

"I banish. I don't kill, Katarina. You know this. I send them back to hell where they belong," Reynard said. He stepped nearer. One stride. Katherine took the same stride back and away. He had always refused to call her by the name her mother had given her. It was as if he attempted to erase her true identity and replace it with one he had created.

But she had nowhere to run. She could still hear traffic and people in the distance. So close and yet so far away. The hum of the city mocked her efforts to defy the man who had dogged her steps from the time she could walk.

"So you say. All I've ever seen is the blood. The suffering. The pain," Kat said.

The boy trembled in her arms. At some point, his small arms had twined around her neck.

"They are deadly. They manipulate us with trickery and deceit. Have you forgotten your mother?" Reynard asked.

Her mother had been killed by a daemon. It was true. They were dangerous. Deadly. But so was the human being she faced.

Reynard held his long blade in a steady hand. She could see the muscle and sinew standing out in his right forearm where his coat had fallen away. He was ready to slit the throat of a child…or her throat if she got in his way.

"A daemon killed my mother. But you were using her to

hunt him when it happened. Would she be dead if it wasn't for you?" Katherine asked.

"She would never have been born if it hadn't been for Samuel. He gave his last breath to resuscitate your grandmother, a stranger he met on a train. He passed his ability to detect daemons hiding among us to your family. And this is the legacy you spurn." Spittle flew with the accusation, and then several sudden steps brought Reynard much too close.

There was nothing she could do. Her back was pressed to the grungy brick wall. Only decades of faded graffiti would mark her grave if she continued to fight him. She had nowhere to go, but then again, she never had.

"It's you I spurn, Reynard," she said.

Slowly she lowered the child to the ground and pushed him behind her legs. Her body was the only shield she had to give. Her cello case had been dropped back where his mother's smoke still swirled in the air.

"Your sister has evaded me for a long time. Too long. I begin to wonder if she spurned me only to be killed by a daemon, too. Perhaps your family legacy is one of failure," Reynard said. The glee was back in his voice, lilting his words.

She thought of her cello, of her mother's and sister's singing. They had turned to music to buffer the bloody killings and to mute the daemon's call. Had they failed, after all? Had all the years of practice and performance been for nothing? Her fingers tingled and ached, reminders of how many times she'd played until the tips bled in order to thwart Reynard.

The boy clung to her legs. She could feel the damp of his tears soaking through the chiffon of her concert gown. It was no suit of armor. No barrier to Reynard's seasoned blade. She was no match for a killer.

When her sister Victoria had flown to Baton Rouge to

take the role of *Faust*'s Marguerite at l'Opéra Severne, she'd told Katherine not to worry. She'd been gone for months, but she'd kept in touch at first. Kat hadn't heard from her sister in a few weeks, but with rehearsals and the rush of preparing for performances, she'd hoped all was well.

"Give him to me, Katarina. End this. Embrace your legacy. Do not embrace a daemon," Reynard coaxed, edging closer.

The idea that Reynard might be right about her sister hollowed out her insides until she echoed. Hollow or not, alone or not, she wouldn't give up. She didn't have a parachute to count on. She could only jump and try to fly.

"My name is Kat," she replied, pressing her hand against the boy's back and lifting her chin. Whether he accepted it or not, she would claim autonomy. She would follow her heart and her instinct to protect the trembling child behind her.

A sound of disgust erupted from Reynard's lips and he brandished his knife. Would he slice her throat or stab her through her pounding heart?

Either way, if Reynard had to deal with her, it might give the daemon boy a chance to run.

She braced to push the child away, but before Reynard's blade descended, an eerie mimicry of his earlier whistle began in the alley behind them. It stayed Reynard's hand and caused Kat's breath to catch in her throat. The boy against her leg lifted his head and turned his face to see.

There were few streetlights nearby. Most had been busted. Barely mitigated darkness enveloped them. Only one flickering holdout, the ambient light of the city against the sky, and the humid atmosphere gave them illumination to see. It was light pollution, but it mimicked fog. Through its violet haze and the floating of particles that were probably Brimstone ash, a figure stepped toward them.

The whistle and the posture of the man were casual. Exaggerated ease. He must see the confrontation he'd interrupted. He must see a woman and child threatened by a larger, stronger man, but he acted nonchalant, as if he was only out for a stroll. He must see the knife Reynard hadn't bothered to hide away.

Man?

Kat's gift wasn't one of sirens and flashing lights. She was pulled toward daemons. It was subtle. The tingle, the thrill that shivered along her veins as the man approached was probably only shock that he would stroll past Father Reynard with barely a glance in his direction. A daemon wouldn't dare approach them.

Closer, she could see that the stranger's tall form was clothed in evening apparel. The flash of white from his shirt contrasted with the inky darkness of his suit or tuxedo. But closer still, she noted his bowtie was undone at his neck and hung on either side of his collar. So easy. So debonair.

It wasn't until he stopped at her side that she knew she'd been fooled. He wasn't relaxed. The tension in his body transferred itself to hers when his arm brushed her elbow. Hard. Prepared. Ready.

He might wear formal clothes, but beneath them he was all warrior. Molded body armor would have been more appropriate to the purpose inherent in every flexed muscle and the energy he exerted to hold himself in check.

"Who are you? What do you want?" Reynard asked.

The blade of his knife had dipped. He preferred an audience of one for his performances. Her. And her alone. Or her sister in turn. Their mother and grandmother before that.

"A bystander who finds himself unable to stand by," the man said.

For her ears alone he added, "I'm John Severne."

Memories of the opera house in Baton Rouge teased her mind, but she pushed them away.

She had no time for nostalgia. Worry for her sister wound tighter until her insides were pulled like cheap strings on an instrument's bridge, stretched to the breaking point. One clumsy finger would cause her to snap.

Severne reached for the boy, but she stopped him. It only took one hand on his hard arm, but touching him felt braver than that. Almost as brave as opposing Reynard. His cultured Southern tones seemed as incongruent to him as his evening apparel. Beneath the polish, he was a man to be reckoned with. She couldn't see his face…only a suggestion of angles and curves, but as he drew his arm back, she felt what it cost him. He forced patience with her interference. A thrill of cool adrenaline rushed down her spine at his stiffness, his anger. It shored up her nerve… barely. The boy trembled against her, not oblivious to the forces at work above his head.

"You are making a mistake," Reynard growled.

"I would say the same to you," Severne replied.

Then he pulled Katherine against him. She'd been right about his tension. She could feel the planned action in his body everywhere it touched hers. Muscle. Energy. Strength. And more adrenaline rushed because she was fairly sure the warning in his words, just like his name, had been for her, not Reynard.

He was warning her it was a mistake to resist his help.

But she didn't snap like the cheap strings she imagined. She held fast. Unbroken.

"Let me take the boy," he said for her ears alone, the flow of the Seine even more apparent in an intimate whisper than it had been in his louder speech. He had a Southern accent, but it was old-fashioned, formal and touched with a hint of Paris. Clenched teeth and a hardened jaw and the iron of his body against her offset the softness of his accent.

He was no French-kissed delta dream.

He was real. And the potential for danger radiated off him in heated waves.

"Hell, no," Kat replied.

She finally recognized Brimstone's fire. She'd felt it only a few times in her twenty-two years. Normally she avoided touching daemons. Pressed close to him, the simmer his body contained couldn't be ignored. He had seemed so cool and collected in his initial approach. He wasn't. Beneath the surface, he burned.

Her rescuer was a daemon, and she was damned for sure because she still refused to join forces with Reynard against him.

"We need more time to negotiate," he said as if they sat at a boardroom table. "I can arrange that."

She'd seen Reynard fight before, but when the energy she'd sensed in Severne erupted, the ferocity of his clash with her lifelong tormentor took her by surprise.

Reynard was in trouble.

Severne used only his body—fists, feet, arms and legs—but he used them in a graceful dance of martial arts moves meant to be deadly. The tuxedo he wore was revealed inch by inch as his coat was shredded away by Reynard's blade.

John Severne was in trouble, too.

When a particularly vicious slice cut the fabric away from his muscled chest to reveal a hard, sculpted body, she blinked the sight away, but not before she cringed at the dark rivers of his blood.

After Reynard, there was always the desperate flight and the need to hide again. This time she'd flee for two. For the first time, she imagined what it must have been like for her mother to protect them from the obsessed monk. It had been a lost cause. But she had never stopped trying.

"We have to go," she said to the boy. The fight was the

diversion they needed to get away. She pulled him up into her arms again and ran. He clung to her this time, wrapping his legs around her waist and his arms around her neck, subdued by all he'd seen.

The absence of her cello made her ache. It wasn't a missing limb. It was a missing chamber of her heart. There was nothing to be done. She couldn't go back for it. She had gone to her apartment for a few necessities, but had sought shelter in the house of a friend who was out of town rather than risk Reynard knowing her current address. She moved often. It never mattered.

He always found her eventually.

While the boy slept, she looked up driving directions to Baton Rouge. She couldn't ignore her concern for Victoria any longer. They'd been out of touch too long, and Reynard's appearance only confirmed her fear. Urgency pounded in her temples to no avail. She couldn't fly because she had no papers for the child. He wouldn't even give her his name. If Reynard defeated the daemon, he would hunt her down. She didn't have much time to save the daemon boy and find her sister. She'd called Victoria's phone again and again. The cheery voice mail greeting became more ominous with every repeat. And what of John Severne? Had he ended up with his throat slashed and Brimstone-burned back to wherever he'd come from, or did she need to fear him as well as Reynard?

"Let me take the boy," he'd said.

But every fiber in her body had resisted. It was her fault Reynard had found the boy's mother. It was her responsibility to protect him.

The boy had refused to talk, but he'd seemed to understand everything she'd said. He'd also refused to let her out of his sight until he finally fell asleep. His dark lashes against his chubby cheeks gave him an angelic mien against his borrowed pillow. She'd smoothed his soft hair back from his forehead to kiss it, finding the extra warmth beneath his skin pleasant instead of frightening.

After that, the loss of her cello didn't matter.

She'd curled her legs under her in a nearby armchair, determined to watch over the boy through the night.

But a noise outside interrupted the tea she'd made to calm herself. It had been cooling untouched anyway. She'd been replaying every word Severne had spoken. She'd even closed her eyes to remember the song of his voice, to gauge what was the truth about the daemon—his drawl or the deadly way he'd used his whole body as a weapon. His anger or the way he'd restrained his impatience with her resistance.

At the sound of a step on the front porch, she rose from the chair beside the boy's bed.

She didn't know whom she most feared to see.

It was ridiculous to feel gratitude to a stranger for his help when he might have his own daemonic designs on her family. The name Severne couldn't be a coincidence. She hadn't heard from her sister since Victoria had gone to the Théâtre de l'Opéra Severne in Louisiana, and Kat had felt the heat from Severne's Brimstone-tainted blood.

She'd been desperate to defy Reynard, and for the first time she had, openly and with no regret, but she'd been successful only with the stranger's help.

The shotgun colonial had creaky floors and high-ceilinged rooms. Kat moved along the edge of the hall where the boards were more firmly nailed to diminish the sound of her feet on the floor. The peach chiffon of her soiled and torn gown swirled around her legs. She hadn't wanted to leave the frightened boy alone long enough to change, and now she padded downstairs on bare feet, pausing only long enough to pick up a bronze statue. It was a cherubic angel.

(

Her friend's decor held an irony she was too tired to appreciate.

"Did you know your ability to detect daemons works both ways? They're drawn to you like moths to a flame," a familiar voice said. Her memory recalled the exact inflections and the intimate way he drawled certain vowels, low as if in a register she felt more than heard. Musical. His voice was musical.

Severne.

He came through the front foyer painted by shadows and soft light.

The door had been locked, but that fact seemed distant. As if she'd expected the bolt to be nothing to him. She feared him. She feared what his intentions might be. But there was a song in his accent she couldn't help appreciating. His voice called to something deep inside her, making her fingers itch to play.

All the lamps had been extinguished. The light from an open laptop and the streetlights outside still didn't fully reveal the daemon's face, but they did reveal the familiar shape of her cello case in his hand.

He came toward her with no hesitation, completely undaunted by the statue in *her* hand until he was only inches away…until she could feel his Brimstone heat. Again, the heat wasn't unpleasant. In fact, in the air-conditioned chill of the unfamiliar house, she could almost lean into Severne's heat if she allowed herself to be lulled by his song or relieved that she wouldn't have to fight Reynard to protect the child…yet.

"Judging by body temperature, you're mistaken about which of us is the flame in that scenario," Kat said.

She'd never had a conversation with a daemon. It was wrong. Against everything she'd ever been told or taught. The trouble was, it was also exhilarating. Part of her was still all adrenaline from the way the night had played out.

She should have been shaky and over it. Ready to hide behind Tchaikovsky and Wagner as safe excitements she could easily handle.

Instead, a part of her wanted to jump off a ledge again with this flaming parachute she'd been given and enjoy the burn all the way down.

Could he sense her exhilaration? How it barely edged out fear? Could he tell she trembled when he moved a little closer?

"I could have taken the boy away from danger," he said, so close now that the statue pressed between them was even more useless than before. He didn't make her put it down. He ignored it. As if he knew she wouldn't give in to fear. As if he expected her to be braver than that.

She would have to be braver, because the real danger was Severne and her reaction to him, and there didn't seem to be any escape from that.

"I don't trust Father Reynard, but I don't trust daemon manipulations, either," Kat said. "Did you kill him?"

He paused. Hesitated as if her words had stopped him. Maybe she shouldn't have spoken her suspicions about him and what he was…but the thought disintegrated when he lifted a hand to touch her face.

"No. He isn't dead. Only slowed down for awhile," Severne said. "I'm sorry."

She let him touch her. She didn't cringe away. As his warm fingers lightly trailed across her skin, Kat suddenly thought of the graceful but deadly way he'd dealt with Reynard in the alley. He was a daemon. It didn't matter that he had helped her. She wouldn't trust him. She hadn't even fully seen him yet in a night of shadows and flickering light…

She could tell his hair was dark. Not whether it was black or brown. His eyes were dark mysteries. They could be any color. They held all his secrets in depths that appeared onyx in the night.

When he leaned down to press his lips to her temple, then to her cheek, then to trail them along her jawline as if to trace her face in the darkness…she didn't protest. Was he comforting her? His lips were warmer than they should have been. The heat caused a responsive flush to rise on her skin. Her affinity kept her from reacting the way she ordinarily would if a man she'd just met had been so bold. It was a secret pulse between them, heightening a natural flare of chemistry, drawing them closer, sooner, than it should.

"Don't be sorry," Kat said. "I think he can't be killed. He's like Death himself, a Grim Reaper I can't escape."

He was all relaxed grace, taking the statue and placing it on a nearby table. She was all adrenaline and trembling sighs, but when both hands were free, she kept them at her sides. Not pulling him closer. Not pushing him away. Only refusing to hold on with all her might. He warmed her in ways that went beyond mere physical heat. Her usual affinity was magnified by his touch. It rose up and rushed through her veins almost as heated as Brimstone until she had the crazy urge to surrender to it and press herself closer into his arms. She saw it again in her mind, the way he'd braved Reynard's deadly blade.

Those images held her still for his kiss.

Or did they? Her body mocked her need for an excuse. This—the heat, the masculine aura drawing her in, the night-cloaked scent that clung to his earthy skin and his hair and clothes—wasn't he enough?

Right now, he was everything.

Because by then his soft, tracing lips had discovered her mouth in the dark, and a more intimate exploration of it had begun—lips, teeth, tongue. So velvety and alive with tremors and gasps and the sudden moist dip of his tongue.

A hot coil unfurled in her abdomen, her nipples peaked and her knees grew weak.

Then Severne pressed the handle of her cello case into

her right hand. Her fingers curled around the indentions they'd made over fifteen years of constant companionship to the leather-bound grip.

"Never trust a daemon bearing gifts, Katherine D'Arcy. There's always a price to be paid," he murmured into her hair when she slumped loose-limbed and faint against the firm wall of his body.

"No," she protested. But it was too late. She'd accepted the cello like a long-lost love. The Order warned against communicating with daemons. Hell was structured around a complex system of negotiating. She could feel daemonic power like static in the air as some unspoken bargain physically materialized around them, beginning with her acceptance of her case from his hand.

He lifted her and the cello easily. He cradled her against his chest, but she couldn't make her body resist or her hand release the cello. He carried her and the instrument upstairs and placed her beside the boy on the bed with the cello case cool and lifeless on the other side.

Then he made the trade.

He picked up the daemon child.

Kat couldn't move. He was no longer touching her, but his heat had remained, leaving her lethargic and weak.

Somehow she had agreed without meaning to. The cello for the child. The daemonic bargain held her in place. She couldn't fight its power.

"Come and play for me in Baton Rouge, Katherine. We have more bargains to make. I can help you find your sister," John Severne said.

"Never trust a daemon," Kat promised her pillow. She refused to let her tears fall. Or maybe it was daemon manipulations that suspended each perfect droplet on her lashes as Severne walked away.

Chapter 2

He could hear the siren song that sounded when her heart beat, when she inhaled and exhaled. But that wasn't what called him to her. It was the subtle scent of her, beneath soap, blended with a hint of verbena perfume. Like cotton warmed by the sun, but cooled by the breeze on a spring day, there was a freshness, a goodness to her, untouched by Brimstone.

Untainted.

And she thought he was a daemon.

He settled the boy with the costume matron, Sybil, who had been at l'Opéra Severne almost as long as he had. She'd always appeared as an older woman with that particular blend of sternness and maternal habits that made everyone defer to her in case she should decide to box their ears or swat their behinds. She looked no older than she'd looked the day he'd been ushered into her care when he was about the age of the boy he'd brought from Savannah.

Katherine D'Arcy was wrong.

No surprise that his Brimstone-tainted blood had fooled her. He wasn't a daemon, but his grandfather had inked a deal with the devil in Severne blood. The Brimstone had come after, scorching their veins with its invasive mark.

He was only an heir to damnation, but Katherine D'Arcy was associated with the Order of Samuel, and in such a woman's eyes there could be little difference.

Once he'd settled the boy with Sybil, he made his way back to the suite of rooms that made up his apartment several stories below and behind the grand opera stage for which the house was famous. The seemingly endless levels of basement beneath the opera shouldn't have existed in a city that itself was beneath the flood plain of the mighty Mississippi, but nothing followed natural law here.

The opera house was a universe unto itself, influenced by its damned denizens and masters.

Its gilded mahogany columns and highly polished boards held ground against elaborately carved wainscoting more baroque than anything else you'd find in the river city. The carvings seemed to gambol and change as you passed, often reflecting your own experiences and thoughts back to you as if some long ago sculptor had chiseled out premonitory dreams in a laudanum haze. And all the shadows were draped in heavy layers of black-and-crimson satin and velvet curtains, which in spite of being impeccably maintained always ended up seeming shabby chic in the candlelight.

Time, distance, reality were softened inside l'Opéra, but the softness didn't mute the cruelty of an eternity in the luxurious chains of candlelit opulence you couldn't escape.

His rooms were more austere, but still overly filled with the detritus of centuries. His prison was made even more claustrophobic by books and art and textiles from too many years and fears to count.

Resisting the oppression of time had helped to harden him as much as his constant training had.

Only his bedroom reflected his true taste for simplicity. In it, the only furnishings were a large black cypress bed and a matching trunk bound with cracked leather straps and a heavy iron padlock.

He opened the trunk with gloved hands, carefully removing an iron cask. Even with the gloves, the heat of the metal fittings of the cask was uncomfortable to his hands. Without the added protection of the Brimstone in his blood, he would have been horribly burned.

He placed the cask on the hardwood floor, noting the scorch marks from it having been placed there before. The trunk was lined with lead or it would have turned to ash. Good thing his task wouldn't take long.

He opened the iron lid, a habitual move that was still momentous every single time.

Inside the box, on a bed of coals, lay a rolled parchment. A curl of smoke rose lazily from one end, but there were no flames. He picked it up, ignoring the prickle of burns to his fingertips.

Slowly he unrolled the scroll.

The first names on the list had been marked through years ago. Their glow had faded to smudged black. But the second-to-last name on the list still shone like an ember in his dimly lit bedroom. It brightened even as he watched, and suddenly a line of fire scratched across the name. The blazing line flickered, flared and then went out.

In time, the name of the boy's mother would fade as the others had before her.

Lavinia.

It would blaze in his mind much longer than that.

This time there was no corresponding pain as a slash of black was added to his scarred forearm like a grim tattoo. He hadn't actually dispatched Lavinia himself. But there were many more marks from his shoulder down to beyond the crook of his elbow. A torturous tally he couldn't ignore. One appeared each time he sent a daemon back to hell. Sometimes he wondered if the black marks reached deep, all the way to his heart. Marks that would stay with him forever even after he was free.

There was only one name left on the list.

Michael.

After centuries of damnation's shackles, he was almost free. More importantly, his father would be free before he died. They'd suffered under the burden of Thomas Severne's lust for success. The only way they could regain their souls was to hunt down the daemons on the scroll.

A being had to be extremely evil to wind up on hell's blacklist. Or so he told himself when the nights grew long.

The boy was sleeping. He'd been reassured by the familiar warmth of Brimstone and by Sybil's welcome. Severne was suddenly fiercely glad the old monk had been the one to dispatch Lavinia. The gladness stung. It was a weakness he couldn't afford. Not now when his father's soul was almost within his grasp before it was too late. He had always been as hard as he had to be. He'd grown even harder over time. His father needed him to stay strong.

He'd sent thirty daemons on the list back to hell. Usually a name was enough. Younger daemons were horrible at incognito. They always revealed their secret at the wrong time, in the wrong place. They shared their true name out of passion or pride, and then he was inevitably there to catch them. Because he didn't rest. He'd watched those thirty daemons consumed by the very fire he feared as a corruption in his own veins. The boy here in his home would be a constant reminder.

Severne allowed the scroll to roll in on itself. He replaced it in the cask and then set the cask back in the trunk.

Only one name left… Michael.

But he might be the one that got away if Severne failed to use Katherine D'Arcy the way he intended. Michael had proved illusive. He was one of the ancient ones. They were much more experienced and discreet and much harder to find.

He rose from the trunk, but stood in the dark for a long time with the glow of the scroll still gleaming behind his eyes. He fingered the network of fine white scars that he'd received over the decades from daemon bites and claws or whatever weapons they could wield against him. Those marks were also reminders. Of what he had done. Of what he still had to do.

Hard.

Katherine's skin had been perfectly smooth. So very soft to his touch.

He didn't touch the tally marks. He suspected they'd scorch his fingers as badly as the scroll. If not literally, then figuratively, because of the guilt each mark represented.

She was coming. He could feel her approach, a distant tug on his senses that was both anticipation and… Her lips had been sweet, flavored by a vanilla lip balm and the champagne she'd been given after her performance. He hadn't had to kiss her to influence her. The Brimstone in his veins gave him heightened powers of persuasion. A touch would have sufficed. He'd tasted her because he'd had to, but he hadn't expected the taste to linger on his tongue. Most flavors were burned away before he could even enjoy them.

She threatened to soften him. He could feel the seduction of what it would be like to ease into her arms. Instead, she was the one who had to be seduced. He needed her to complete his task and end his imprisonment. The contract Thomas Severne had inked with hell must be fulfilled before Levi Severne died.

He left the bedroom to pass into a room that looked more medieval torture chamber than exercise room. He'd crafted most of the equipment himself to test his limits and push his body to become as iron as it could be though still flesh and bone. He began what would be hours of training with one thought burning in his mind.

When he was finished with Katherine D'Arcy, she would be scarred, as well. His seduction and betrayal would irreparably mark her heart.

Chapter 3

When Kat made it to Baton Rouge after driving the rest of the night and into the next day, she couldn't shy away from her memories any longer. The city was a blend of modern glass and steel from the present and neo-Gothic architecture from times long past. It wasn't hard to find the opera house because it sat on Severne Row, a street time had forgotten to touch. While much of Old South Baton Rouge had been claimed by poverty and, later, revitalization, Severne Row had stayed the same for decades.

They'd been to l'Opéra Severne as children accompanying their mother on tour. Even then, the theater was infamous for being devoted to a darkly Gothic version of Gounod's *Faust*, its most popular draw. Their mother had been a contralto Marthe for several nights while they'd watched in awe on velveteen seats of pale, faded scarlet.

She pulled up to the theater and parked the nondescript sedan she'd rented with a friend's help so her name wouldn't be on the paperwork. Later the rental company would come to claim it. Kat was an old hat at traveling quietly and lightly. She had only a couple of suitcases in the trunk.

She carried them to the side entrance, where Victorian-style signs directed employees away from the main portico. She did pause to look up at the grand porches with their arches and massive stairs. The curving style of the rails was both beautiful and intimidating, oversized to denote the palatial quality of the building they pointed to.

When she moved to the side door, it pressed inward easily, and the shadowed interior sighed a welcome to her travel-weary senses.

The scent of the place evoked sudden visceral memories: swinging her legs clad in white tights, her feet tucked into polished Mary Janes, the scratchiness of her ruffled tulle skirt with its wide satin belt far too fancy for fidgets, and Victoria humming along, lost in rapt enjoyment of their mother's inspired performance.

She could sense again the hush, the thrill and the music swelling until it claimed her to the marrow of her bones.

That night she'd known she would never sing.

It was the polished maple that called to her, the hollow reverberations coaxed to fill an entire room—lofted cathedral ceiling and all—in spite of humble nylon and steel beginnings.

Dust. Lemon floor polish. Wax and powder. As soon as she breathed the air in the two-hundred-year-old opera house again, she knew she'd missed it. She'd been in thousands of auditoriums, theaters and even more magnificent venues.

But it was the Théâtre de l'Opéra Severne that had shown her the way in which she could hold Reynard at bay.

She'd been fascinated by the orchestra pit, but especially

the stringed instruments. The sound and movement of the musicians had transfixed her, and when they had plucked at the strings, they had plucked at her soul.

Her first cello came soon after. Then lessons. Then obsession. Her calloused fingers, the muscles in her gracefully bowed back and her well-shaped arms all because of Severne's opera house.

Had she recognized its echo in him? The interior of the whole building was as expectant as John Severne was coiled and prepared. The same ready-for-what-was-about-to-happen filled both the theater and the man.

The daemon, she corrected herself. Lest she forget. The residual heat that still made her movements languid and slow—it mocked her.

Kat walked through the side mezzanine with her cello case, though she'd left her suitcases in a pile by the door at the usher's urging. Now the same usher led her through the building to Severne's offices.

Compared to the humid outdoors of Baton Rouge—more moistened by the Mississippi River than cooled by it—the interior of the opera house was shadowed and cool. The atmosphere was close down the columned corridor with almost too many details to make out in the scant light of midafternoon, when no candles were lit and few lamps glowed. She could see the rough texture of carvings on the wainscoting, but she couldn't pause to make out exactly what the carvings were about. It was only her imagination that made it appear as if hundreds of faces rendered in the wood turned to follow her movements as she walked by.

She was escorted. It was formal and old-fashioned, but she didn't want to be rude to the eager-to-please uniformed young man. Whether he strived to please her or his employer, she couldn't be sure. But she thought the latter because there was an urgency to his steps slightly more colored by fear than a young woman in a sundress would inspire.

As she followed, his mood was contagious. She thought maybe her old tulle and satin would have been more appropriate for a job interview in this vintage setting than the light cotton dress she'd worn for travel between one hot Southern city and another even hotter. She recalled with perfect clarity John Severne's hard, deadly form beneath his shredded evening attire, and as she did, she also recalled the velvet tease of his tongue.

Her arms and legs might be gauche and exposed, but she'd already been more intimate with the daemon than she'd been with another man. It was impossible to forge relationships when your lifestyle was one of running, constantly running. She couldn't trust intimacy. She avoided it at all costs. Oh, she'd had hurried kisses in moments when her guard had fallen, but she'd never allowed herself to fall fully, to indulge fully in desires to touch and taste.

And now was probably not the best time to wonder why a daemon had been able to breach her usual defenses.

The usher opened the double doors of what she supposed to be John Severne's office. With a flourish and a bow, he stepped aside. Her wedge sandals on the Persian carpet didn't fit into this sudden 1863 in which she found herself.

She wanted to play her cello. She could make music that would fit, music that would fill, no matter the time or place or her attire.

"The boy is fine," Severne said. He walked into the office from another room. The desk, the polished cabinetry and gleaming glass, the dark cherry floor covered in luxurious woven rugs no doubt created decades ago in the Middle East—none of it prepared her for *this* John Severne.

She'd thought his evening clothes had given a false impression of sophisticated ease. She'd been more right than she could have known. She'd felt the hardness of his form, his energy and his heat. She'd sensed his preparedness.

Now she saw what she'd only sensed before.

He wore a pair of low-slung shorts; all else was bared to the lamplight and her stunned gaze. She'd been to gyms. She'd seen people ripped for appearance or for health. This was so obviously not that.

Severne walked into the room wiping his chest and arms and the back of his neck with a snow-white towel. He came around a beautiful desk that would have looked at home in a French palace, and Kat instinctively placed her cello case on the floor in front of her. She didn't hide behind it…exactly, but she blushed when Severne saw the move for what it was. Defense. His gaze flicked from her face to the case and back again. Green eyes. Deep, dark green that had looked black when she'd seen him before at night.

"I want to see him," Kat replied, looking at John Severne during the day for the first time.

He was still shadowed. There were few windows to let in outside light. Those that existed were heavily draped in black and red satin. But she could still see him better than before. What she saw confirmed what she'd already supposed. He was no polished gentleman. Almost nude, his hard, muscular body was too seriously honed to be called athletic.

How had she ever supposed him to be human?

She wasn't a sculptor, but if she had been, she would have wept because Michelangelo was dead and a master should memorialize John Severne's body. Yet the leanness of him, the lack of one ounce of spare flesh, was as painful as it was beautiful.

He took not one second of ease.

His tension was absolute.

She knew this about him as surely as she knew how to coax the perfect note from a string.

His pale skin, so harshly honed, was marked by more than exercise. There were faded scars across his chest, abdomen and back. She tried not to trace them with her eyes. Whatever suffering he endured—or courted—wasn't hers to see. The black slashes of numerous tattoos down one arm from his shoulder to his elbow were almost as sacrosanct as the scars. Something private. She tried to look away, but the marks gleamed darkly like his hair and his eyes.

"He's having his lessons right now. I thought a semblance of normalcy would help him adjust. He seems bright. He's definitely had schooling in spite of his unusual circumstances. But he'll join us for dinner. Later tonight," Severne said. "I'm glad you accepted my invitation."

The fine-cut lines of his lips stood out, or was it only the memory of the taste of them that made them seem noticeable to her?

She could feel his Brimstone heat even at this distance. It prickled her skin as if she was in the same room with a roaring fire.

How could she have stayed away?

With the boy involved, it wasn't a choice to her at all. But deeper parts of her had to acknowledge the pull of John Severne had influenced her decision to come to Baton Rouge as much, or more, than the child.

He stood across from her, but he wasn't even pretending to be relaxed. Not like before. His energy was there for her to see, barely contained. As if he might take her in his arms again if she said or did the wrong thing. Or the right thing. Depending on how you looked at it.

The thought made her stand frozen, a rabbit who sensed a predator and feared to twitch a whisker in case the movement would lead it into a leap for the fox's mouth rather than standing idle and waiting to be devoured.

"What about Victoria? Where is my sister?" Kat asked.

"I travel often," Severne began. "Various business interests require my diligent attention. I wasn't here when your sister disappeared, but I'm told she was—is—a brilliant Marguerite. The first performance of the season is two weeks away, and…"

"She's gone," Kat said, as any hope that Reynard might have been wrong evaporated.

"I came to you in Savannah and invited you here because there's no evidence of foul play. She was performing under an assumed name, as I understand she often does. She told us she has a stalker. My manager was more than happy to accommodate her wishes to engage her stellar talent under an alias. I'm assuming I met this stalker last night? He seemed completely ignorant of her whereabouts. The only hope of finding your sister is in the clues she might have left among her life and friends here at l'Opéra Severne. If you follow in her footsteps…" Severne suggested. "I'm afraid there's a distance between me and my employees that prevents me from discovering more about her disappearance."

He was a daemon. He couldn't be trusted. And yet she was so conditioned to fear Reynard that this seemed better. Not safer, but better. He'd asked her here because Victoria had disappeared. There was more to it than that. There had to be. But walking away wasn't an option. Not when the last place her sister had been seen was this opera house.

"I might vanish without a trace, as well," Kat said.

"No. That won't happen. I'm here now," Severne said. "I won't be called away again. You'll have my undivided attention."

As if his mere presence would keep her safe. He was

a daemon. Not a bodyguard. He might look like he could take on an army of Reynards, but it would be a mistake to trust him. Why should he stand at her back and protect her from the Order of Samuel and other daemons while she tried to ascertain what had happened to Victoria? He couldn't have perfectly altruistic motives. He was a daemon. They weren't known for noble intentions.

"Play for me. Let me see what I've done in offering you a seat without an audition," Severne challenged her.

His bare muscular body stood out in stark relief against the polished antiques of his office. On the desk, several deep purple calla lilies sat in a crystal vase. Like Severne, the lilies stood out. A hint of passion, life, color…but their petals were stiff and perfect like Severne's physique.

Kat hesitated. She should walk away. Where better to leave a daemon child than with a daemon? But the memory of the boy's angelic face and the hope of finding clues to her sister's whereabouts held her in place.

And pride.

There was no denying the frisson of need that rose up in her when he said "Play for me" in his deep voice, smoothed by a creole accent less influenced by modern inflections probably because it had been influenced by Parisian émigrés decades ago. Daemons weren't immortal, but they lived a very long time. If she played for him, she would be playing for someone who had heard celebrated masters play.

Now he reined in his energy to appear more casual. He moved closer. She could detect a hint of smoky sandalwood, sweat and a lightly concentrated scent that was the heated air of the opera house itself settled on Severne's hair and skin. The sensual impact of that recognition made her knees turn soft.

She loved the theater scent. To breathe it on him messed with her equilibrium.

He couldn't be trusted. He smelled like heaven, but his veins flowed with the fires of hell.

"Play for me, Katherine," he repeated, and this time her eyelids closed against the compelling drawl in his words.

"I'll play for Victoria," Kat said to cool whatever charge there was between them.

Severne sat on a straight, tall-backed chair as if it was a throne. He'd placed the towel around his neck, and it hung there like a gentleman's scarf. He waited for her to sit on a chair arranged across from him and open her case. She took out her cello and her bow. The familiar motions were a meditation even under Severne's watchful eye.

This was her best defense against the fascination building in her for this daemon she couldn't avoid. She'd always used music to fight the pull that drew her to daemon blood. Maybe it would help her against the pull she felt for lips and lean muscled heat, for the musical history he'd lived through.

But she couldn't dismiss the fascination of centuries or the ears of a connoisseur.

When she sat, when she played, it couldn't be for Vic... not with Severne in the room.

From the first note, she could feel her affinity vibrating the air between them as if the strings of her cello also invisibly existed between her body and the inhumanly hard body across from her. Whatever drove him to discipline his body, inch by inch, sinew and tendon and skin as taut and smooth as untouched steel, didn't stop him from feeling her song.

She chose Victoria's favorite concerto. The first she'd learned all those years ago. A simple Beethoven piece that was nonetheless lightly intricate when played by an expert. She meant to keep it light and airy, but it deepened with Severne as its audience.

The music wasn't a barrier between them. It was a conduit for the electric connection that was already there.

She closed her eyes and remembered the flash of his bare chest when he'd fought Reynard and the heat of his arms around her when he'd cradled her and carried her to bed. Betrayed, but with a tenderness that didn't seem possible from such a hard creature.

She played every note perfectly…for him. She infused every movement of her bow with emotion…for him. Years ago, she'd decided the instrument had called her to play at l'Opéra Severne, and now she played it as it had never been played. The striated maple and polished spruce were more a part of her than they had ever been, and the music twined between her and Severne's Brimstone blood only a few feet away.

While she played, the water around the calla lily stems rippled, though the perfect petals remained calm.

She didn't.

Her skin flushed.

Her thighs tensed.

Her breathing and heartbeat increased.

This was no audition. It might be a test for him or for her, but it was no audition.

Music had always been her protection. Now instead of sheltering her, the sound rose up and filled the room, swelling out to envelop a creature who obviously held himself apart as if she would embrace him and seek to soften his iron edge.

In spite of his obvious discipline, Severne was touched. She could feel his response. Could see his chest expand and contract.

She wouldn't believe it. She couldn't. His tenderness

had to be a lie. The truth was in the muscle and tendon there for her to see and the fire in his blood she could feel.

She told herself that this was a bargain. He would offer her a place and she could search for her sister while being close to the daemon child if she played well enough to pass muster. But she didn't want simply to perform well. Always before, when Reynard found her, she fled, she hid. Not this time. This time boldness had led her here to help the boy, to find her sister.

And to John Severne.

Something was different in her. She could feel the blood rushing in her veins as if she'd come alive for the first time.

She wanted to touch him.

Though her hands were on the neck of her cello and the bow, it was Severne she tried to reach. His cheeks above his perfect, angular jaw darkened with some emotion she couldn't name. His eyelids lowered to half-mast over his deep green eyes. His hard chest rose and fell as if he needed oxygen to cope with what her music made him feel. His response was heady. More so than a theater full of patrons. Her life was about hiding. Subsuming herself in the music of her cello so she couldn't be found. But, here, now, she played to be felt, seen, heard, and her music was a call for the intimacy she'd always avoided.

"Enough," he ordered, and her hands faltered. The bow dropped from the strings and her fingers stilled. But her body continued to tremble. She wasn't used to reaching out. She moistened her lips. It was as if they'd been in a heated embrace and he'd been the one to break it off and push her away. "Enough," he repeated, and he stood abruptly.

Katherine stood in response. Again, it was more adrenaline that came to her rescue than courage. She wouldn't slump defeated in her chair. The rush she experienced in his presence wouldn't allow it. Her best defense had failed because of that rush. She lifted her chin. She held her cello to the side so she wouldn't seem to cower behind it again.

Severne's gaze froze her in place in spite of the heat she could feel from the Brimstone. He looked angry. She had played for him just as he'd asked, but he looked like he might want to throw her out of the opera house.

Never mind the boy.

Never mind Victoria.

She couldn't let that happen.

"I'm not leaving," Kat said.

Severne met her wide-eyed stare. He didn't soften. He didn't ask her to leave or to play again.

"A bargain, then. You'll stay. You'll…play. But only in the orchestra pit with the other musicians or for personal rehearsals. Not for me. And I'll help you find your sister," he said.

He crossed the room until they were side by side, but it wasn't until he walked away that she realized his nearness had distracted her from the calla lily he'd dropped into her open cello case. Its deep purple bloom looked almost black in the dim light.

Never trust a daemon.

But the lily wasn't a gift. It was only a payment for her song.

Her playing hadn't displeased him. He had liked it. More than that, he'd been affected by it.

He'd paid for her performance because the music had touched him.

Kat sat again before her trembling legs could give out beneath her. The cello she gripped in one hand wasn't nearly as comforting as it usually was. Her best defense hadn't only failed against this particular daemon. It had become something else between them…a seductive promise.

He didn't want her to play for him again because her song breached his defenses. Her inhalations still came quicker than they should. Her skin was heated though the fire had left the room. She shivered in the sudden chill. This was a mistake. But it was one she had to make. For the boy. For her sister.

She had to brave John Severne in order to find her sister even if her music was no shield against him.

Quietly she slowed her breathing and calmed her heart. She vowed never to play for him alone again and to guard against her fascination with the daemon master of l'Opéra Severne.

Because the calla lily hadn't only been payment for her song. It had been a last-minute substitute. Her lips tingled. He'd been as hungry as she was for another kiss.

Chapter 4

Her bags were taken to a room off the corridors that surrounded the opera hall itself. They wound in concentric circles with the apartments set like the spokes in a giant wheel. It was dizzying, the walls a kaleidoscope of rich cherry wainscoting filled with elaborate carvings like the first hall she'd traversed to reach Severne's offices.

Her passage was lit by flickering sconces that made her wonder if the almost subliminal hiss her ears detected was air conditioning or gas to fuel primitive lamps. The dancing light made the carvings gambol around her in tumbling shadows. But it was her playing for John Severne that had upset her equilibrium. The music echoed mockingly in her ears. *Too*. Too hungry. Too evocative. Too needy of his reaction. Any reaction. The uncertain light made her path waver, but she wouldn't have been firmly grounded even if there had been bright runway lights.

He was hard. Both physically and mentally. To touch

him with her music, even for a second, had been too heady for her own good. He wasn't a man. He was a monster. He was a being all human souls had been taught to fear for centuries. But as the night deepened, the flutter in her stomach didn't feel like fear. Not exactly.

Her room was beside her sister's. Supposedly Victoria's room had remained untouched. When Kat tiptoed hesitantly in, not wanting to disturb the dust and silence, the room taunted her. It wasn't empty. Seeing the normal, everyday mess her sister was prone to create—silk slippers tossed to the side, smudged tissues on the vanity table, the pale ivory stockings from her costume rinsed out and long since dry on the bathroom rack—tightened Kat's lungs until each stale breath hurt. The air tasted bitter on her tongue.

If Victoria had been free to sing and build a reputation under her own name, she would have been a much bigger star than a regional theater would hope to hire, but Vic loved to perform. It didn't matter how or where. She could almost feel her sister's anticipation for performance in the air.

Gone.

She'd known it. But seeing it was too final, too real. She sniffed the faint, weeks-old hint of Victoria's perfume, and tears prickled.

She stopped in the center of the room and willed them away, widening her eyes. She was not going to hide behind tears. She was here for a reason, and grief wouldn't help her sister now. Katherine waited until her eyes were so dry they hurt. Then she forced an inventory of every detail.

What had happened?

There was no evidence of violence. All was painfully normal and undisturbed. Victoria could walk in at any second complaining about the lack of honey for her tea. But as the seconds ticked by, Katherine knew waiting for her sister's familiar tread was in vain.

Gone.

On the bed, nestled on Victoria's pillow, was a pair of opera glasses. They were the only item in the room that seemed out of place. Kat walked to her sister's bed and picked up the binoculars. The opera glasses were white porcelain with gilded edges. The handle she used to flip them over and hold them up to her eyes had a grip on the end of a brass extension that matched the porcelain around the lenses.

The lenses were meant to bring the action onstage closer to the viewer's perceptions. They distorted her view of the room.

She lowered the opera glasses and opened her hand on the grip, where she could feel a brass plate. It was engraved with a letter and a number corresponding to the box and seat from which it came. Each seat in every private box at l'Opéra Severne had a slot in the right armrest where the opera glasses rested when not in use.

It wasn't normal for one of the company to have taken a pair back to her room.

Suddenly, fatigue was a more solid barrier to press through than emotion. She'd been driving for hours. With her travel-fogged brain, she would surely miss important clues if she tried to ransack the room tonight.

Other than removing the opera glasses that were an intrusion of the room's hushed normalcy, she couldn't go through Victoria's things yet. She couldn't snoop in the closet or the drawers. The room waited for her sister's return. She would let it wait one more night. It wasn't rational, but she had a sudden fear that if she disturbed the room's silent vigil, her sister would never come home.

* * *

Her room was as perfect as Vic's was messy. And much more ornate. Decorated in French rococo style, the whole space was full of white and gilded furnishings and etched glass. Butterflies, thorny vines and rose petals decorated the mirrors in white, only to spring to vibrant, noisy shades of color on the walls in one large continuous design. Plush creams and pale pink with splashes of scarlet and lush green were echoed in the heavy damask bed coverings and carpets on the floor.

She told herself she'd return the opera glasses to their rightful place in the private box high above the auditorium when she had the time. For now, she placed them in the drawer of her bedside table.

She was startled again and again as her movements were reflected in the glass wall panels in jagged interrupted pieces because of the etchings. She showed up as a disjointed leg or arm, a flushed cheek, or a quick glimpse of shadowed eyes. Her equilibrium might never right itself in this place. She couldn't find her footing, mentally or physically. Every thought, every move needed to be carefully calculated. Which meant the evening was going to be a test. Severne threw her balance off even without the aid of strange surroundings.

Finally she was unpacked and changed for dinner.

She'd brought no tulle and satin this time, but she did wear pearls with a pink shell of shimmering crushed silk and a long ivory pencil skirt with matching heels. The boy might be afraid to see her. He might instinctively fear the woman responsible for his mother's death. Dressing for dinner might be inadequate preparation to face him, but it was the least she could do in this aged atmosphere.

She unclipped her hair and let it fall in heavy curls around her shoulders, hiding the pallor of her cheeks behind chestnut waves.

It was stalling and she knew it, but curiosity was a good excuse to pause in the quiet hallway and step closer to examine the wainscoting. In the dimly lit corridor of l'Opéra Severne, the elaborate carved murals were a jumble of faces and forms. From the grotesque to the sublime, on the walls beautiful angelic figures embraced mystical beasts and monsters, all entwined. The artist had been both mad and brilliant. So lifelike were the figures, Kat blinked against the feeling that they peered into her face as she tilted it closer to examine them.

Around her, all was silent. The whole opera house was expectant and still. The building along with everything and everyone in it waited for noise to rise up and fill its grand salon with music.

But something pricked at her senses…

Kat held her breath as she pricked up her ears to pick up a distant murmur. There were likely hundreds of rooms and chambers in l'Opéra Severne. Closets and offices, attics and catwalks, scaffolding beneath the stage for trap doors to allow entrances, exits and costume changes. This must account for the murmur. Not gas or air conditioning, but people. Many people going about some manner of business, but respecting others who slept at odd hours to accommodate schedules kept during the opera season.

The great swirl of carvings was still and silent. In spite of the trick of her eyes that brought it to life as she stepped closer, it was as immobile as it should be. Hundreds of faces were frozen in wood even as they cried for a hundred years. Cried or screamed. She could also discern lovers embracing amid the chaos of passionate battle. Murder, kisses, tears.

So many tears.

The mural in front of her was filled with weeping. Why hadn't she seen that at first? Face after face contorted by poignant emotion. Kat moved even closer, drawn by the pain. Why, she couldn't say, but she was compelled to see, to…hear?

The distant murmur was no longer a hollow echo from the dark reaches of the opera house. There was a whispering quality to it now. A sibilance. Gooseflesh rose on her bare arms. The close, still, dusty air of the theater had gone suddenly chill. The hallway darkened and then lightened in turn as if a shadow passed in front of light after light. The dimming and lightening progressed closer and closer to where she stood.

There must be a thousand eyes in this mural. And suddenly they all shifted their focus to her. Staring. Beseeching. Drawing her closer.

Kat lifted her hand, ignoring the strange behavior of the lights and the tremble in her fingertips. She would touch the mural. Prove it was nothing but inanimate art created long ago. As one shaking finger neared the closest face—a masculine angel perfectly captured in the gleaming shine of carved wood—a very real and immediate noise superseded the whispered murmur.

A low growl sounded behind her, and Kat dropped her hand to turn and face its source.

Adrenaline warmed her goose bumps away as a flush of blood flowed to her extremities from the sudden leap of her rapidly beating heart.

The murmur had stopped. Her pulse rushed in her ears.

A black dog stood with its feet braced apart and its head down. Though its teeth weren't bared, a growl rumbled from deep in its chest again, and its bushy black hair stood on end at its hackles, showing paler pewter beneath.

The dog was out of place. The opera house around her—while vintage—was all slumbering opulence. He was a nightmare hallucination from a dark fairy tale where wolves appeared larger than humanly possible.

"Okay," Kat soothed. The shaky syllables scared her more than the growl. Instinct warned her not to show weakness to this angry creature of shadows come to life. Its eyes gleamed yellow in the gaslight flicker as she tried again. "I was only looking at the mural. Nothing to get upset about," she said.

The dog didn't relax. But it didn't growl again as she edged away from it toward the west wing, where she'd been told dinner would be served.

"No one warned me about you. I'll have to talk to Severne about that oversight."

The dog disengaged from the shadows of the adjacent hallway, but as he stepped into the light, he brought clinging darkness with him rather than leaving it behind. He was black, but there was a gray, sooty quality to every hair on him as it shifted over his muscles, remnants of a dark fog roiling around him as he walked.

"I'm on my way to dinner. Perhaps there'll be a bone for you there," she suggested.

Preferably a bone not attached to me.

The animal was as tall as her waist, and its snout was long and broad. Its muzzle indicated a powerful jaw, a deadly bite. It couldn't come to that. She had to keep it from coming to that. She couldn't afford an injury now when Vic depended on her to stay strong. The dog was no longer growling. She'd willed her breathing to slow. She forced herself to walk slowly, as well. Now that she'd stepped away from the mural, toward the dining room, the dog padded with her, silent and slightly calmed.

It was an odd escort to have down hallways that must have seen much fancier processions. Kat was reminded of Little Red Riding Hood in a black forest with a giant trickster wolf at her heels. The dog was more German shepherd than wolf, but his size was twice that of any wolf, and there was no woodcutter in sight. She saved herself, step by step, refusing to show her fear to the tense animal looming beside her. They came to the entrance of the dining room. She paused to smooth her skirt.

It was good that she'd had to calm herself before entering the room. Truth was, the beast at her heels was no more frightening than the man she prepared to face.

The table glittered with crystal, china and silver, but it also welcomed with more intimate warmth than she'd expected. Half a dozen candles glowed in the jeweled centerpiece at the table's heart, throwing off colored shadows of ruby, emerald and sapphire. The boy was already seated, drinking from a large glass of milk held in both hands. He greeted her with big dark eyes and a white moustache.

"Ms. D'Arcy has found us, Eric," Severne said.

Their host reclined at the head of the table in a large, straight-backed chair with red velvet upholstery and a scrolled wooden frame, very throne-like and fitting to his authoritative demeanor. And yet, the tilt of his finely shaped mouth drew her eyes. She thought about soft silken petals he'd given her. She'd imagined them a substitution for a kiss. Had she been correct? Had he wanted to kiss her because her music had moved him? She'd been certain before, but facing him now she was no longer sure she could read him at all. She noticed the swell of his lower lip was fuller and more sensual than she'd first imagined, a hint of softness in an otherwise hard line.

Now that she'd tasted it, she couldn't forget it was there.

The dog showed itself behind her and Severne's smile disappeared, interrupting her thoughts. He went from indolent royal to intimidating man in seconds. He stood as the semblance of a lazy royalty fell away.

"Grim," he said. There was no doubt it was a warning.

Katherine hadn't relaxed with the monstrous dog, but she had convinced herself it was safe. Now, with her intimidating host reacting to the dog's presence, she wasn't so sure.

She moved to position herself between the boy—who had obviously felt comfortable enough with Severne to share his name—and the dog. Severne stepped forward, but not before his glance took in her brave move with a slight shift of eyes that gleamed in the candlelight from the table. All the green she'd seen before was lost. His eyes were black in this light and, if possible, his jaw firmed before looking back at the dog.

He stared the dog down, and its eyes widened and flared. Her body tensed. Every muscle quivered as she prepared to react to the result of the unspoken communication between the dog and his master. It was so ferociously tense that it might lead to blood.

But if it was a challenge, John Severne came away the victor. How had she doubted for a second he would? The dog's head dipped, and he stepped back several paces before turning to disappear the way he'd come.

"Good boy," Kat said. Her voice was an adrenaline-soaked quiver. That sign of fear was embarrassing, but she stood tall. Her body might have been a poor shield, but she'd offered it to Eric one more time.

The child at the table lowered the glass he'd held frozen to his lips during the confrontation. Severne stepped back to the table and held out her chair. Still not as relaxed as he'd seemed when she came in the room, but pretending to be. He met her gaze as she moved to take the proffered seat. Met and held, his stare giving away nothing of why the dog was banished from the room, but not the opera house. His eyes were still dark in the candlelight, without a hint of green. She had the sudden urge to edge even closer to him to rediscover the softer moss hue around his pupils that she'd seen before.

"Grim? Isn't that the name of a mythological hound that's a portent of death?" she asked, though it was Severne's nearness she truly questioned. Why he lingered near her, why she cared, why an invisible force tingled across her skin when the mere cuff of his suit brushed against her with his movements to help her sit. Better to turn the subject to the large dog, even though it and the death it represented didn't seem nearly as urgent as the scent of smoky candle from Severne's skin. "They're supposed to frequent places of execution in England."

"And crossroads. They traverse ancient pathways. They're seen as guardians in many cultures," Severne said. "Grim is actually a hellhound, and he takes his job too seriously at times. He's the protector of this place and of me since I was a child."

She hadn't felt protected by Grim. More like he was protecting someone or something from her. But what threat did she pose to the master of l'Opéra Severne? What secrets did Severne's Grim guard?

Severne moved back to his seat and sank down. But this time he didn't recline. He appeared hard against the velvet, as if its decadent softness couldn't entice him to relax ever again. Eric watched one of them and then the other silently.

"I wonder, was Grim guarding me from something in the corridor outside my room, or…?"

"Protecting something from you?" Severne finished. His eyes shifted to take in Eric's stare, and he seemed to stop himself from saying more. Out of consideration for the boy's feelings and his recent loss? The loss that she'd played such a horrible part in?

Her own chair swallowed her. She didn't feel like royalty at all. Now she felt like Little Red Riding Hood staying for dinner in the wolf's lair. No mention was made of putting the dog outside or what she should do if she encountered him again.

Several servants brought in the courses in silver tureens and on shining platters as the evening progressed. They were dressed in immaculate uniforms of black and white, their pristine shirts starched, their trousers pressed.

During the meal, she saw the boy put several scraps in his pocket. She wondered if they were bribes for Grim. Safe passage through the elaborately carved corridors of l'Opéra Severne didn't seem possible. Could he buy it from the giant dog with honeyed buns and cake?

They consumed exquisitely seasoned pheasant and savory gravy. The meal was presented as if John Severne was a restaurant critic, yet he ate with no relish or apparent discernment. Rather, he watched her eat as if every bite was performance art. When she nibbled the edge of a puff pastry with pleasure, his eyes widened, then narrowed in concentration, as if he wasn't chewing the same treat but only tasting through her reaction to the dessert, which failed to impress his palate.

Her cheeks warmed beneath his scrutiny. How could such perfect food fail to catch his attention?

Eric ate with more enthusiasm than both adults. He gobbled. She noted his place setting was simpler with a more colorful napkin. Who had gone to such consideration for him?

"I'm sorry about your mother, Eric. I'm sorry I couldn't save her," Kat said.

The boy didn't look up at her. He stared at his plate. But then he spoke. "Her name is Lavinia. She's glad you saved me."

Eric was obviously still processing the loss of his mother. He'd referred to her in present tense as if she wasn't gone.

The conversation was stilted after that, with "More, please" being the predominant phrase until an older woman came to the door.

Her tea-length skirt was perfectly pressed and flared but fifty years out of fashion, its tiny polkadot print and lace trim a style reminiscent of black-and-white television.

Severne rose, and Kat followed suit. She was jumpy. In spite of the fine meal and beautiful table, she wasn't at ease. Because of her guilt over Eric's mother, her uncertainty with Severne and the confrontation with the hellhound, she waited on a razor's edge for disaster to happen. For all she knew, the woman in polka dots might have a machine gun under her skirts.

"Matron," Eric greeted her.

"Bath and bed, young sir. I believe you've had your fill," the woman said to the young daemon boy after a curt nod to Severne. She seemed to see nothing different about the child. She didn't act nervous about babysitting a daemon. When Eric smiled at the woman, Kat finally relaxed about his being at the opera house. He was welcome. Cared for. Her chest tightened with emotion, thinking about Reynard's blade cutting into his mother's throat.

The older woman glanced at her, but instead of looking away again to her new charge, her gaze held. It became a penetrating stare.

"You are like her. Very like. The same eyes. Same hair," she said.

Kat's heart leaped to her throat, but the woman wasn't referring to her sister. She and Victoria were as unalike as could be. Vic was taller, her hair auburn and her eyes the palest blue. She'd taken after their father, a man they'd barely known.

It was her mother the woman referred to. It had to be, though twenty years had passed since her mother had performed here.

"She was lovely. And talented. Drew them like a flame. Her voice was an angel's voice. But…" Her eyes narrowed as she looked closer at Katherine. "She wasn't as strong, I think. You are the strong one," she concluded. She toyed with an iron ring of keys that dangled from her belt as she spoke.

Kat clenched her napkin in her hand. Strong? Was love strong? It was the only weapon she had in the fight to find her sister.

"Yes. Definitely stronger," the woman noted.

"Sybil has been costume matron at l'Opéra Severne for many years," Severne said.

She hadn't come into the room or approached them as she spoke. She held herself apart. The soft candlelight didn't fully illuminate her face. She must have been older than Kat had first assumed if she remembered her mother that well. The keys hung beside a small sewing pouch with a pincushion full of needles incorporated into its design. A bit of measuring tape peeked from the top of the pouch. Altogether, she seemed a woman used to taking care of business, one who didn't need a machine gun to do so. Was she the one who had set a special place for Eric at the fancy table?

Eric had paused near her chair, and now he flung himself at Kat's legs in a tight hug reminiscent of last night, when they'd fled from his mother's killer. His move distracted her from Sybil. Her chest tightened as she felt his ferocious hold again.

"He won't find you here. You're safe with Severne," she said.

Their host heard the exchange. He stood straighter as if

she'd surprised him. His whole hard body stiffened. Eric let her go after a fierce squeeze that made her eyes burn. He went happily with "Matron," his pockets bulging with pilfered food.

And then they were alone.

Severne didn't reclaim his seat, so she remained standing, as well. She forgot her pastry—in fact, she forgot everything—as he suddenly moved. He came toward her in a slow, steady approach very like a stalk, as if quicker movements might scare her away. Did he consider her strong? How soft she must seem to him. How mortal and easily broken.

She tried to convince herself she was stronger.

Her heart beat faster in her chest, an urgent pulse she could feel in her whole body. The heat in her cheeks flushed hotter and spread until she was sure the low neck of her silk blouse revealed her consternation.

She was frightened. But she didn't run.

He was a daemon.

Dangerous.

And so inhumanly hard. He was dressed in a modern, fitted button-down shirt that hugged his chest. Its white fabric was only slightly paler than his skin, but the candlelight caressed his skin to a golden glow, whereas his shirt was left stark in shadow. Or maybe Brimstone caused the color, a more subtle tan than sunlight? He also wore straight-legged black pants that were tight against muscular thighs. Suddenly the idea of feeling his form like perfectly sculpted marble beneath her hand invaded her thoughts.

Could he be made to blush? Or sigh? Could his heartbeat be quickened? Would his breath catch as hers did when he stopped millimeters from where she stood?

With Grim, she'd mastered a calm that Severne shattered.

"You can see I've helped Eric. Just as I intend to help you find your sister," he said.

His voice was a vibration on her skin. His face tilted toward her. There was the green she'd wanted to seek, but it glittered. Dangerous, not soft. Getting close enough to see the colored striations in his dark irises was a compulsion she should have been sure always to deny.

There was bold and there was crazy. Severne inspired mad impulses she should have resisted.

She imagined it for only a second—her hand fluttering softly over the plane of his chest, his stomach and his thighs—but the vision was undoubtedly braver than one she would previously have had. The flush her vision inspired spread more intimately until her knees grew weak.

Again, she could feel his heat. Maybe he would blame Brimstone for the blush he could see in the candlelight? The candles' glow was cruel, causing more warmth and intimacy in the room than she was prepared to handle.

She drew in a quick breath when he reached out toward her, but his hand went past her to the table. She held the sudden gasp in her lungs because to exhale might cause her body to brush his reaching arm. And one touch might betray her. The air filled her chest, tight and unexpressed, as he lifted a tiny pastry from her plate and brought it to her lips. When it was so close to her mouth that the scent of vanilla cream teased her nose, she exhaled softly, meeting his eyes over the proffered treat.

It was a confession, that exhalation. And his eyelids drooped over his eyes in response.

"You didn't enjoy your own pastry," she said.

His gaze dropped from her eyes to her lips and back again.

"I've eaten them a thousand times a thousand. But you chew as if nothing so perfect has ever touched your lips and tongue. They're dust to me. Watching you enjoy them is delicious."

Katherine's head grew light as blood rushed to her lips and the tips of her breasts. He knew. He must. His jaw relaxed, and he brought the pastry to her mouth. He touched the pursed bow of her lips with a light, teasing tickle of sugary cream.

She licked out, instinctively dipping into the residue of icing with her tongue. He watched as she tasted it once more. It was even more decadent when combined with the intensity of his attention.

"I've tasted cream a thousand times a thousand, but I've never tasted it on you," he said.

Had she known? Had her head gone light because she knew her nibbles of delicate pastry had overwhelmed any decision on his part to keep his distance? Or on her part to stay calm and controlled?

Earlier in the evening, he'd given her a calla lily instead of a kiss. The lovely flower had been no substitute at all. Its soft petals were nothing compared to...

He sucked the sweetness of cream from her lips. He sought its remnants on her tongue. He pressed into her until her bottom was on the table and his impossibly muscular body was between her legs. The pastry was forgotten as his mouth took its place, a much more decadent treat. Forbidden. Bad for her. Crazy. She tasted sweet cream and pastry and fire and a wicked hint of wood smoke that must be the never-before-tasted burn of Brimstone heat on her tongue.

She opened to him. She didn't resist. Their tongues twined. Their bodies melded as closely as clothes would allow. He tasted her completely, plundering every gasp, every sugar-sweetened sigh.

And when he finally pulled back, as she clung to him so she wouldn't fall, she finally saw the flush of pleasure on his face and neck that the pastry alone had failed to give him. Heaven help her, but she instantly ached to give him more. It wasn't his marbled perfection she wanted to caress; it was his vulnerability. She wanted to explore the chink in his armor that had allowed him to taste her.

"Good night, Katherine. You heard Sybil. It's time for bed," Severne said.

He backed away. She straightened. In his deep, smoky voice, the suggestion of bedtime was much less utilitarian.

It had been only a kiss.

Only.

She walked by him on quaking legs. He let her go. But between them was so much more heat than could be blamed on hell's fire.

Her whole life she'd hidden in music. Perhaps being excellent at hiding made her also long to seek. Severne hid many things behind his mystery and his muscle. His hardness was his armor. But he was capable of softening. He'd softened tonight. For one stolen moment, his mouth had softened on hers. She couldn't risk losing herself in the search for the softness he hid from her and from the world.

Victoria was missing, and she couldn't afford to lose herself in John Severne before her sister was found.

Chapter 5

The next day John left the opera house as much to escape the memory of Katherine's taste as to fulfill his duties. The house he visited was small, but neat, in a row of older bungalow homes in Roseland Terrace, a part of Baton Rouge's Garden District that had been carefully maintained. The elderly man inside the historic Craftsman was happiest in a home with few rooms and big windows to let in the sun. The navigable home kept him from being confused as he moved from room to room with poor eyesight, failing legs and a cane in a stoop-shouldered shuffle.

And the big windows kept the shadows at bay.

He didn't like shadows.

He didn't remember why.

At first John Severne had tried to correct his father's failing memory. He'd consulted the best doctors. He'd experimented with homeopathy and modern medicines. But then he'd seen the grace in Levi Severne's forgetfulness. The relief.

His grandfather had been killed by one of the daemons he'd been charged to hunt. He'd died a doomed man. He'd known hell had come for him. Though only a young teen, John had seen him consumed by Brimstone's fire until nothing was left but dust. His father had seen it, too. He'd taken John's hand, helpless to prevent for them both the same fate unless they were successful in their task.

Down to the last name on hell's most-wanted list.

John Severne had visited with the father who hadn't known him for decades. Every time he came, they met for the first time. A nearly immortal man with Alzheimer's was a pitiful sight. But it was also a respite. They spoke of other things. The hydrangeas were blooming. Levi Severne liked blue. The big clusters of blooms made him smile.

Severne had left his father on a chair in the backyard, where the flowers swayed in the breeze. The nurse would collect him in time for an afternoon siesta. No more killing. No more strife. He had no memory of the damnation that had once plagued him with nightmares.

"We'll beat it, John. We'll beat it. I promised your mother before she died I would see you saved. I promised her my father's terrible contract wouldn't damn you."

How many times had his father repeated that pledge to him?

How many times had he stood watching the frail old man he loved and quietly vowing the same pledge back to him?

"I'll beat it. I'll save you. You have my word," Severne said.

The burn in his throat wasn't Brimstone.

The evil old man who had been his grandfather had deserved the agony that had devoured him. He'd brought it on himself. His father had been an innocent child when Thomas Severne made his deal with the devil. John had been sacrificed to the Council when he'd been barely old enough to survive the burn of Brimstone that had claimed his blood.

He had been playing with jacks when his grandfather came for him. It had been his favorite game, to bounce the ball and swipe up as many metal crosses as he could before the ball came down. He'd wiled away many a lonely afternoon in solitary play, too grand of parentage to be approached by servants' children or the children of performers. He was often alone while his father was away on hunting trips.

He'd been too young to imagine that his father hunted monsters. But he'd often wondered why his father hunted when their cook visited the butcher for all the meat that went into his oven and pots.

He bounced his ball, and Grandfather caught it before it came down. Only then did he notice the shiny boots that had crushed the tiny jacks he'd not scooped up in time. His grandfather hauled him up roughly with his other hand, and the jacks John had managed to scoop fell from his fingers, prizes he would never come back to retrieve.

His time of childhood play was over.

He was five years old.

His grandfather had taken him down several flights of stairs too quickly for him to follow safely. He'd fallen several times. Skinned both his knees. His arm had felt almost ripped from its socket each time his grandfather had pulled him to his feet.

"It's past time. The Council grows impatient. Your father should have done this well before now," the old man had growled.

He'd had a booming voice up until the very end, when its deep resonance had morphed into high-pitched screams.

He'd done his best to keep up. His father had always warned him not to anger Thomas Severne. With his bushy brows and wild hair over ruddy cheeks, the old man had featured in many of John Severne's nightmares even before that night.

More than once, in fevered dreams, his grandfather had picked him up and tossed him into a roaring fire.

John didn't dare cry even when his knees bled. He didn't dare protest even when his elbow popped out of joint from a jerk too hard and sudden to anticipate. Agony flared, but he didn't cry out loud. Instead, he hurried as fast as he could, all the way down to where his father had always forbidden him to go.

The secret catacombs beneath l'Opéra Severne.

These dark, endless caves were filled with chill shadows his father warned him might not be as harmless as they should have been.

The giant door protested when Thomas Severne pushed it inward and open.

John had mindlessly held back. His instinct to fear the catacombs was greater than the order always to obey his grandfather when he couldn't avoid him.

Thomas Severne jerked even harder on his arm. The dislocated joint screamed. He bit through his lip to keep from crying out at the pain. He stumbled after his grandfather, knowing he was in great danger, and his father couldn't save him.

"It's a good thing your mother is dead, John," his father always said. "She would weep to see what has become of us."

But John prayed for the angel of his mother to save him from his grandfather that night. They'd practically run through the catacombs to answer the Council's call.

"You will serve them, as your father serves them and

as I have served them. It is the price we must pay for our success and longevity," Thomas Severne said.

His grandfather's shadow was thrown crazily onto the walls by the lantern he'd taken up in his other hand.

John thought his legs would give out before they reached their destination. He'd thought he would pass out from the pain. He knew his grandfather would continue to drag him on the hard, uneven ground of the catacomb's floor. He'd run his first marathon that night, his legs pumping, his scuffed boots flying. His knees would hurt worse if he didn't stay on his feet. His arm might actually be ripped from his body. He focused on those two horrors rather than shadows and his grandfather's crazed urgency.

Finally Thomas Severne stopped in front of what John thought at first was a door as black as pitch. Only there was no door. Instead, there was only an opening made of flat, solid darkness. He never would have tried to walk through it if his grandfather hadn't tugged him roughly into the black.

But it was the pause before the tug that made his stomach fall away. This was the first time he'd seen his terrifying grandfather afraid. Thomas Severne squared his shoulders and took a deep breath. His fingers tightened around John's fingers.

Then they stepped through the doorway.

His arm was a white-hot agony most adults couldn't have endured.

His knees bled.

But in those moments, as he passed through the doorway with his grandfather, every cell in his body screamed in pain.

They came out on the other side, into a high-ceilinged chamber that had no end to his child's eyes. His grandfather pulled him forward to a long pathway that stretched far out of sight between two rows of stadium seating filled to capacity with a silent, faceless crowd. John felt the weight of thousands of eyes. His grandfather ignored them. He pulled the tiny child at his side along.

But they walked beneath those stares. Calm and slow. With only his grandfather's tight grip to show that the calm was a lie.

Thomas Severne was still afraid.

To John, the dais they finally reached with its massive table was made for giants. But the men who sat along its intimidating length were normal-sized.

They spoke.

His grandfather replied.

And then he was grabbed under his armpits by Thomas Severne and lifted high off the ground. He cried out at last. The move cruelly wrenched his arm, and it was almost a relief to shout. His grandfather didn't care. The man at the head of the table came to take him. As he was lifted even higher, he saw the bronzed wings hanging on the wall above the Council.

He'd thought of his mother and of angels, but not for long.

The other men at the table rose and came to where their leader held him. They wore plain black clothes, but when they rolled up their sleeves and drew blades across their wrists, their blood was brilliant flame.

He screamed and screamed.

The Brimstone entered him though every opening in his skin. His pores. His nose. His mouth. That moment supplanted his nightmare of being thrown into fire.

He choked on the hot coals of his breath turned to embers.

That's when he knew the men were not men. As he choked, he heard Thomas Severne laugh.

His father had wept when he'd come home. But his training had begun. Grim came soon after, a dark gift that nonetheless soothed his pain.

Levi Severne hadn't saved him. But he'd tried. Where Levi had failed, John was determined to succeed.

His grandfather might have deserved to be completely consumed by Brimstone's fire, but his father didn't deserve the torture that lurked, waiting to claim him if his son failed to fulfill the contract before he died.

He wasn't sure how much time he had. His grandfather had signed his deadly deal just after the Revolutionary War. Levi Severne was only five at the time. Such a small boy. Innocent. But condemned by his father's greed. His mind had started to fail when he reached two hundred twenty-five years old. The Brimstone prolonged their lives, but it didn't hold off the price of age forever.

Severne clenched his fists against the damnation looming so close to his father. The sun had gone behind a cloud, and Levi Severne had called for his nurse in a small voice that seemed to come from the boy he'd been so very long ago.

He'd done his part. He'd hunted daemons for decades. He'd taught his son how to fight. He'd shown him how to handle the terrible burn of Brimstone in his blood. He'd taught him to look away from the walls of l'Opéra Severne as the burden of years and souls began to weigh him down.

He'd tried to teach him how to hope. Levi had always been an optimist. He'd met and married a beautiful Southern belle, thinking he'd be free from the contract before they had a child.

He'd been wrong.

She'd died in childbirth believing his promise that her son would be saved.

Severne didn't believe in hope. He'd never allowed the softness of hope. He believed in perseverance, determination and pain. He would need all three things to save his father before his mortal body failed.

And maybe one day he'd be graced with the ability to forget all he'd done.

The nurse had come to check on her charge. She must have rushed out as soon as she'd heard him call. John was pleased by her quick response. The best that money could buy. Her tone was kind and patient as she responded to Levi's fear of the darkened day and the shadows that stretched toward his seat from the bushes, which had given him pleasure only moments before.

The nurse helped his father up with the aid of his cane, and the two slowly made their way toward the house. He resisted the nurse, though, forcing a pause beside the hydrangea bushes. Severne watched his father reach out and take a cluster of blossoms in his hand. Levi Severne pressed the bloom to his face and inhaled, but then he dropped the crushed flowers, and John could tell by the nurse's consternation that the old man cried.

The nurse urged Levi to come with her. She soothed him with soft assurances of safety. Severne knew from experience that inside, many lights and lamps waited to be turned on. All Levi's caretakers knew the house needed to be aglow during a storm.

His father's fears would fade. His tears would dry.

To be sure, John waited and watched until light after light came on. Even as fat droplets began to fall and sizzle on his skin, he waited. His temperature dropped, but he ignored the chill. He paid no attention to the wet seeping into his hair to run in rivulets down his face. He waited until he was sure the house was lit and his father snug inside before he turned and walked away.

* * *

Kat should have known she couldn't be quicker on the draw than John Severne. She'd thought she would return the opera glasses before anyone missed them. But the next day when she climbed the stairs to the third-level balcony and quietly approached the box corresponding with the number on the porcelain handle, she found the opera's master in the seat she searched for.

She tried to halt her entrance in time to go unnoticed, but he rose to turn and face her. He'd heard her steps, or he'd felt her approach as she suddenly felt him. She'd tried to tune out the pull of his Brimstone blood, which followed her wherever she went in the opera house, but rather than helping her avoid him, it had placed her in a compromising position.

He was both everywhere she walked and here, where she least expected to find him.

"Where did you find those?" Severne asked.

The box was small. It held only two seats. And the opera glasses were obvious in her hands.

He didn't seem to mind the close quarters. As the curtains she'd parted closed with a whoosh in her wake, he moved even closer while she tried to think of what to say.

Was this his box? Were the glasses his? Why had they been in Victoria's room?

All those questions assailed her along with his nearness and the unusual appearance of his rumpled clothes. He wore a white oxford shirt and black pants, but his jacket was missing, his sleeves were rolled up and his tie was loosened.

"They were on my sister's bed. Left on her pillow," Kat said. "I thought I should return them. She must have accidentally carried them away. I assume they belong to this box."

Below, dancers practiced for the ballet often omitted from performances of *Faust* by other opera companies. At l'Opéra Severne, the ballet was a favorite of fans. It represented the temptation of Faust by the greatest and most beautiful women in history that had been offered to him by Mephistopheles.

So far, from what Katherine had seen of rehearsals, this version was suggestively choreographed while still seeming subtly playful in its eroticism.

"This box is like the other boxes in the house. Elite patrons own them all. Some families have kept them for generations. Politicians, celebrities and foreign aristocracy all float in and out in relative anonymity. To be honest, I thought this one was abandoned. Many seats are kept by the elderly and passed down to heirs who prefer sports arenas or video games," Severne said. "I'm here only temporarily. Captivated by the view."

So she'd found the stoic yet sensual master of the opera house looking down on his lithe dancers? Her cheeks warmed. "They are captivating," she agreed.

The dancers practiced with an old stage piano more suited for vaudeville than opera, but they were talented. Once their moves were paired with costumes, lighting and the full orchestra accompaniment, the ballet would be sublime.

"I'm proud of every aspect of the show, but I do enjoy this dance—the temptation, the resistance, the surrender," Severne said. It was almost a confession. He was a daemon professing his fascination with the dance of damnation.

He leaned toward her and her breath caught, but he was only reaching for the opera glasses. She released them from her fingers at the same time as she released a—she hoped—unnoticeable sigh. He didn't turn back to the dancers. He held the glasses and continued to look down at her.

"These levels are closed until performances. Performers don't enter the boxes or wander around. I'm not sure why your sister had these," he said.

"You don't know who owns this box?" she asked.

"There are records you could search, but they haven't been computerized. I'm afraid our offices are Victorian by today's standards," Severne said. "Decades of papers and dusty files are an immortal's prerogative."

Behind him, several stories below, the dancers writhed and undulated for Faust's pleasure as Mephistopheles pretended to hold their strings like they were marionettes. Kat felt a little bit like her strings were being tugged by a fate that would have her dance for John Severne.

How would she ever find her sister in the purposefully ambiguous atmosphere of l'Opéra Severne? The owner of the box might have nothing to do with her sister's disappearance. In spite of what Severne had said, the boxes were curtained, not locked. Anyone might have slipped in and out of them unseen.

Severne had stepped lightly to the side. He was offering her a seat. Because she didn't want to seem intimidated or afraid, she took it, and he sank down beside her. Thankfully, the dancers were now separately working on individual elements of the ballet so the overall suggestive effect of the piece was lost. Unfortunately, the only suggestion left was the full force of her affinity for Severne, closed in the curtained-off box where her seat and Severne's were so close that his arm brushed hers.

He moved to place the opera glasses back in their slot. He had to lean across her body to do so. She couldn't will the affinity away. This close, it was impossible to ignore. Even if she could, his natural magnetism would have called to her with or without Brimstone in his blood.

It was the end of the day. Whatever he did in his Vic-

torian offices, he'd literally rolled up his sleeves. The
hair on his arm brushed hers. The tattoos she'd seen before peeked from beneath his white sleeve. This was his
leisure—overseeing rehearsals, pondering damnation
and torturing her.

He sat back from returning the opera glasses to her
chair, but the scent of smoky sandalwood still teased her
nose. She wouldn't meet his penetrating gaze. He hadn't
looked back at the dancers since she'd arrived. While she
avoided his eyes, she noticed the longish black waves of
his hair were slightly damp and curled against the open
collar of his shirt.

She was familiar with temptation and resistance. Surrender was a new possibility. She was afraid if she spent
too long in John Severne's company, her limits might be
tested. He was a daemon, but he had taken the guise of a
very attractive man. She was drawn to the burn beneath
his control. She was drawn to what he might hide beneath
the hardness he cultivated for the world. His penchant for
sugary kisses and his reaction to her cello music gave her
a glimpse at what vulnerabilities he might hide.

He wasn't a forthright man, but a daemon. His every
move screamed those truths to her even though his words
and demeanor were enigmatic.

"Your music will make this dance impossible to resist.
The audience will be captivated," he said.

And yet he also made raw confessions at every turn.

She lifted her gaze from the dancers below to Severne's
eyes. The shadows were too deep to see any green, but he
tilted toward her as if to accommodate her search, and a
shaft of stage light fell over his eyes. The rest of his face
was still shadowed, but his eyes were fully illuminated
and as green as she'd seen them before.

His eyes and his shadowed mouth drew her.

But she quickly rose before she fell further under his daemon spell. Or his masculine spell. Or both.

She wasn't here to be seduced. Surrender wasn't an option.

"I enjoy the music. I appreciate the dance. I don't want to captivate. I just want to find my sister," she said.

She mumbled to excuse herself as she tried to navigate gracefully past his long, lean legs. He stood, but he didn't try to stop her. She pushed through the heavy curtains behind their seats, but as she did she heard him reply.

"As do I, Katherine. As do I."

He said he wanted to help her find her sister, but she wasn't certain what he wanted most. He was a bottomless pit of wants and needs she couldn't quite ascertain.

Chapter 6

The sun was only a pink hint at the edges of the city's dark silhouette against the sky as he ran the Thames path away from Central London. One of the benefits of damnation and a hellhound for a constant companion was that he wasn't limited to mortal means of transportation. He rarely had to use more than a word or a glance before he materialized where he wished to be with Grim's help.

He'd always run in the dark even before it was a common sight, nothing to note, a man with a drive to beat the cheeseburger and beer he'd consumed last Sunday. It was nothing now to pass other runners in the fog and shadows, them with reflective strips on their shoes or blinking LED bands around their elbows.

He had only Grim, a great, hulking shadow among shadows loping on silent paws that hardly touched the ground.

He seemed to be using this means of escape more and more often since Katherine had come to l'Opéra Severne.

Severne's own feet pounded pavement, then dirt; real enough, a solid, mortal man with a life extended by Brimstone blood rather than the exercise that was his absolution, his penance and his salvation. He ran farther and harder this edge-of-day. Every time his heel hit the ground, he tasted sweet cream and musky woman. She'd been frightened, but exhilarated. Her heart pounding so hard he could feel it in his own chest.

Sybil had called her strong. Katherine's strength caused her to be enticingly bold.

Sweat poured from him. Everything that could burn did—calories, fat, energy—until he was left with nothing but lean, honed muscle and memories.

Then he ran some more. Toward Hammersmith.

Grim didn't whine or complain.

He was silent.

He'd been a constant companion for as long as John could remember. Which was far longer than most men could recall.

The longer run was as much an apology to Grim as a punishment for himself. His conflicts and mixed emotions over Katherine D'Arcy had confused the daemon dog, so in tune with his master that he usually knew instantly whether someone was friend or foe.

With Katherine, it was…complicated.

But Grim had held himself in check.

Good dog.

Good, good dog.

Bad master.

He'd exercised way less control.

She was all soft, sensual emotion in his arms. Desire, need, fear, sadness and a poignant hope he could almost feel like a veil of gossamer illusion against his skin. If shadows clung to Grim, hope clung to Katherine, an invisible aura that drew him too close. So close his Brimstone threatened to sear it away.

When he tasted her, the hope tried to envelop him, too, in spite of all he'd done and seen. His whole body felt the thrill of coming alive to it until he wrenched back before he scorched it *and her* to ashes.

No wonder Grim was confused.

He had need to stand the dog down with clear mental orders to guard and protect, but not harm the very obvious threat in their midst. No. That was his job. To harm. To hurt.

He turned his thoughts from the lovely, enticing bloodhound of a woman to focus on one foot in front of the other. His path inexorable. Burned into being decades ago.

He'd told Katherine that Grim was a portent of ancient pathways. It wasn't a myth. It was true. Grim was the key he used to traverse the globe on his deadly mission to eradicate the names on the daemon scroll. The hellhound had been a gift to the Severne family when his grandfather had signed a deal in Severne blood with the Council that had overthrown Lucifer.

He followed Grim easily through the shadows in between this location and that on pathways through the world no one else could see. He'd often come here to run, far from home. This time he realized he'd come too often. Two figures detached themselves from park trails flanking his on either side to veer toward him. Their move was sudden and aggressive and far too coordinated. They were together even though they ran apart. His path would put him between them. Their legs pumped with purpose and a sudden burst of speed unlikely to indicate a casual change of direction.

They meant to intercept.

Grim was ahead of him, somewhere in the mist evaporating off the black river. It rolled wetly across the park, thick and hazy, providing enough cover that no one would see what happened when the two approaching runners converged with him.

He didn't slow his stride. He didn't speed up. If he'd wanted to outrun them, he could have. Even drained from a long workout, his Brimstone blood would give him an edge unless... Closer now, he could see their speed was inhuman. Just this side of a blur. He noted that the dark clothes he'd assumed were sweat pants and hoodies were actually combat trousers and hooded snoods he'd seen before, a glint of familiar metal at their necks. They would have crisscrossed daggers at their backs in hidden sheaths close to their bodies.

Lucifer's Army.

Assassins sent to stop him from fulfilling a centuries-old deal with lower-caste daemons that had ripped the greatest of the fallen from his throne. A Council now ruled in Lucifer's stead. His mighty shorn wings were encased in bronze as a gruesome symbol of fraternity. The Council sought to eradicate all his loyal followers. Severne had stood before them once as a child. He'd never forgotten the burn. It didn't matter that it had been Severne's grandfather who had chosen a side in a hellish revolution.

Now John Severne had to fight.

When Brimstone-tainted blood met the same, it bubbled and sizzled as if the individual cells fought to occupy the same place. The sound hissed in the air as blood was let on all three sides. John felt the slicing burn of a blade across his shoulder, but the other three blades met daemon flesh as he deflected them back on the creatures that brandished them with well placed blows to their lower arms. One sank deep enough into the sternum of the left daemon that he cried out as all the Brimstone his body contained flared out and up in a column of fire. He was consumed completely until nothing but dissipating smoke remained.

"Good talk," Severne grunted as he grappled with the remaining assassin.

Grim was more than a key, more than an omen of cross-roads and pathways. He was a guardian. He was death. As John held the wrists of the daemon that struggled to bring two wicked blades with serrated edges down to impale him through the vulnerable flesh at the points of his collarbones, Grim leaped from the mist.

His great gaping maw closed on the daemon's throat. The hellhound wasn't fazed by the inferno of released Brimstone. It barely singed his charcoal fur. John was left with daemon blades and an ancient brooch at his feet. Forged of a metal like iron with a bold, stylized *L* in its center, the brooch had been what had gleamed at the assassin's throat. Another lay a few feet away, where his partner had vanished in a flash burn.

John gathered the brooches and the swords while Grim watched with a curl of stinking smoke rising from his muzzle, joining the morning mist rising to the brightening sky.

"Nice entrance, big guy. Worthy of Rin Tin Tin," Severne said.

It was always the same after the frenzy of kill-or-be-killed: the need his body had to shake, his mortality evidenced by his reaction. He refused to allow the shudders. He threw the daggers in the Thames. The water bubbled and boiled and then settled to gentle ripples as the blades sank to the murky bottom and cooled, forgotten. He kept the brooches. It seemed more honorable than throwing them away.

He'd been forced onto a side of this ancient fight, but he felt no allegiance to the daemons that held his soul and his father's soul ransom. He fought for a father who no longer knew him. The Brimstone in his blood couldn't negate the coldness of that. He was only surviving so that one day his father might live out his remaining days and die in peace.

The silent daemon dog turned and led the way back to Baton Rouge.

The offices of l'Opéra Severne were housed in an octagon-shaped room behind the main box office. Kat hadn't expected the room to stretch up to as many floors as the balcony levels of the main hall, or for the only way to reach the levels to be wrought iron ladders on wheels like you'd expect to find in a Victorian library.

Severne had told her she was welcome to search out the paperwork involved with the ownership of the private balcony box where the opera glasses had been returned. He'd also warned her the search would be more easily offered than done.

The next day, when she made her way to the offices after rehearsals, she didn't know where to begin. Although the walls were lined with wooden drawers, the rows of drawers extended all the way up, floor after floor to the ceiling, which lofted in a frescoed peak high above her head.

As she paused to decide where to begin, the chirruping of birds could be heard in the rafters and from perches and nests in the nooks and crannies of the half dozen four-story-tall ladders, which had landing platforms at each floor.

"I warned you," Severne said. He came from behind a stack of loose files taller than her head. Taller than his head, come to think of it. He had nothing in his hands. She couldn't imagine him doing paperwork as part of his job. He was master, not assistant. He was a king, not a clerk.

"There are several employees who tackle the books

from time to time. But they mostly click their tongues and despair," he said.

Kat looked at the daemon she knew to be wealthy and successful. He looked more capable of waging war than accounting.

"You're free to wade through as much of this as you'd like, but I'll warn you that it's more a sentimental collection than a useful resource. My father was an optimistic hoarder. He always thought he'd have time to organize," Severne said.

"Was?" Katherine asked. It was an intrusive question. Her curiosity made them both pause as if they'd been caught in a sudden, actual conversation against their will.

"He still lives, but he's not himself. He doesn't remember his time at l'Opéra Severne. All of his keepsakes would be strange to him now," Severne said.

He'd tensed, and the whole room all the way to the rafters seemed to note the change in atmosphere. He nudged the ladder nearest to him, and a small flock of brown sparrows rose up, startled and protesting.

"So this cluttered office was his domain. That makes sense; I couldn't imagine it as yours," Kat said.

The restless man across from her suddenly quieted and focused on her. His entire attention fell on her face.

"Do you spend much time imagining things about me?" he asked.

She'd blundered into a trap, and her unwitting confession had given him an excuse to change the subject from the warm clutter of the room and his father.

Kat traced pictures in the dust of a nearby desk. She drew a feather with a long sweeping quill.

"I was only comparing this office to your personal office and your gym," she said.

She felt it when he began to move toward her. It might

have been her affinity that made her hyperaware of his placement in a room in comparison to hers. It also might have been pure physical awareness as if he was only an attractive and charismatic man.

She and Victoria had both been on the run for a long time. Victoria wasn't the only one fascinated with the subject of star-crossed lovers. She'd done her share of dreaming and wondering. And she'd recently found the subject more fascinating than before.

He stopped beside her and looked down at her dust drawing.

"Dreaming of feathers means you long for freedom and happiness," he said.

"I was only thinking of the birds," she said, looking up beyond his handsome, hard face to the sparrows that still swooped in the rafters.

"We've tried to net and release them, but they always get back in somehow," Severne said.

"L'Opéra Severne is a hard place to escape. I've thought of it often although I haven't been here since I was a child," Kat confessed.

"It's a part of me," Severne said.

She lowered her gaze from the swooping of the birds just enough to meet his dark eyes. In this dusty place, they were even harder and more alive with shadows. She wouldn't tell him how her feelings for the opera house had merged with her feelings for its master, leaving her more confused than comforted in spite of her nostalgia for the old theater.

"I can call in the clerks and have them search for the information you seek, Katherine. You don't need to bury yourself in the dust of this place," he said.

He brought his hand near hers and wiped the dust from the desk, erasing her feather drawing at the same time.

The birds above their heads had settled. Either they didn't believe in freedom and happiness or they had found their share in a small world sheltered from all the predators outside.

Katherine's hand was still on the desk, separated from Severne's by mere millimeters. His fingers lingered in the dusty place he'd wiped as if he waited for her next move. She breathed lightly and easily. Dust motes floated in the air between them. They sparkled with possibility, but then they fell, settling back down to earth before either of them moved.

"Thank you. Please tell them I appreciate their help," she said.

She took her hand from the desk, and only then did he remove his, as well.

The birds had gone silent, with only an occasional rustle to indicate that the roosting creatures had the potential for flight.

He'd meant to keep her busy digging through the paper detritus of the past century, but when he'd found her in the office, he couldn't bear the thought of his beautiful, musical Katherine trapped with the birds and the dust. It would accomplish the same thing if he had his employees comb through the disorganized records. Let her feel that the human owner of the box had something to do with her sister's disappearance, when all the while she would be inadvertently leading him to the daemon he needed to find.

His.

He had no doubt that the daemon he sought had spent time at l'Opéra Severne. He'd been drawn to the opera house because of its proximity to the hell dimension. He'd been drawn to Victoria D'Arcy as all daemons were. Severne had been away hunting other daemons, and

Michael had made himself at home, coming and going through the private boxes of the balconies and the private rooms of a woman who should have been under Severne's protection.

It wasn't safe for a human woman to consort with daemons. Or with a man who was damned.

That was a reminder he needed to embrace. He'd failed Katherine's sister. She would be hurt by what he had to do if she'd taken Michael as her lover. He couldn't afford to care. Not when he had to use Katherine and endanger her heart in much the same way.

Chapter 7

Backstage could be volatile, and a seasoned company welcoming new players could flare from volatile to combustible. Katherine tried to blend in, but it was tricky. L'Opéra Severne seemed to have less turnover than most theaters. Urgency helped her persevere. For Victoria, she had to find her place quickly and well because she needed to spend the majority of her time searching for some clue about her sister's whereabouts.

Just because she didn't have to tackle a century's worth of dusty papers in the opera house offices didn't mean she was free only to rehearse and perform. She had to continue to keep her eyes open and question the other musicians and performers. There was a good chance she could learn more from conversation than disorganized records. She also had to maintain her distance from Severne while still trying to understand what drove him to help her.

How much time did she spend imagining things about

him? Way more than she should. But no one ever needed to know it.

Victoria had used an assumed name to avoid Reynard. As one cello in an orchestra of five, Katherine didn't feel the need for such measures. She wouldn't be on the marquee or the playbill. She wouldn't be named in advertisements. She was one of a whole. Here she was still Katherine D'Arcy and no one batted a lash.

"Julia was an understudy until a couple of weeks ago," one of the seasoned prompters shared. Tess Vaughn was quiet, punctual and good at her job. A woman in her forties, Tess was the backbone of the production without longing for the spotlight of a part onstage. Prompters fed the singers their words on the upbeat, moments before the actual lines were required. They kept the production flowing smoothly in spite of performers who might be nervous or ill or just suffering a momentary memory blank.

Kat was naturally drawn to Tess because soft conversation could often reveal what urgent interrogation couldn't. Tess seemed to have nothing to hide. No dark ambitions. No rivalries to put her on guard. Everyone liked her. "She's not as gifted as her predecessor and she knows it," Tess said, "so she's making simple mistakes from trying too hard. Beatrice felt the music. Every word. Every note. Julia is singing a part. Bea *was* Marguerite."

Tess was turned away from her while Kat limbered the muscles and joints in her fingers, arms and midsection, where strength of core centered her playing. She hoped her hands didn't tremble at the praise for her sister. Victoria was brilliant. No matter what name she'd gone by. Her singing had been her escape from blood and death. But had her song betrayed her in the end? Had it failed to keep her safe?

"I'm surprised someone made for the part would quit and leave l'Opéra Severne," she ventured.

"We were all surprised. And disappointed. Bea's performance would have elevated the whole company. It seemed unlike her. She didn't have a cut-and-run temperament. But…" Tess trailed off, and Kat noticed an uncomfortable glance her way.

"But…?" she prompted. She hoped her expression didn't show how her heart was hanging on every word the other woman spoke. Tess was right about her sister's temperament. Kat had been the expert at cut-and-run. Her sister had always chafed at hiding.

Victoria D'Arcy was still dressed as Juliet. Katherine had dreaded the final performance. Her sister was always the least consolable when she sang the tragic part of the young star-crossed lover. Not because she had to play the part of a young woman who had loved and lost, but because Victoria had never had the opportunity to love at all.

They had no time for romance. Not with Reynard constantly hounding their footsteps.

She hurried to Vic's dressing room following the final curtain call, barely pausing to wipe down her precious cello with hurried swipes of a soft cloth. Even her treasured instrument wasn't as dear to her as her only sister. There was a crush of press and fans waiting outside the stage door, but Katherine was able to enter the dressing rooms through the backstage tunnels of the Cincinnati Theater. She was glad she'd gone to the trouble even though she was exhausted from her own performance when Vic turned from her dressing table with tears streaking the pale makeup on her face.

"I keep doing this to myself. I'm always drawn to Juliet. I don't know why," Victoria said.

Kat ignored her aching body and hurried to hug her crying sister.

"Because you're a lyric soprano and you're perfect for the role. And because you're a brilliant actress with a feel for the part that most modern performers can't really empathize with," Kat reminded her. "You are the young virgin who can't have the man she loves. Or any man, for that matter."

Victoria laughed through her tears just as Kat had intended.

"Aren't we pitiful? Blessed and damned all at the same time," Vic said.

What she said was true. The affinity in their blood gave them an even greater gift for music than they would have had without it. But it also kept them from experiencing the emotional connections they played and sang about.

"I still don't regret it, Kat. Not even Juliet. The role hurts me, but I somehow need to sing it," Vic confessed.

Her sister's need to play the tragic role of the doomed lover bothered Katherine more than she ever let show. She was afraid that it was somehow prophetic of pain and loss to come. And they'd already endured more pain and loss than most.

"You were beautiful tonight. I cried. The conductor might not welcome me into his orchestra pit again," Kat said.

Victoria laughed once more and hugged her tighter. After the embrace, she was able to rise and begin to take off the costume stained with Juliet's fake blood. Kat fell silent, staring at the blood. This time her feelings of an evil portent were not so fanciful.

"We've stayed too long, haven't we?" Victoria asked. She had stopped. The makeup wipes she'd been using to cleanse her face fell to the table.

"Yes. I saw him in the crowd. We won't be able to lose him tonight," Kat said.

"I'm sorry, Kat. It's my fault. I linger. I hate to give up great roles. I hate the constant running," Victoria said.

"I know. I hate it, too. But we can't give up. Mom is gone. It's only us now. We have to try to escape. We have to resist," Katherine said. "Just as she taught us to do."

Victoria nodded. She took a deep breath to will away the last of her tears. There would be real death before the night was through. She could waste no more energy on Juliet. Her sister hated to run and hide, but she always did what needed to be done in the end for them to survive. Kat helped Victoria take off the rest of her costume before she changed out of her own concert dress.

They had to be ready for Reynard. He would be following them on the hunt. And, when it was over, they would need to be prepared to escape one more time.

Always one more time.

"She was seeing someone," Tess said.

Her voice tore Katherine away from her memories.

"One of the company?" Kat asked.

"No. There was gossip that he was from old money. A patron of the arts. Maybe even European royalty. I guess anyone could be lured away from all this by a prince." Tess gestured to the dusty backstage dressing area and shabby velvet curtains faded from red to pink ages ago. "There was definitely something going on. I worked with her every day. She was distracted at the end. Excited. But she didn't talk about her personal life much, so I didn't ask."

"Seems odd someone so serious about her work would leave before the season ended," Kat said.

"It depends on the man, doesn't it?" Tess smiled, and an unexpected dimple showed at her chin.

Kat's heart fell. She suspected foul play, not romance, but she couldn't forget Victoria's many portrayals of Juliet. She hoped her sister hadn't been drawn to the romantic tragedy for prophetic reasons. She had to force a smile for Tess's benefit. The friendly woman had no idea she might be joking about a deadly situation. Perhaps this "patron of the arts" was the owner of the private box where the opera glasses had been returned.

"All the patrons will be at the preseason masquerade two nights before our first performance," Tess said. "Michael might be there, too. She never mentioned his last name. Only Michael. I'll point him out to you if he's there. We're expected to attend, but no one minds. It's the hottest ticket in Baton Rouge. It's a hundred-year-old tradition. Sybil always allows us to choose a costume from the collection. Last year I was Marie Antoinette."

Kat thought about John Severne in formal wear and a domino mask. She could perfectly envision the potential for green to glitter in his eyes. They would seem dark to everyone except the person who got close enough to see more. She could also too easily imagine how the black silk of a mask would highlight the cut of his jaw and the swell of his sensual lower lip.

She closed her eyes and swallowed. One more challenge for her to endure.

"Mr. Severne serves the best champagne that night. Always. We look forward to the masquerade all year," Tess said. "And there's always a buffer of recovery time between the party and the first performance."

A daemon she desperately needed to resist at a masquerade. The possibility of meeting a man involved in her sister's disappearance. And a high-profile party where the Order of Samuel could easily stalk her unawares.

Her first week on the job was revealing multiple ways in which she might fail before she'd even begun.

Their conversation ended when rehearsals began. Tess had to make her way to the tiny spiral staircase that led up and into the hooded prompter's box, where she performed her vital role with only the performers as a grateful audience.

Kat took her place down in the orchestra pit. All the other musicians waited for the conductor to wake and move slowly from his chair to become suddenly animated and vigorous as if the music brought him to life.

After rehearsal, Katherine could no longer put off the inevitable search of her sister's room. Forewarned was forearmed. She needed to learn more before the masquerade. She swallowed her fear and her pain. She forced herself to ignore the dust and stale perfume. If her sister had disappeared because of this mysterious "patron of the arts," it had to have been against her will. The opera glasses might be only the first of many clues she uncovered, but only if she braved her pain.

The scariest question plaguing her was whether or not Michael was a daemon.

Alone, without Reynard, without the Order of Samuel to help her or even her sister at her side, Vic would have been in terrible danger if her gift had led her to a daemon that didn't want to be found.

And what of Severne? Had he known the mysterious man? Severne was supposed to be helping her find her sister, but she could only doubt his motivations. How could she trust a daemon? Maybe her sister had been killed by a daemon at l'Opéra Severne and its master didn't actually want her to be found. Maybe she would join her sister in oblivion when Severne decided it was time.

On the night of the masquerade, she was sure to face dangers even darker than she could imagine. The opera house was filled with secrets. Perhaps her sister had stumbled upon some secret that had ended up being too dangerous for her to handle alone.

The room was less poignant and vaguely threatening this time when she unlocked the door. What terrible things might lay in a drawer or cabinet?

Kat breathed deeply, somehow fortified by the hint of freesia Vic always wore. It was faint, but still there, as if determined to bear witness to Vic's having been in the room not too long ago. Her resolve wavered as she faced intimate reminders of Vic at every turn. She forced herself to go through the drawers. She found her sister's favorite scarf. Kat picked it up, and underneath its silken folds she discovered a photograph of their mother. In the photograph, her mother was achingly familiar. Kat recognized the clothes she wore and the way she styled her hair. It must have been taken just before she was killed.

The photo made Kat pause.

She held the delicate paper in her hand. It was pale and faded, representing a moment captured in time now long, long gone. In it, her mother stood in front of a flowering hydrangea bush. The shrub was covered in drooping blossoms. Kat imagined the damp summer day. She wondered if her mother had cared that the humidity had lightly frizzed her usually smooth blond hair. Her mother looked at the person taking the photograph with a soft, sad expression on her face. One Kat had often seen. A faraway look in her eyes. Sybil had said she looked like her mother. The expression in the photograph was too familiar. She saw it every time she looked in the mirror.

But in the photograph, her mother held one of the blossom clusters in her hand so tightly its petals were crushed.

Not a posed shot, but one snapped when she'd been taken unaware.

Why had she crumpled the flower in her hand? The fist and the flower conveyed a tension in the shot that her face belied. And why had Kat never seen the picture before this moment?

Inside the drawer of the bedside table, where the photograph had been left, was also a key. It was an old brass skeleton key with an artistically scrolled stem and a faded crimson tassel hanging from its handle. It had no distinguishing marks on its surface to indicate what it might unlock.

Kat picked it up and put it into her pocket. She also kept the photograph. Somehow she couldn't leave it behind in the room as if it, too, along with her mother and her mother's life, had been abandoned and forgotten. She placed the scarf back in the drawer, determined that one day her sister would return to reclaim it.

She found nothing else beyond the ordinary until she opened a small drawer of a secretary desk that had been almost hidden behind a folding screen. The table was buried under a small hill of Victoria's discarded clothes. Inside, nestled on a soft handkerchief, was a heavy brooch made of iron that was tarnished at its rusty edges. A stylized *L* decorated its center. The monogram was eerily familiar. Katherine picked up the brooch, and a cool rush of gooseflesh prickled along her arm.

The iron was cold against her fingers, but its chill didn't account for the frisson of fear that followed.

Suddenly she felt as if she was being watched from the shadows.

Kat wrapped the brooch back in the handkerchief. She closed the drawer and glanced around one more time. No other belongings seemed unusual. She refused to let her nervousness rush her away. But she found nothing else during one last, quick sweep of the room.

She tried to ignore the tingle between her shoulder blades and the chill on the back of her neck.

The feeling was even worse in the corridor, where hundreds of eyes stared at nothing for eternity. She passed them quickly, trying to ignore the observation from inanimate eyes that were too real.

She took the brooch, the key, and the photograph of her mother back to her room.

Only when she closed the door did the feeling of being watched fade.

Chapter 8

The enclave nestled on the side of a mountain in the Western Carpathians on a range that ran through Slovakia, Hungary and Ukraine. Formerly an Eastern Orthodox monastery, the Order of Samuel had reclaimed the deserted castle-like structure for their training. Young novitiates were brought to the Order by train to Poprad-Tatry. Then they moved on to electric tram to reach High Tatras. From there, they proceeded on donkey up steep, winding trails to the enclave.

The strenuous journey was the first trial Reynard had conceived to test the strength and determination of those he called to serve. The wind, rain, ice and snow contributed to the monks' education.

There were many more trials, some so cruel they resulted in permanent scars or even death.

The abandoned castle wasn't the only abandoned thing Reynard used to fuel his obsession.

He traveled the world to recruit for the cause. The devout, the driven, the orphaned, the abused and neglected—all proved fertile ground for his teachings, lost boys made devoted servants when they were found. He gathered them to him like a pied piper, and all of them danced to his tune.

All but the members of the D'Arcy family.

They had been of Samuel's choosing.

Their reluctance to serve never allowed Reynard to forget it.

He'd come back to his mountain sanctuary to heal after the daemon attack that had left him near death in spite of his special blessings. His men had nursed him with special medicines and poultices and prayers, but it was his calling that had begun to close his wounds and strengthen his heart. He'd made a pledge to those who would help him to fulfill it. This cause now burned in him where a soul no longer resided.

Katarina had escaped with the child, sheltering the daemon's spawn against her blessed breast.

His pen scrawled on the page of parchment. The sound was loud in the room in spite of the wind and rain that lashed the thick antique bubbled glass of the windows in his high turret study. Occasionally he coughed and the spasm shook his body, jarring his wounds.

Once, monks had transcribed biblical teachings on similar parchment in this place.

His own missives were just as holy.

He dispatched instructions to his men around the globe. His hand shook with righteous fury he hadn't been able to express because of the physical weakness that still claimed him. That weakness also contributed to his shaking until his usual dark script was pale and scribbled on the page.

He would recover. He always did. He had done what was necessary to ensure his survival and success.

The ungrateful bitch.

As worthless and treacherous as her mother.

He had let the D'Arcy women roam free with only strands as fine as fishing line to bind them to the Order they should have been fervent to serve. All he asked was for them to lead his monks to their prey. They did not have to sully their delicate hands with Brimstone blood.

But he'd been too lenient.

As he'd lain close to the death that would have been the torturous end to all his plans, he had vowed to change that.

He scribbled and he planned.

This time, he would use real chains, not the symbolic bracelets that had failed to hold them. They would never be free again.

It was time for this D'Arcy generation to beget the next.

The letters he currently wrote were instructions for his best men to return to the enclave. From the thirteen he called home, he would choose the hardest and the most devoted to bed the D'Arcy sisters. This time he would have the men run a gauntlet of trials to prove their worth.

And if none of them rose to the top, he would take on the task himself.

He paused in his writing.

He sat back in his chair and closed his eyes as the idea made him lightheaded with possibility. His fountain pen slipped from his fingers. Ink flowed from its tip and pooled like a premonition of blood. At all times, he was conscious of his responsibility to lead the monks in the way they must go. He balanced fear with revelation, love with pain and righteousness with fury.

Perhaps only his seed would sire Seekers who deserved the affinity Samuel had wasted.

He rose from his chair and limped to the narrow window. The whole world stretched out beneath his domain, beginning with the sloped edges that formed the mountain pass. He'd begun his life in one of the modest villages in these Carpathian Mountains. Now he ruled an empire that begat life or death, depending on his whim.

No. Not his whim. His calling. His cause.

He was the true Father of the Order of Samuel, after all.

Chapter 9

The cello lured Severne through hallways haunted by the souls of the damned. They watched as he walked by. The woman's blessed hands deftly coaxed out the notes with a well-placed bow drawn over perfectly tuned strings, and the sound tortured him. More so than the doomed observers.

He'd lived a half life for a very long time. The music—her music—woke feelings in him he never allowed. Longing, desire, hunger. It was homesickness for the man he might have been without his grandfather's wicked bargain. He was a beast drawn to a beauty so poignant it caused his chest to fill with emotion he could only repress because there was nowhere safe for it to be expressed. But the emotion drove him as the music drew him. She lured him closer and closer to a place he'd forbidden himself to go.

She'd practiced all day. He was the opera's master. He knew the hours of the orchestra and the company. He'd avoided her siren song. After his dawn run, he'd slept fitfully, and then he'd gone to several meetings in a perfectly tailored suit that hid the tally marks on his arm and the dagger slash on his shoulder. He'd left Grim to wait and watch over her. He'd thought to miss her playing and thus its effect on him.

To no avail.

She never rested; therefore, nor could he.

He'd heard it wafting through the corridors as he'd loosened his tie.

He could have ignored it. He could have changed into shorts and hit the gym he'd specially engineered to hone away every ounce of softness in his flesh until he dimmed the ache of his bartered soul.

Could have, but didn't.

Instead, he walked barefoot down shadowy hallways with his suit loosened and his whole being less tamed by weights and ropes and old-fashioned medicine balls than it should have been.

He craved a different, sweeter penance.

Not one of lifting and pulling and sweat and blood, but one of kisses that could go no further and a soft, feminine body he didn't dare corrupt.

The cello, mellow and low, spoke louder and louder. He could feel its reverberations on his skin as if she touched him when she drew the bow again and again across its strings. He came to her door. He leaned his forehead against the cold wood.

Grim whined once and fell silent from the shadows, perhaps only half-materialized with his forepaws in Baton Rouge and his hindquarters in Paris.

Katherine paused in her playing, and he held his breath. Would she come to the door? Would his resolve be tested to an impossible degree? The moment stretched. Its tension was tighter than the cello's strings. His chest was so full, he had to expel his pent-up breath or the emotion, because there wasn't room for both inside him.

The woman on the other side of the hard wood against his face resumed her song and air escaped in a sigh through his parted lips. It was safe to breathe. Emotion was the dangerous thing to allow after all this time. Feeling had to be denied.

He was using her to fulfill an evil bargain signed in Severne blood. It was madness even to imagine tasting her lips again…or more. Her skin would be as soft as petals against his mouth. Her sighs as sweet.

No. Hell no, to put a finer point on it.

He backed away from the door without knocking. He left her alone with her music. Several hours in the gym would set him on course for victory. Damn him forever if he now felt hollowness in his chest that had been so full. He must succeed in this quest to save his father. He had to free him. Even if the price of that freedom meant he had to continue to suffer alone.

She'd felt him outside her door. He'd stood, resisting, then he'd gone away to bleed. Kat let him go, but her playing slowed and stuttered to a stop once he'd gone far enough. Or too far. Her affinity felt the loss of his presence. Keenly. She was compelled to put her cello in its case. She allowed the pull toward Severne's Brimstone blood to urge her out into the hallway to follow in his retreating footsteps.

He wasn't calling her.

He had resisted and rejected the connection between them. But his resistance called as surely as the damned beats of his heart.

She listened. She followed. It was always like this. She

could ignore the call, but not forever, and Severne's call was stronger than any she'd heard before. Worst of all, she didn't have Reynard on her heels contributing to her need to resist. Why not follow the magnetic pull of Severne's blood? So many logical reasons. None strong enough to obey.

When she found him, he was in his torture chamber of a gym. She hesitated when she saw him. His every muscle flexed as he lifted and released the weights on an oversized wooden contraption with an inhuman amount of heavy iron disks on massive chains.

She wavered in the doorway.

But she didn't turn away soon enough to avoid being frozen by what she'd seen. She might never turn. She might stand and ache to her bones for the torture he inflicted upon himself forever without being able to look away.

His jaw was set.

His body trembled.

He'd obviously taken his physical form to the brink of what it could do.

It was horrible and it was beautiful. She was caught at the door of his monk's cell where he'd come to hone his body rather than knock on her door. And there was no way she could do anything but follow the pull of his blood and her fascination over the gym's threshold. Only then, when her soft satin nightgown's sheen stood out against the wood and iron and chains, did she realize she'd walked through the opera house in her nightgown to respond to this daemon's call.

"Katherine?" Severne asked. He rose, allowing the weights to slam back down into place. The floor shook beneath the impact. She'd surprised him. She'd shocked herself. He'd already warned her away. But his blood called and her affinity for daemons answered. At least, that was the excuse she could claim. Stronger needs and urges had contributed to her entrance, but she wouldn't admit it.

"Tess said there was a patron named Michael who was interested in my sister," she said.

His dark eyes shone, as did his bare body beneath a sheen of perspiration.

They both knew she wasn't here because of Tess. Or her sister.

Severne reached for a towel and wiped down his chest and abdomen as he rose and came toward her. She didn't avert her eyes. Despite the surroundings, this wasn't 1852. She could look if she wanted to. And who wouldn't?

"You're learning more, just as we hoped you would," he said.

"Tess says he might be at the masquerade," Kat said.

"Everyone will be there, but I doubt the solution to your sister's disappearance will be that simple," he replied.

"I've never had the luxury of simple solutions," Kat said.

He was so hard, honed, as if he'd attempted to become stone, inside and out. Because her muscles weren't as obvious and her past was unknown to him, he assumed she was soft. He was wrong. She'd seen horrible things. She'd endured. She hadn't been soft even when she'd been in hiding. It was her strength that had allowed her to survive even then.

"I'm used to complicated," she continued.

Severne smiled. It was as tight a smile as a woman would expect from his angular face. But she saw something others might not see. In a face with eyes nearly black and lined with fine, white scars, his mouth was full and sensual. She'd tasted his kiss, and it had been a hint of softness in an otherwise steely man.

She wanted to taste it again.

He saw the direction of her eyes. If possible, the black in his eased to a hint of green. Only a trick of the light. A reduction of pupil that allowed striations of iris to be seen. It might cause his expression to soften to match his lower lip, but she couldn't read softness toward *her* in that.

The logical pep talk about the science of irises and how they reacted to light didn't keep her stomach from lightening, as well. She lost the firm footing of his hard, daemon appearance because of that subtle shift from hard to soft. It seemed to occur just for her.

He reached a calloused hand up to brush her hair back from her collarbone. Then he traced a gentle touch down her bare arm to her wrist. She trembled, but she didn't turn and run. He threaded a finger into her bracelet and lifted her wrist with it, carefully, gently. The Samuel medallion tinkled against its silver chain, a comfortable, familiar sound. But the sound contrasted with the moment, because he held the bracelet up to his daemon scrutiny, and his eyes had gone dark once more. They glittered beneath one raised brow.

"The Order of Samuel has chained you to a duty you detest, but you haven't removed their chains," he said.

"I'm not allowed to remove it. I've worn it since I was a small child," she said.

The silver glimmered in the light beneath Severne's dark gaze.

"Your chains are all around us," she reminded him. His gym looked like it had been built decades before modern equipment. Heavy iron chains and wood looked more like medieval torture devices than fitness machines. She could see the smooth surfaces of worn wooden handles indicating his long obsession.

"I don't wear them," he said.

"But you are marked," she noted. The tattoos on his arm

stood out starkly on bare, uncovered flesh. She reached with her other hand to touch the black slashes. He didn't pull away or drop her bracelet, but he did stiffen as if her touch on the marks pained him in some way.

"Mine wouldn't come off as easily as this," Severne said, tugging her closer with the tiny chain on his finger.

The scorched marks on his arm did seem permanent. Her delicate bracelet was slight in comparison. Until she remembered the mad glint in Reynard's eyes when he'd placed it on her arm. She still relived that moment in her nightmares.

They hadn't known Father Reynard was coming. If they had suspected, Mama would have packed up all their belongings so that they could flee. Kat had her own special travel case in the palest pink leather, and she'd been taught to keep it packed with necessities like underwear, a toothbrush and socks.

Her mother had sewn a special pocket into the lining of the suitcase for her doll, Lucie. She had bought the porcelain doll in a Parisian shop. Kat loved the red bow of Lucie's mouth and the blush on her cheeks. The dress Lucie wore was as finely made as a costume in one of her mother's productions.

But Lucie hadn't been packed safely away that night because Reynard caught them by surprise.

Her case was under the borrowed bed in a flat they'd stayed in the night before, after their mother sang in one of the grandest opera houses they'd ever seen. She'd had only a very small part, but it had been quickly accepted so that they could leave London in a hurry.

Katherine knew it was because Reynard had been closing in on them.

Now he had found them, and Katherine was old enough to know this kind of hide-and-seek wasn't really a game.

"Anne, you led me on a merry chase this time. Sydney? And only a bit part? But never mind. Here we all are, together at last," Reynard said.

Katherine stood with Victoria at attention like toy soldiers. Mother had told them to never argue with Reynard. Not because of love and respect, the way they didn't argue with her when she told them to eat their sprouts or wash their hands.

Reynard had madness in his eyes.

He was a bad man.

The worst Kat had ever seen in all her five years.

"I have a gift for your daughters. A gift for them and a reminder for you. Their father would have given it to them if a daemon hadn't killed him. Now it's up to me," Reynard said.

"No. Leave them alone," Anne D'Arcy protested.

Victoria had gasped.

Katherine could still hear the sound of her sister's shock. Their mother had broken a very important rule. And they saw her pay the price.

Reynard backhanded the petite contralto. He knocked her against the table holding Lucie, and both the doll and their mother had fallen. Lucie's cheek had shattered, but it hadn't been the jagged hole in the beloved face of her doll that had made silent tears course down Kat's face.

It had been the blood on her mother's mouth. The lovely face of Anne D'Arcy was suddenly unfamiliar as it swelled.

Neither of them rushed to their mother's side. She held up her hands to warn them away. They stood, quivering, good little soldiers, while Reynard turned from the woman he'd knocked to the ground.

"Your mother disappoints. Always she disappoints us.

But I have high hopes for you. High expectations of what you can do for the Order of Samuel," Reynard said.

They heard the tinkle of the silver medallions and the chains that would become so familiar to them as Reynard pulled them from his pocket.

"One for each of you. See the medallions? It is Samuel's figure upon them. He will go with you wherever you roam. To remind you of your gift and your sacred duty," Reynard said.

He fastened Victoria's around her wrist first. She didn't protest. Their mother stood. She didn't try to stop him again. She only watched silently and bled while they cried.

When Reynard took her hand, Kat grew lightheaded and weak. Repulsed by his evil, but confused by the affinity she hadn't learned to control or direct. He fastened the bracelet and stepped away, but not before Kat thought she detected the scent of a match, sulfuric and sickeningly sweet.

She coughed. She gagged. Reynard only laughed.

"And now we will go hunting," he said to their mother.

Katherine tucked Victoria in that night. She patted her shoulder as her sister cried. Lucie slept in the pink suitcase, a bandage carefully applied to her broken cheek. They would run again in the morning. Kat was small, but she knew how to be prepared.

It didn't matter that this time they would run in chains. They would run, and only running mattered.

"Sometimes being able to remove the chain makes its weight harder to bear," Katherine whispered.

"I know," Severne whispered back.

There were only inches left between them. He'd tugged her closer and closer, and she hadn't pulled away. The heat from his body easily penetrated the thin satin of her gown. From Brimstone or his workout or both, he was an inhuman torch. She sucked in her stomach and held her breath, sure that an inadvertent brush of skin to skin would burn.

Yet she craved the burn.

She'd been so careful for so long. Hiding. Silent. Severne called her from her protected places. And he knew it. She could see the knowledge in his eyes. He had decades of experience reading others. He could see why she hadn't pulled away. He kept himself hard and untouchable, but he was playing a game with her.

He'd tugged her closer to see what she would do.

"I'll find my sister in spite of the Order of Samuel. We'll walk away when we're ready. Together. That's why I'm here. We've run long enough. It's time to cast off our chains," Kat said.

"Easier said than done, but I'm fascinated by your determination," Severne said. He glanced down at the medallion in his fingers.

"I don't expect it to be easy," she said.

"Good. Nothing is easy at l'Opéra Severne. Trust me. Nothing. You've come to a hard place to make your stand," he said.

"Hard doesn't scare me," Kat said.

Finally, when he still didn't release her wrist, she pulled, and he let his finger slip from her silver chain. He let her go easier than she'd expected, quicker than she'd wished.

"You should have kept running," Severne said.

"The Brimstone is always there. No matter where I run or where I hide. The Brimstone is with me always," Katherine said.

She backed away from Severne's magnetism. He let her go. They were still the hardest steps she'd taken. Her feet felt like they slogged through nearly dried cement. Her body yearned to press toward his. She forced it to obey her will and move in the opposite direction.

John Severne lowered the hand that had held her bracelet and clenched it into a fist as if to stop from reaching out for her again.

"I know," he said.

Kat continued to force herself to move away from a daemon pull she hated to resist. She wanted to go back to him and magically wipe the marks from his arm and the scars from his flesh. She thought of her mother's long-ago injury and of Lucie's shattered cheek. She couldn't help Severne any more than she'd helped her mother or her doll all those years ago. She could only help the sister who needed her now more than ever.

She left John Severne standing with clenched fists surrounded by heavier chains than she'd ever borne.

Chapter 10

The orchestra pit of l'Opéra Severne was deeper and wider than most. It dipped between the auditorium seating and the stage like a moat, which would swell with rivers of dynamic sound rather than stagnate with water.

When the pit was full of musicians, it flowed with rivulets of body movement to create the mood and emotional sense of shows that were often in a language the audience didn't fully understand. It wasn't the printed translations that truly conveyed the meaning of opera. It was the music itself.

Opera, more than most other forms of theater, was about feeling. The size of the orchestra at l'Opéra Severne showed the intention of its master to encompass the hall with emotion.

Funny that.

A being as hard as stone ruling over a theater and an art form that was in its essence the very opposite of the face he showed the world.

Kat was alone in the orchestra pit.

Rehearsals were over for the day, and the conductor had retreated to his chair in the passage between the pit and the halls, where he nodded with the heavy breathing of deep sleep. The lights were low, mimicking the gloaming of twilight that occurred in the outside world.

Tess had tried to get her to go out for dinner with some of the other performers and musicians, but she'd stayed behind. She hoped the house would empty enough in the night that she would be able to spend some uninterrupted time with the key she'd found in Victoria's room.

For now, she played alone.

She'd managed to avoid John Severne for several days, but she couldn't keep him from her thoughts.

She didn't play any of the pieces from Gounod's *Faust*. Instead, she played "The Swan" from *The Carnival of the Animals* because the piece was elegant and fun and very French. The beauty of the music reflected the beauty of the opera house while holding back its shadows. Though she sat in darkness, "The Swan" surrounded her with light.

She didn't play to call Severne.

She intended no siren's song.

Yet, as her bracelet pressed against her skin beneath the long-sleeved shirt she wore to keep it from interfering with her bow, she couldn't help remembering the way he'd held her chain. He'd pulled her closer with the reminder of her service to the Order of Samuel. The irony of that was seductive. As if he'd made a direct challenge to the Order itself. The crook of a sexy daemon's finger tugging at her chain was hard to forget.

She didn't consciously shift to a darker piece, but emotions drove her when she played, especially when she played alone, and this time her feelings led her into Elgar, a yearning, melancholy concerto that reflected her thoughts of Severne more than it should. She played it through, then stopped, too overcome to go on.

"It's as if you knew when I'd arrive," Severne said.

Katherine relaxed back from her playing position. She dropped her bow hand and breathed out in a long sigh to release the air she'd been controlling while she played.

Severne stepped from the tunnel into the orchestra pit. His dark suit was pinstriped charcoal gray, but even with its modern sheen, it hadn't revealed his presence in the shadows. Had she felt him approach and subconsciously changed her song? Probably. Would she admit it? Never.

"The light has diminished. Night is falling outside," she said. It was perfectly true, just not the true reason her song had changed.

"It's always night in the theater," Severne noted.

He'd paused at the doorway when her playing halted, but now he placed his hands in his pockets and approached. His suit jacket was unbuttoned. The white shirt beneath looked lavender in the dimmed hall's lights. His tie, though probably black, seemed a darker purple.

She was reminded of the calla lilies in his office. Which, in turn, reminded her of the taste of his lips.

"The hush of an empty pit appeals to me. I love the size and depth of l'Opéra Severne's pit. I like to fill it. To play in the silence," Kat said.

She stood to put her cello away, but he was already close enough to get in her way. He stood between her and her open case with exaggerated ease.

As usual, his casual posture was a lie. His true emotion was in the tightness of his jaw and the rigidity of his shoulders. He had come to her, but he didn't like that he had.

"The Théâtre de l'Opéra Severne was built in the seventeen hundreds. It was one of the first major buildings in Baton Rouge. The city rose around us. Severne Row has always been kept sacrosanct. The other neo-Gothic buildings in this district were all built to my grandfather's specifications. Some say he even influenced the architecture of the capitol," Severne said.

The impromptu history lesson became seductive in his smoky accent. Her cello was no barrier between them. His body leaned toward hers as if he imparted a confession or was about to.

"I share this because even though it was built long before you were born, I would like to go back and personally construct it, stone by stone, with my bare hands, to give you the perfect place to play. L'Opéra Severne wasn't built for you. But I wish it had been. You fill the silence well," Severne said.

As confessions went, it was a killer. His hands were still in his pockets. Hers trembled. Her lips had gone numb from all the things she couldn't say.

"It pleases me that you like this orchestra pit. It shouldn't. I should wish you away from this place," Severne said. "You should go."

His hands came from his pockets, and she held her breath. She needed him to be dark and dangerous. This gentle appreciation, though reluctantly given, was dangerous in a far more enticing way.

This time, he didn't search out her bracelet. He simply took her hand. Only when she felt the warmth of his palm did she know hers had been cold.

He cupped her hand, palm up, in his and lifted it to the soft light nearer his searching eyes. With his other hand, he traced calloused fingers over her calloused fingertips. He lightly touched each permanent crease caused by her cello's strings.

She forced herself to breathe. It was a triumph to appear

calm. To take in air, lightly and normally, while her entire universe narrowed to his touch on her hand.

She should have pulled her hand away. When he touched her fingers, he plumbed the depths of her soul. Her greatest strength and weakness was written in the indentions on her hand.

"Art is pain, but you wear it well. You have a soft, feminine body, but when I hold you, I discover hidden strength. You have to be strong to play as well as you do. Physically and emotionally. You have to be able to climb and plummet and coax the depths and heights from the strings," Severne said.

She was hypnotized by his perception. She couldn't pull away. When he leaned closer to her hand, but looked up to make contact with her eyes, she held her breath again. Weak in the knees though he perceived her as strong.

"But it's the marks from the strings that show the true sacrifices you've made. You've given flesh and blood to song," he said.

She couldn't help it. When he pressed his lips to her calluses, one by one, brushing each digit with a kiss, she released her pent-up breath in a long, shaky sigh.

He watched her.

Yet she couldn't pretend to be aloof and untouched. Her eyes closed with each press of his lips and opened in fear and expectation of the next.

"Don't tremble, Katherine. I'm not here to seduce you. I shouldn't be here at all. I know that," he said.

The hot coil in her stomach tightened as he paused over the last finger before gifting it with a brush of his lips, as well.

Then he lowered her hand and lifted his head, and she took possession of what he had temporarily claimed.

He was not a modern man. In spite of the contemporary cut of his suits and his painfully sculpted physique, Severne was a daemon that had lived through past times. He had made love to her by those old-fashioned standards. Her body might stand in the twenty-first century, but every inch of her throbbed nearly replete from the touch of his lips on her hand.

And the wicked, worldly creature knew it. He had the experience of decades with which to read her response.

He smiled.

"I've had a long day, and I need to retreat to my gym before we both regret my…lingering," he said. He punctuated the words with a very Gallic shrug.

"Good night," Kat managed to reply.

But she didn't try to put away her cello until he had stepped aside and walked away.

Chapter 11

She'd asked Tess about the key. Tess had explained that all the private dressing rooms had keys like the one she'd found. She'd advised Kat to turn it in to the costume matron because one of the principal players must have misplaced it.

Vic's dressing room hadn't been reassigned, though some of the costumes had been shifted to her understudy's room.

The key was heavy in the pocket of Katherine's silk pajamas tonight.

She'd played her cello in her room after leaving the orchestra pit long after midnight, when the opera house slumbered around her. Except for Severne, who had probably labored in his gym longer than she labored over her strings. Now she quietly clicked open her bedroom door and crept toward the hidden hallway beneath the stage that was lined with private dressing rooms. She'd decided against dressing in something other than her sleepwear.

If anyone saw her, let them assume she was sleepwalking or headed to the kitchen for a midnight snack. She hadn't visited the cook's domain yet, but others who lived in the opera house treated it like the kitchen of their own home.

Severne would have given her a formal tour, but she didn't want his audience. She couldn't trust him not to mislead or misdirect. She was drawn to him, but it was an impulse she couldn't safely indulge.

John Severne was the opera's master. If a wealthy patron was involved in her sister's disappearance, then he might not be as interested in helping her find her sister's abductor as he intimated.

It wasn't only l'Opéra Severne that had mysterious shadows. Its owner was shadowed in his own right.

Kat slipped through the dark opera house. She moved with silent steps on slippered feet through passages that watched her progress with wooden eyes. She purposefully avoided looking at the murals. They gamboled around her, chaotic and indistinct in the darkness.

Somewhere a hellhound prowled and a daemon brooded. She was only a silent wraith wandering in search of the truth. If only she didn't suspect that the secret she probed was bigger and older than Victoria's disappearance.

She came to the room she searched for, still marked with a placard bearing her sister's assumed name. She took the key from the pocket of her silk pajamas and fumbled to insert it into the slot in the dark.

Kat cringed when the key slid home.

The rattle of metal against metal was loud in the silent corridor.

She held her breath.

Her heart pulsed in her ears, an embarrassing whoosh that mocked her. *Go get back in your warm, safe bed*, it said.

But her shoulders stiffened in response. Her spine went to stone. She stood her ground. She waited.

No growl. No steps. No whispering sibilance came from the sconces or the vents or the walls.

She turned the key farther, and oiled tumblers responded smoothly. In the quiet hallway, even the easy operation of the mechanism shouted her presence to a malevolent world. *Here she is. What is she doing? Why is she here where she doesn't belong?*

She opened the door anyway.

The dusty cool air of the hallway met the rush of stale, closed-up air from the abandoned dressing room. Powder, freesia, hair spray…her sister's professional persona of wigs and stage makeup and elaborate make-believe wafted out to envelop her. It was subtly different than Vic's personal scent, but just as familiar to a beloved sister who worked side by side with a lyric soprano.

The opera was an escape for Victoria as it had been for their mother, but it was an escape that hinted at dark fantasy and the undercurrents of melodrama they lived with every day, both gorgeous and awful, both life and death, filled with lush, deadly beauty.

Their life, and the work that hid them from that life, were both music and madness.

Kat slipped into the room and shut the door behind her. Only then did she click on the lights. They sputtered to life in a flickering, unreliable glimmer from a mirror framed by glass bulbs that seemed almost as old as l'Opéra Severne itself.

Besides the dressing table, there were two lounges in the style of seventeenth-century fainting couches. Their upholstery was a faded tapestry that indicated they were authentic antiques. She jumped when the other denizens of the room were revealed. Several tall, headless dress forms stood naked to the side.

She calmed her heart, and then ignored a sudden pinch of emotion as she realized the barren forms had held her sister's costumes that had been taken to the understudy's room.

Kat walked over to one of the dress forms and placed her hand on its shoulder. The cage beneath its waist would have supported the heavy bustled skirts and petticoats of Victoria's costume. Now it looked skeletal. The papier-mâché bodice felt hollow beneath her hand.

The dress form was nothing without her sister.

Victoria D'Arcy would have been the most famous name in opera if she hadn't had to live a life in hiding. She'd taken smaller roles in smaller theaters than her talent deserved. She'd had to use assumed names, often changing her appearance and losing roles because she auditioned without her full résumé.

Kat turned from the form and stepped toward the mirror. In its wavy, vintage glass, the room behind her was emptier and darker. What had this room seen? She suddenly wished the shadows could whisper their secrets. Behind her, layers upon layers of old posters and playbills plastered the walls. Like the dress form, she felt papier-mâchéd by a hundred years of dramatic make-believe. What truths were hidden behind it all?

She forced herself to sit at the dressing table and open the drawers one by one. Tons of cosmetics and toiletries rattled and rolled at her touch. Among the jumble, an anomaly stood out.

Kat's gasp was more of a choked exclamation. She forced herself to reach out and scoop up the unmistakable charm bracelet her sister never removed. The matching bracelet on her own wrist tinkled gently like chimes whenever she moved.

But her sister's bracelet was drastically altered. It had been blackened until the Order of Samuel medallion hanging from it was charred. The sound it made as she turned it this way and that to examine it was dead and dull.

Her fingers shook as she held Vic's bracelet up to try to ascertain what had caused the damage. Fire? Brimstone? They had never removed the bracelets. They'd been afraid to. Just as Katherine always wore sleeves that pressed her bracelet to her skin to keep it from interfering with her bowing, Victoria altered her costumes to hide the chain whenever it was necessary.

Had Victoria removed it herself, or had someone ripped it from her wrist? And did the condition of the blackened metal tell a terrible truth about her sister's condition? Was she hurt…or worse?

Kat held the bracelet in her fist for a long time. Tears burned behind her eyes. She willed them away. She carefully placed her sister's bracelet in her pocket. She refused to give up hope. The bracelet wasn't a warning or a premonition. It was only another clue. A piece in a puzzle she would solve to find her sister, safe and sound.

Victoria was fine.

Kat would find her.

The only thing the bracelet revealed was that she was on the right track. She would pick up every precious bread crumb until she finally reached her sister's side.

She put her elbows on the powdery surface of the table and rested her face in her hands, but just as she began to close her eyes, the reflection of a name caught her eye.

Kat stood and turned.

Not only a name. She recognized a face and a particular set of eyes she'd known as well as she knew her own.

She moved toward the wall with hesitant steps.

From the vanity to the poster, she traveled back in time

twenty years. Her mother had been a lovely Marthe. It was the fluttering corner of her poster that had caught Kat's attention and drawn her eyes to her mother's name. The paper was yellow and curled. She reached to touch the face she'd lost before she'd lost Victoria. Her sister had done the same. Kat knew she must have. Vic had stood where she stood now with her fingers trembling and tears on her lashes, with her heart trapped in the tightening cage of her chest. Had her sister remembered the full contralto swell of their mother's voice singing lullabies to her children as easily as she sang her dramatic roles?

Victoria must have peeled back the loosened corner. Kat peeled it back, as well. The move revealed a seam in the wood that ran down to her knees. It was a cupboard, one that had been papered shut decades ago.

But it had been loosened much more recently than that.

Kat slid several lacquered nails down the seam to edge it open. Inside was a shallow enclosure built into the wall. Perhaps it had been installed for costume jewelry or other small valuables, but the only thing in it now was a small bundle of folded letters bound in a faded satin sash.

She recognized the old belt to her childhood dress.

As she reached to close her hand around the stack, she glanced at the mirror over her shoulder. In it, her reflection looked small and humble and completely dwarfed by a hulking shadow on the wall. She reached for the stack of letters, and as she did, the shadow shifted and changed. The black mass of it swelled bigger and bigger. Large wing-like projections unfurled and stretched from corner to corner of the room. In the reflection, she was sheltered or threatened beneath those shadowy wings.

Kat left the letters where they lay and whirled. She stared at the shadow to determine where it came from. A flood of instinctive energy rushed to her legs, urging her to flee. Was it adrenaline that made the room seem colder? She could see nothing that would cast the shadow, and neither dress forms nor couches had moved. The lights around the mirror flickered and flashed. The wings stretched as if they would envelop her. But it had to be a trick of the light. She was in no danger from darkness.

As she tried to calm her heart and ignore the urge to run, the tip of one wing lifted from the wall.

The translucent shadow that was no mere shadow reached out to her and touched her cheek in a feathery slide down her face.

These black feathers would never give her freedom or happiness.

Her body went suddenly cold. Ice radiated outward from the shadow's touch as if flowing superchilled through her veins. She cried out, and the sound escaped from hard lips in a puff of white. A tingling numbness was following the ice. Her body was freezing while she tried to tell herself it couldn't be.

The whole room dimmed. The shadow was detaching itself from the wall. There were whispers now, all around. Urgent shushes and hushes she no longer wanted to hear.

She could think of only one person who might be able to combat the freeze.

Kat flung herself forward and away from the shadow. She wrenched open the door and began a stumbling run down the hall. It was desperate and probably foolish, but in that moment, John Severne and his Brimstone's fire seemed a salvation.

Whatever peace he'd achieved from hours of weights was shattered when the woman he'd tortured himself to forget rushed into the sanctum of his private gym. Grim leaped to his feet from his place at the door, but he didn't

confront Katherine D'Arcy. He faced out toward the hallway instead, his hackles raised and a growl rumbling deep
in his chest. The dog's hind legs dug into the floor until
his claws pitted the rug as if he expected to be met and
slammed with great opposition.

Severne was lathered, spent, self-flagellated to nothing
but muscle and bone.

Still, he rose.

He met Kat as her momentum brought her to his side,
but he didn't take her in his sweat-slicked arms. Instead,
he faced the hallway as Grim faced it, planted, prepared,
an unuttered growl filling his chest.

Kat stopped. She turned to face the hallway, as well.

"C-c-cold. S-so c-cold," she stuttered.

It was only then that he saw she quaked until her teeth
chattered as she tried to speak.

He had nothing to give her except the damnation in
his veins.

While Grim guarded the door, Severne turned to the
woman beside him and took her in his arms. Hours of
forced separation and austerity fell away. This was what he
most wanted and most feared. She was shivering, and her
soft skin was ice against him beneath the delicate silk pajamas that provided no warmth. Thankfully, they provided
no barrier, either. He hissed from the pain as their bodies
came together. Her ice and his fire. Immediately he felt
the drain as her frozen body absorbed his Brimstone heat.

More pain of a different sort flared when she touched
him, both palms coming against his chest. Only strength
of will kept him from dropping to his knees. The ice was
agony. The contact was worse. Her reaching for him in
need was torturous.

In spite of the pain, or maybe because he needed the
lash of it to keep from feeling her softness, Severne pulled

her closer. She'd been touched by a banished daemon, one that wasn't fully contained in the walls. His lean form pulsed with Brimstone. Banished daemons were completely drained of fire. How had one managed to free itself, and why had it reached out to Katherine?

Kat pressed into him, seeking his warmth.

Torture? He'd been tortured his whole existence, but Katherine hungry for his damned heat was worse than any hardship he'd ever endured. He gave it to her while holding an untouchable part of himself back. Here, now, he burned for her. He saved her with hell's fire.

He'd been right that her skin would be perfect and soft. He had reason to caress it now. Her cold was the perfect excuse to slide his Brimstone-heated hand over her skin. She trembled, but she didn't ask him to stop. Cold, fear, desire—what fueled her shivers? He held her with a strong arm behind her back while he ran his other hand gently over her arms, each one from shoulder to wrist, purposefully ignoring the tinkle of her silver chain.

A flush rose in response to his touch. Her pale, frozen flesh was brought back to heat and life. The silk of her nightclothes was nothing compared to the softness of her.

From her arms, he slid his hand over each leg, torturing himself at the tremble of her thighs and the seduction of silk in the V between them. But he devoted himself to giving her his heat without demanding anything in return. No more intimacy than this. She would be cradled in his arms and accept the heat of his touch and him. The pleasure of nearly innocent exploration was a test for his control.

Noting how her nipples peaked the silk of her top wasn't innocent, nor was his swelling erection.

But he ignored his ache to tend to her. She trembled in his arms. She warmed. She relaxed.

He brushed his hand against her face, and she sighed.

She leaned into his palm. She didn't stop him when he moved his hand to her bared neck. She only opened her eyes and watched through her lashes as he slid his fingers from her neck to her chest, where he spread them between the fullness of her breasts.

Her heartbeat was rapid but steady.

Not frozen.

Not anymore.

His Brimstone was a blessing for just this night. He was no daemon. But he was also no saint. He lightly teased his palm over and under one heavy breast, and she gasped, but she didn't pull away. He tested the weight of her in his hand, but only for a moment before he slid his palm to her stomach.

There, beneath her ribs, she was still far too cold.

He gathered her closer. He pressed his hand tight. He willed his heat into her. He wasn't afraid. His fear had been burned away long ago, but he was suddenly desperate to warm her.

"You're safe," he said. As he held her and healed her, he would have accepted eternal torment rather than let anything hurt her. He would hurt her. One day soon. He would betray her. But he held her now and helped her. He gave her all, if only for a few moments.

"That's a lie, but I'll risk it. I don't want to freeze to death," Kat said.

Too soon, but not soon enough, she flushed in his arms. He sensed when her body temperature was closer to normal. Her shivers stopped. She sighed.

"Is l'Opéra Severne haunted?" she asked against his shoulder.

"No. There are no ghosts here that I've ever seen, and I've walked these halls a long time. There are only souls doomed to a limbo even the damned don't deserve," he replied.

"The walls…the murals," she said. She no longer shivered from the cold, but she did shudder as she comprehended one of the opera house's darkest secrets.

"Don't look. Don't touch. There's nothing you can do for them. This is a war that began before you were born. Before I was born. They're casualties of war. Gone but never forgotten," Severne said.

"They're suffering," Kat said.

She trembled now. His body felt every subtle reaction to his touch. She was no longer cold. She didn't need his Brimstone heat. There were other needs shifting into focus.

She was warm now.

His body beneath her hands was a living furnace. Her shivers had stopped, but she still trembled. Severne was back in his workout shorts. His black hair was damp against his forehead. His muscles beneath her fingers were honed and hard.

She tilted her chin to look up at his face. His cheeks were flushed from exertion, from Brimstone, but also, maybe, from her touch? He'd shielded her from the door with his body. Grim had crouched down, warily watching the hall, but silent now. The icy threat had been burned away by Severne's fire.

It was momentary. This truce. This shelter. This shield. But she gave in to appreciation anyway.

Kat lifted her hand from his chest to his face. Such a perfectly chiseled cheek and jaw. No softness. Had immortality worn it away or had he been nothing but hard and harsh from birth? Yet…he tilted down. He leaned over her. He cradled her body in his arms. How could she not take advantage of the curve in his spine? She rose on tiptoe before he knew what she intended. That had to be the explanation for why he allowed it. First she pressed her lips to his hard jaw, and then it was only a whisper of movement to taste his mouth. Sweet, salty, smoky skin. Full, firm, slightly open lips. Once. Twice. She brushed her mouth against his. Again, then deeper again.

He sighed, but it was an exhalation of protest. More like a moan. As if her hesitant lips hurt him. Still, he sank into her. He met her hesitation with the sudden dip of his tongue. It was a stolen moment. He pulled back from her too soon. Never really softened. Tasted but not fully touched. At least, not for long enough to last.

"Don't be grateful. I don't deserve it," he said. "Grim, show us the way."

He took her hand and pulled her out the door. The way was shadowy and long. At times she thought they were no longer in the opera house at all. There was a strong scent of crushed pine needles beneath their feet and the rush of cold air from a coniferous forest at night. There was the soft nip of snow, warm compared to the ice she'd felt before.

But Grim responded to Severne's commands. Stop. Go. Run.

Finally, after a long journey, much longer than if they'd taken the normal route, they stood at the door to her room. The corridor was blissfully too dark for her to see the faces.

"We'll guard your door until morning," Severne promised. "I said you were safe, but you aren't. You're in danger. Never more so than when you willingly step into my arms."

"I'm not cold anymore," she responded.

He watched as she stepped into her room. She slowly, slowly shut the door against him. She leaned into the wood, feeling his heat from the other side.

He said she was in danger. But she was warm again.

In many ways, she felt warm for the first time.

Chapter 12

Kat huddled over a steaming cup of chamomile tea, neither soothed nor warmed as much as she'd hoped to be by the cozy brew. She'd left the letters in the cabinet, abandoned, because of the shadow. In the light of day, her retreat would have seemed ludicrous if not for the deep ache of chilled marrow in her bones.

She couldn't go back to the room during the day, when the whole opera house was full of people bustling in the halls. She had no legitimate reason to have and use the key in her pocket. Did she dare go back at midnight?

She wasn't sure she'd survive another brush with the shadow's frigid wings.

Kat couldn't seek out Severne's heat. Not when he'd warned her away. The tea was a meager substitute. Her fingers wrapped around the cup, almost as if to keep themselves from seeking more dangerous things.

She couldn't retrieve the letters. She couldn't approach

Severne, but what of Sybil? The costume matron had a ring of keys at her waist like a housekeeper from a hundred years ago. She must have been in all the dressing rooms a thousand times.

A thousand times a thousand?

She remembered Severne's confession and just like that, the hot tea on her lips was a reminder of Severne's much hotter mouth. A rapidly cooling reminder that wasn't helping at all.

She rose, abandoning the useless tea.

Sybil might have seen the shadow. She might have felt its chill. Maybe she could shed some light on Katherine's dilemma. Though as Kat left her room to seek out the woman she'd seen only in candlelight, finding illumination at l'Opéra Severne seemed an impossible quest.

Several technicians directed her down a winding spiral staircase beneath the main stage. It led to a hushed space with a cramped, low ceiling and bare bulbs sparsely placed along a long hall. When she thought she couldn't stand the claustrophobic confines of the long wooden tunnel any longer, the hallway led out from under the stage and opened up into a much more cavernous room.

Double doors sat across from her—seven-foot-tall wooden doors with heavy iron fittings and a closed-to-all-intruders feel that made her hesitate to approach. She squared her shoulders, took a deep breath of dusty, stale air and walked up to them anyway.

She reached for the latch and creaked one door open enough to slip inside. Her chest expanded when she saw the interior of the room stretched out impossibly deep before her. The room was lined from the double doors to the distant shadows with racks of textiles. Three layers of racks with the topmost ones accessible only by rolling ladders like those she'd seen in the opera house office. Several ladders had been left waiting should they need to be used. They were crafted of scrolled iron like the staircase she'd used to reach this level.

Suits, dresses, petticoats and hats. Her eyes strained to widen and focus enough to perceive the entirety of contents on the racks. Cloaks, gowns and crowns. She saw everything and nothing because it was a mass of structured confusion, a whole conglomeration of separate parts pressed together in rows that couldn't be distinguished from each other. Feathers, silk, satin, poplin, crepe, muslin, wool, cotton, batiste, calico, brocade, lace…and she knew who must be in charge of it all.

Suddenly *costume matron* didn't seem like a pretentious title.

Kat's eyes were dazzled and her senses dizzied by the riot around her. She stepped forward between the towering rows, an Alice in a dark wonderland of make-believe as colorful as any fantasy garden, but blanketed in shadows.

Polished boards protested under her feet, and far above her head, the rafters also evidenced the crowd of performers passing to and fro upstairs. The racks seemed neverending. They disappeared in a blur of unlit recesses she couldn't quite see.

Mephistopheles loomed beyond a far row of costumes. She could see his ram-like horns and his arched brows. The warehouse wasn't only for costumes. It held a props town of discarded giants. They created gruesome shadows in the distance. She didn't head that way. The great devil's head with its grinning maw repelled her.

Instead she chose a path down the costume rows. The only illumination came from a distant source of light she couldn't see. It wasn't bright enough. She began to hope a helpful caterpillar would show up in a cloud of smoke to help her with tricky questions that might ultimately reveal her way.

"What exactly have you come looking for?" Sybil's voice came from behind a long row of red coats with tarnished brass buttons. Her voice came from high and then low as she climbed down a ladder and wheeled it into sight.

Somehow she'd expected the costume matron to be as hard to deal with as Alice's caterpillar.

"I'm not sure," Katherine said.

How did she ask about threatening shadows on the walls? The question was ridiculous now as she faced a woman who lived and worked in these shadows every day.

"I wondered when you'd find your way here. Most of the women and even the men have already chosen. Only a few stragglers haven't been here, and they'll be left with moth-eaten rejects," Sybil said.

She came into the light wearing another old-fashioned dress with a nipped waist and full skirts. This time she had her pincushion on a strap around her wrist and a measuring tape draped around her neck like a jaunty scarf in addition to the jangle of her keys.

Her mention of moths was a joke. In spite of the age of the collection around her, Kat would bet there wasn't a moth nibble to be found in the whole warehouse. With Sybil on guard, they wouldn't dare.

"I saved something for you. Eric insisted and I agreed," Sybil said. She smiled, and it was a *Mona Lisa* tilt of her lips.

"Thank you. Tess said I should ask you about a costume for the masquerade, but I've been busy with other things," Kat said.

She followed as the other woman wordlessly nodded and led the way down one packed row. Instead of ending in darkness, this row curved into a well-lit alcove where an old theater ghost light had been left burning. She'd seen its light from a distance before. She wasn't surprised that one large globe was the only light in the warehouse. It was fitting. Sybil wasn't afraid of shadows. It also amused her to see that the dust motes that swirled in the glow of the light resembled smoke. Sybil was no caterpillar in wonderland, but she was as confounding. The ghost light's glow revealed a ball gown that was out of place among the old costumes.

Constructed of delicate, uneven layers of ivory tulle and white satin, the voluminous skirts were more modern than vintage, an almost sculptural masterpiece. Above the skirts that had been calculated to be jagged—a fairy-tale dress, but one with dark Gothic edges—there was a gossamer bodice constructed of thousands of tiny, clear gems.

The gown was perfect for a masquerade at l'Opéra Severne.

Kat wasn't sure if she was bold enough to wear it.

To wear this dress would be to embrace the very things she should have been resisting—Severne, mysterious shadows, daemon desires.

When Sybil lifted the dress from its form, which was eerie in its mimicry of Katherine's own figure, the fabric shimmered in the ghost light like a candle's soft champagne glow come to life. The fluttering edges of fabric as Kat took the dress in her hands mimicked flickering flame.

"Severne will be all in black, of course. Unrelieved as usual. I admit I had that in mind when I designed this dress for you," Sybil said.

"You made this for me?" Katherine asked.

"For you," Sybil said. "From the day you arrived."

"That's impossible. A gown like this would take months to construct…" Kat protested.

Sybil turned fully toward her. She'd been hidden behind the folds of dress, but now she was illuminated by the ghost light's bulb. Kat felt it only then. The burn of Brimstone. Dim, banked, a fire that had been allowed to turn to ash, but definitely there. Beneath Sybil's beautiful skin, far less lined than it should have been if she'd served as costume matron of l'Opéra Severne as long as it seemed.

Kat stepped back. The dress was no shield between them. The light of it no protection from Sybil's darkness.

"Don't be afraid. You have nothing to fear...from me," Sybil said.

"But from others? From icy shadows? From Severne?" Kat asked.

"Much to fear from those things. Much to face. But you can do it. Eric told me how you saved him," Sybil said.

"His mother died," Katherine said.

"She isn't dead. You can still save her. And all the others," Sybil said.

"But Severne..." Kat began.

"Fear him. Definitely. You are a pleasure to him, and he cuts pleasure from his life, ruthlessly. No quarter given even if it causes him pain. Especially if it causes him pain. He's determined to be damned, you see. It's his price to pay. His personal penance. He believes in redemption only for others. Not for himself."

"Daemons can't be trusted," Kat said.

"Never. You've taken the ball gown I designed for you, Katherine D'Arcy. I have sewn it with my own hands. You owe me something in trade. I will tell you when it's time to pay," Sybil said.

Her words rang out with a formality Katherine recognized. The moment stilled and crystalized just as back in Savannah, when John Severne had traded her cello for Eric. She couldn't move. She couldn't drop the dress. She suspected it would cling to her fingers like a glistening spider web even if she could force her digits to open and release it. She'd made another agreement with Brimstone blood. It was too late to reject the dress. Her heart had accepted it. Her skin already flushed against the tickle of tulle and satin. The bejeweled bodice might as well already cup her breasts. It would fit her perfectly.

The costume matron had the experience of immortal eyes.

"There's always a price to be paid," Katherine said.

She was as she had been in Savannah, under the influence of a daemon bargain she hadn't meant to accept.

"Please feel free to explore for shoes or accessories. I must see to Eric before nightfall. He wanders around the opera house more than he should," Sybil said.

"Would Grim bother the boy?" Kat managed to ask. Sybil had taken the dress from her hands and placed the gown back on the dress form while Kat still struggled to make her body respond to her will.

"No. I don't think the hound would harm him. He's in no danger…from Grim," Sybil said. The new knowledge Kat had gained about the costume matron's daemonic nature made every word from her mouth seem mysterious and vague. But the daemon woman covered the dress she'd made for Kat with a sheet using regular, unhurried movements, taking care of business as usual before she nodded a goodbye.

Kat watched her leave until only a rattle of keys in the distance proved she'd been there in the first place.

She was left in the warehouse.

Alone.

The sheet-draped figure was almost sentient beside her. It stood, keeping the secret of what Sybil might want in exchange for its Gothic beauty in the future. It took several more long minutes before she could breathe normally. Before she could move.

Kat backed away. She didn't turn off the ghost light. It was the only illumination she had. She didn't intend to search the gloomy warehouse for shoes with Sybil gone. The discovery that the costume matron was a daemon with hidden motives and desires had given the warehouse a creepier atmosphere. Now its shadowy depths were threatening, the looming props more grotesque. Mephistopheles grinned and seemed all-knowing as if the giant papier-mâché devil had foretold the surprise of Sybil's nature and enjoyed Katherine being trapped into another bargain she hadn't intentionally sought.

But as she made her way back down the aisle, footsteps interrupted her progress. They were slow, measured and unhurried.

Someone else was in the warehouse.

Probably another performer who had been encouraged to look for accouterments for the masquerade or a technician who had come to hunt for a replacement for a prop that had failed. Definitely not dress forms or papier-mâché come to life to intercept her retreat.

Kat stopped and turned to confront whoever or whatever controlled the steps that approached.

Somehow, a few seconds of waiting told her heart who the other person in the warehouse would be.

John Severne came out from the shadows surrounding the jumbled props town. He wasn't in workout clothes or a suit. He wore jeans and a faded T-shirt, form-fitting but more casual on him than she'd previously seen. He looked dusty, ordinary and too approachable. His approachability was far more frightening than a shuffling dress form or an animated prop with evil intentions would have been.

"I heard Sybil leave. Did she give you a key?" Severne asked.

The only key she had was hidden in her pocket. She didn't want to admit the key to Victoria's dressing room was still in her possession.

"She wouldn't lock us in," Kat said.

"Wouldn't she? Sybil often has her own agenda," Severne said. He seemed intrigued. Maybe amused. But not alarmed.

She hurried to the doors she'd opened to enter the warehouse. They were shut tight. When she tried the handle, it wouldn't budge beneath her fingers.

"I'm supposed to be looking for shoes," she told the door. She almost hated to turn around and face Severne, though she could tell he had walked up behind her.

"I'm sure someone will come down to let us out soon," he said.

Locked in a deserted warehouse with an approachable Severne. Kat tried to breathe normally. She willed her heartbeat to calm. It wasn't claustrophobia or panic. It was anticipation. Okay, maybe a little bit of panic.

She turned to face him. Better late than never. She was cautious, but she was no coward. In fact, just like the night when he'd come to her with her cello in Savannah, she felt an adrenaline response to being near him when she shouldn't have been. Being trapped near him was a whole other level of temptation. She couldn't flee, so why not enjoy the fall?

"We could call for help," she suggested. "Maybe Grim would come?"

"There's no danger here. I don't think there's cause for alarm. Let's finish what we started and see if someone comes by the time we're ready to leave," Severne suggested.

She should leave. Now. Because she didn't really want to go.

This down-to-earth Severne was worse than the stoic opera master. His raven hair was liberally sprinkled with dust. His handsome face was smudged. His jeans were worn until they fit his hips and thighs like a well-loved denim glove.

"And what were you doing down here?" she asked.

"I was revisiting old friends from *Turandot*, *Parsifal* and *The Nightingale*. I usually choose what the company performs after the summer's *Faust*," Severne said.

He'd named a few of the most popular operas for children, dark fairy tales full of fanciful music and colorful costumes.

"Shows very different from *Faust*," Kat noted.

"Yes. They are," Severne said. "They were my favorites once. I like to recall a simpler time."

They stood face-to-face in the shadows, and she suddenly wished for more ghost light. A nostalgic daemon was intriguing. Too intriguing. It hinted that she'd been right. Severne might have a heart beneath his hard, muscled chest.

"I'm here for the masquerade. Sybil gave me a dress. I still need shoes," Kat said.

A daemon drawn to operatic fairy tales was a dark contrast she didn't dare explore. Not when her eyes already searched his for traces of green.

"Ah, speaking of fairy tales, *Cinderella*, then," Severne said.

Unexpectedly, he reached and took her hand. She didn't pull her fingers from his. She didn't jerk away to pound on the door and demand her release. She probably should have. In Severne's strangely playful company, this dusty prison might prove too decadent.

But it was only shoes, after all.

How dangerous could that be?

She followed where Severne led.

Thankfully, they avoided the all-knowing smile of Mephistopheles.

Instead he pulled her toward another row she'd yet to see, where floor-to-nearly-ceiling racks of cubbyholes were filled with shoes to accompany the costumes. They'd passed the alcove where the dress was still covered in its sheet. The way Sybil had revealed it to her made her feel that Severne hadn't seen it before.

Yet he seemed to know exactly where he was going.

With no hesitation, he searched the racks of shoes until they came to a numbered slot with too many digits for her to note. He left her standing near it until he disappeared around the corner and then reappeared with a stool.

He unfurled its folded legs and set it near her. He nodded toward the seat, but she remained standing while he turned to retrieve a pair of shoes from the cubbyhole. They weren't glass slippers, but Kat stared at the delicate pumps made of gossamer strands as if artistic spiders had woven them with sparkling thread. The heels looked insubstantial, as if she'd be expected to walk on air.

She sat.

The dark opera master of l'Opéra Severne knelt in front of her, a daemon Prince Charming with dusty hair and faded jeans, as if the fairy-tale shoes in his hands were a practical offering and not some kind of unexpected magic so perfectly suited to her dress.

He placed one to the side and lifted the other for her to see.

They were closer to the ghost light's glow than they'd been at the door. It illuminated the waves in his hair and the very green glitter in his eyes when his gaze met hers.

Not a practical offering, then. Not if it inspired the light of unspoken emotions to show in his dark irises.

She should refuse, but she couldn't break the spell of the find, not when she wondered how the perfect shoes could possibly fit her feet when chosen from their hiding place among thousands of others.

Kat bent to remove her everyday shoes. The worn ballerina flats came off easily while Severne watched. But when she reached for the shoe he held, he shook his head.

"No. Allow me," he instructed. He was on one knee. His tone was polite. But it brooked no refusal.

He took her bare foot in his warm hand and slipped the gossamer shoe on her foot.

It fit.

He continued to hold her foot in his hands, and their eyes met again.

"Fairy tales are dangerous. In *Cinderella*, the stepmother danced until she fell down dead," Kat said.

She needed the reminder.

Any magic John Severne possessed was damned. Daemons couldn't be trusted.

"Still, I do believe l'Opéra Severne would be the perfect place for deadly dancing," Severne said.

He placed her foot back on the ground. He stood and paced several steps away with his back to her. Kat slipped the shoe off her foot and put her own shoes back on. She left the perfect shoes lying on the floor beside the stool as she stood.

"Maybe we should call for help now," Kat suggested.

There was tension between them that couldn't be blamed on Heaven or hell. It was a purgatory of unexplored feeling somewhere between paradise and devastation. She couldn't accept the shoes, no matter how badly she ached as she left them behind. It wasn't safe to indulge in happily-ever-after dreams with a daemon. Even if the shoes weren't a daemonic bargain, they were a heart's bargain she couldn't afford to make.

"Help never comes, Katherine. We have to save ourselves," Severne said.

He ignored the shoes as he turned back to face her. He pulled a key from his jeans pocket.

"You had a key all along," Kat said.

In spite of her distrust of daemons, she hadn't expected him to be playfully tricky.

He led the way back to the door and easily unlocked the latch. The opening yawned wide enough for her to pass, but she hesitated.

"Why?" she asked.

"Would you have stayed if the door had been open?" he asked.

She was afraid of the answer. He suspected that she wouldn't have stayed. She was fairly certain he was wrong. He didn't move aside as she passed. She brushed lightly against the wall of his chest, all steel once more. He closed the door behind her once she had stepped outside. She heard him turn the key.

As she made her way back upstairs, she worried about Sybil. Severne had said the daemon woman often had an agenda of her own. What favor would Sybil require of her now that their bargain was sealed? And how did her agenda collide with the secrets surrounding her sister's disappearance? The costume matron was a fixture of l'Opéra Severne. She must know something about Victoria that she hadn't seen fit to share.

Katherine tried not to think about John Severne shut in the shadowy warehouse with all his fairy tales that could never be.

Chapter 13

The men stood before him.

Many of them had traveled hundreds of miles to reach the enclave. He could see their exhaustion in the way several of them swayed on their feet. One had suffered a daemon bite that festered on his neck. Black ooze didn't stop him from standing tall with his stoic face firm and his shoulders squared as he faced his master. Another had a broken leg. He hadn't even gone to a hospital to have it professionally tended by a doctor. Instead it was splinted, and Reynard could see how it pained the monk because of the sweat running down his face and staining the robe he wore.

His chair was positioned on a dais so he could peruse their ranks from above.

They stood at attention while he inspected them. They had changed from traveling clothes into the robes that they were expected to dress in while training in the enclave. Many of them wore the robes even when they were away. He wouldn't have been surprised if these, his best men, wore them always, even though he'd chosen the material for the roughness of the cloth. Most of the men had permanent skin conditions from the wool rubbing their skin raw for decades.

In spite of the obedience and devotion that had brought them here so quickly in response to his summons, Reynard found fault with them all. They were too tall, too muscular, too young, but he didn't share his disappointment at their perfection.

He would relish the opportunity to wear them down.

He would enjoy breaking them.

His heartbeat had quickened. He shifted in his chair. His current favorite, Joshua, stepped closer with a tray, and Reynard reached for a hammered copper goblet, which held his wine. The wine was bitter, mixed with an herbal cocktail that would soothe him.

If he broke them, the duty of fathering the next generation of D'Arcy Seekers would fall to him. It was a temptation and a trial at the same time. He must not be greedy or presumptuous although anticipation hummed beneath his healing skin.

He drank the full goblet of drugged wine and sat back in his chair. Joshua took the goblet from his slackening fingers. Like a good servant, Joshua also gave the signal for the monk near the stairs to sound the gong that would allow the sparring to commence.

It would be a sacred duty to father the next generation of Seekers, not a forbidden fantasy he indulged in late at night when the blood ran too hot in his veins. He was healing. He could feel the blood strengthening him and making him whole once more.

He was a man with a divine purpose untainted by the sacrifices he'd made to survive.

That night, Reynard had the heavy silver chains brought to him in his chambers. He inspected the links, one by one. He imagined what it would be like to see their shine pressed tightly into soft, rebellious flesh.

Chapter 14

A piece of yellow paper fluttered to the floor when Kat opened her cello case to practice that evening. The rest of the orchestra had finished for the day and left the opera house to enjoy Baton Rouge nightlife before performances began and their social life was reduced to Monday mornings and a few hours each afternoon.

Kat had to be careful. Reynard had eyes everywhere. Baton Rouge was a musical city only forty-five minutes from New Orleans. It wouldn't be beneath his notice. She had to lay low even as she turned every stone looking for Victoria.

She bent to retrieve the small square of rough-edged cardstock. She turned it over to read the print on its front side. The Blues Queen. It was a riverboat ticket stub for a cruise earlier in the spring. Kat fingered the perforated tear that indicated the ticket had been used.

How had the scrap found its way into her case? It hadn't been there earlier in the day. The black lining of her case wouldn't have hidden the bright yellow paper. Printed along with the words was a tiny rendering of a showboat. The kind that had offered cruises up and down the Mississippi since before the Civil War. The drawing included whimsical clouds of steam from smokestacks that would be mostly decorative in these days of gasoline-powered engines.

Kat closed her case and placed her cello in the corner. Someone had put the ticket in her case. Sybil? Tess? The find wasn't accidental. It was a deliberate hint. But it also felt like a lure. It was dangerous to leave l'Opéra Severne. Vic surely had in the months she'd been in Baton Rouge, and now she was gone.

Katherine decided against going to Severne with the ticket. He might not understand the tug of intuition she felt as she looked at the tiny stub. And she needed to avoid him as much as possible. A night on the town did not figure into the strategy. He might try to persuade her not to go, or he might decide to go with her. Neither of those were options she wanted to consider.

Kat rummaged for clothes to blend in with a riverboat party crowd. Even with her decision made, she wondered what she might encounter alone on a sultry Louisiana night.

She chose a simple belted shift dress she could pair with wedge-heeled booties. Sleeveless in a soft watercolor pattern, the dress wasn't eye-catching, but a sheer wrap of pale green chiffon matched her belt and the leaves on the print, showing enough effort that she wouldn't stand out in the opposite direction. She didn't want to be over- or underdressed. She clipped her hair up in deference to the humidity and added a swipe of matte lipstick.

The yellow clutch she grabbed felt ironically un-weapon-like in her hand. She wasn't as prepared to find and rescue her sister as she should have been. She was unsure what dangers she might face. But she didn't have time to become a ninja or proficient with guns or knives. She was a cellist, and a cellist had to be enough.

The walk out of l'Opéra Severne was interminable. She expected Severne or Grim at every turn. She'd called a cab to avoid lingering on the street and flagging one down. Leaving the opera house and stepping out into the city was like trading one world for another.

Suddenly glittering lights and traffic, the sound of distant music and horns, enveloped her with seductive warmth. Somewhere Reynard stalked, and her sister... She tried not to imagine what was keeping her sister from calling. The pull of Severne's Brimstone blood didn't diminish. It was so strong it followed her into the Baton Rouge night, an attraction she tried to ignore.

The cab took her to the river and the quay, where several paddle wheel cruisers awaited their departures for dinner cruises. She paid the driver and got out to walk down the boardwalk as if she was only a tourist. But the light wind fluffing her skirt didn't charm her. She was too nervous. Her motives for being here were too urgent to enjoy the happy sounds of the throng.

When she approached the window of *The Blues Queen*'s booking booth, she saw others being turned away.

"There are no more seats available for the evening," she heard the agent at the window say.

She could see the large showboat gleaming with lights in the distance. It dwarfed the other boats tied nearby. She could hear the music already playing to welcome its passengers. Beautiful blues piano played by expert hands floated across the water. So near and yet so far. She couldn't sneak on board. There was a narrow ramp with several crewmembers taking tickets from orderly boarders.

She stopped. Instinct still urged her that only *The Blues Queen* would do, even though other potential passengers in front of her were easily moving away to purchase tickets for other boats. Last minute partiers couldn't be picky.

Just as Kat decided she would purchase a ticket for another night, a familiar figure stepped around her to talk to the agent at the window. The agent was obviously familiar with John Severne, as well. She smiled, nodded and picked up a phone.

Severne turned around and approached her. Kat could only stiffen her spine and stand firm rather than retreat.

"I like to let them know when they can expect me. We'll be putting their preparations to the test tonight. Let's see if they stand as ready as I expect them to be," Severne said.

The daemon held out his arm. She noted his perfectly tailored suit. Very different from the shorts he wore in his gym. Yet its fitted lines revealed as much about his physique to the observant eye. She tried to observe less. She failed. He wore the suit casually with a loosened shirt and no tie. Her eyes were drawn to his bare neck. It was so very human of him to seem vulnerable in the loosened collar in spite of the hard body below it.

"I own *The Blues Queen*. My table is always reserved. Will you join me?" he asked.

His pants were slim-cut and low on his lean hips. Painfully sexy and modern for a "man" who had probably stood on this same quay a hundred years ago as casually as he did tonight.

"I'm not sure that's a good idea," Kat said.

It wasn't a date. He must have followed her here to help her find her sister. No more. No less. But she could see in the fairy light glow that the green was already apparent in his nearly black eyes. She hadn't meant to match the moss

there with her wrap. Or had she? When had green become
a color that appealed to her?

"It isn't safe for you to go alone. I'm not the only one
who followed you tonight," Severne said.

Kat looked around. Her affinity was focused entirely
on Severne. He had moved closer to her as she hesitated.
She was blind to other threats just as she'd been blind to
Sybil's true nature. She felt no other pull.

"Is it Reynard?" she asked. She tugged her wrap close
even though the night held no natural chill. Her goose
bumps were prompted by her emotions, a physical rejec
tion of the evil that stalked her always.

"He and his Order are always a possibility. You know
that. But I was referring to other threats," Severne said.

He had reached to take her arm. Solicitous to onlook
ers, but she could feel a tension onlookers might not see.

"Is that why you followed me? To protect me from…?"
she asked.

She looked up into his eyes. The shadows had reclaimed
them as black. She couldn't read the tight line of his lips
or the clenched angle of his jaw.

"I'd like to be able to give you an unequivocal yes to
that question," he said. "Shall we?" He indicated the move
ment of the crowd down the quay and up the ramp onto
the showboat. It was a happy, boisterous line up of couples
and small groups.

"Well, we're here. I'm not going to turn back now,"
she said.

She slipped her hand into the crook of Severne's arm as
if they were a couple, and he led her on board. She prob
ably should have walked away. Chances were her other
stalkers might be dangerous, but in ways she could fight
Severne was the true danger. Him, she might not be able
to beat. He felt far too good by her side.

John Severne was the master of l'Opéra Severne, but that wasn't his only realm. It was obvious from the moment he climbed the ramp up to the waiting boat that he was also the king here on the river. The staff and crew of *The Blues Queen* welcomed him onto the deck with practiced deference, and they treated her royally as his guest.

They were led past rows of bistro-style tables to a more private setting in an alcove that overlooked the gleaming river from a private balcony. Severne held her chair and she stood stiffly, not knowing what to do. She was here to look for her sister. She wasn't here to explore the flutter in her stomach when Severne watched and waited for her to act. Every time, every minute, every move, she felt him teasing her to action. Just as when he'd held her silver chain, he held her chair, almost daring her to resist... or not to resist.

"This isn't the time for chivalry," she said. It was a standoff. Him offering the chair. Her standing even though she was drawn to him and his company.

"But it needs to appear to be. We are being watched. Seeming to be here for any other reason than enjoying my hospitality would be a very bad idea," Severne warned.

He was nothing but a handsome playboy enjoying an evening with a willing woman. No one else would see the tension in his shoulders or the tight grip of his hands on the chair. No one else would see the unmitigated black of his eyes or know that their lack of color indicated his level of tension.

Once again, Kat glanced around. The crowd was an elegant one seeded generously with tourists. She saw no monks. Felt no daemons. Then again, she could feel only Severne when he was standing this close. She decided to accept the proffered chair if for no other reason than to get Severne to move away from her to the other chair.

She tingled with the pull of Severne's Brimstone from head to toe. Or maybe that was the response to the perusal of his eyes. He took in her appearance, lightly, but the approval she thought she saw in the slight softening of his mouth made her heartbeat in her chest seem obvious. Its sensual rhythm would increase with the brush of his hand.

"It's dangerous for you here. In ways you can't see. I'm unpopular with some. Used by others. It's a deadly dance between two factions that will be fighting long after you and I are gone," Severne said. "And your affinity…"

"…is completely unreliable around you," Kat confessed.

They spoke about a technicality, but it was also an intimate truth. Kat could feel her face grow warm. She knew when the flush spread because his dark gaze followed it to her chest and lingered before rising to meet hers.

Their gazes held. His said he wasn't a cad, but he enjoyed his effect on her. He enjoyed her attraction and the hold he had over the affinity she'd always had for daemons.

"You are free to go. At any time," Severne said.

"I'll never leave without Victoria," Kat replied.

She raised her chin and broke the spell of his eyes. She looked away. She would resist the pull Severne had over her senses. Quietly, without meeting his eyes again, she told him about the ticket she'd found in her cello case.

"You came here tonight because you thought someone had left you a clue. I thought you were trying to get away from l'Opéra Severne. It can be a dark place to linger too long," he said.

"But it's also beautiful. Dark and lovely. When I was a girl, I discovered the cello at your opera house. No matter how dark, I'll always love l'Opéra Severne for that gift," Kat said.

"I've learned to be wary of gifts. But your music is very like the opera house. Seductive. Dangerous," Severne said.

"My music? Dangerous?" Katherine asked, incredulous.

"Distraction is dangerous. I have no time for beauty and ease," Severne said.

No time for beauty yet so beautiful in the glittering lights of his steamboat that he made her ache. No time for ease, yet he sought out the comfort of a child's favorite fairy-tale operas in a cavernous warehouse where he had memorized the placement of every shoe.

"But you have time for blues and champagne?" Kat asked.

A waiter brought them a bottle without menu or consultation. Severne nodded, and he popped the cork with very little sound. Kat sipped what she'd been given, but when the flavors hit her tongue, she paused and savored the obviously aged vintage.

He said she was being watched. He said she was in danger. But she suddenly felt the need to enjoy. She wanted to stop the fear and the worry and make Severne relax his guard. He still looked at her as if she were a beguiling specimen that fascinated him, but his tension indicated more than danger. He held himself apart. Always.

The boat beneath them had separated itself from the dock. As they talked and sipped, they floated down the Mississippi, easy and slow. In the distance, the cantilever bridge that was a famous part of Baton Rouge's skyline was aglow beneath a rising moon.

From the stage where they'd passed a shiny baby grand, a jazz standard played. The sound made it to their table. The other passengers talked or danced, enjoying a perfect Southern night for a river cruise.

But Severne was apart in more ways than their alcove position. He was tense. He was stiff. He was cold and controlled in spite of the Brimstone burn urging him to be other, less controlled things. His aloofness was as much an enticement as his daemon magnetism. This was why she should avoid him. His call to her wasn't only Brimstone. He called to her in other, more human ways.

He had fire in his veins, but he needed her warmth.

She needed to find Victoria. She also needed other things. Starting with this daemon's kiss.

"I'm not afraid," she said. In that moment, she meant it. She saw his need and she responded to it as a woman, not as a tool for the Order of Samuel.

"That's what frightens me," he said.

Kat rose from her chair. She moved to Severne's side. But he'd already risen to his feet, as well.

"There are creatures in this room that would burn you for eternity if they knew you helped me or hindered me. They need to see you simply dance with me. As any woman would," he said.

He took her hand and led her onto the dance floor. Her fear came then because she hadn't worn a suit of armor. There was not enough between their bodies when they came together. His broad chest pressed to her soft breast. She could feel his heat. His hand at her back was firm, but she could feel a tremor in his fingers.

This wasn't about disguise. He was putting on a show for whomever or whatever watched her. There were other daemons here, ones invisible to her senses because her senses were full of Severne. But he held her because he wanted to and because she wanted to be held.

"You have nothing to fear as long as you're with me. I'm in the middle of a revolution. You're just along for the ride," he advised. He pulled her closer. Kat relaxed her body and melted into him. It was a capitulation, but not to him or to the plan to appear like an ordinary date. She gave in to her need to feel him and to breathe in his wood smoke scent as she buried her face in his neck.

His hand stiffened and pressed into her back. His fingers gripped her warm skin beneath her light dress. His hold became too fierce. He was definitely not casual, cold or in control. He knew. He could tell she didn't give a damn about disguise. He could feel her let go of all the reasons to hold herself away from him.

"Careful," he said. It was a warning so guttural and low that it vibrated against her.

"I lied. I am afraid. But I'm still not running away," she said.

He inhaled in a hiss, then exhaled through his teeth as her lips brushed his skin.

"You should know the daemons that watch us now don't care if I seduce you. Their surveillance is no excuse to play with fire," he said.

"You should know I don't care if they're watching. I've had to live with stalkers my whole life," Kat said. "And who says *you* will be the one to seduce *me*?"

"This riverboat could turn into a battlefield at any second, engulfed in Brimstone and blood. And all I can think about is having you, tasting your kiss one more time," Severne said.

To have her.

To taste her.

Kat shivered with need and anticipation. Life and death had always hung over her as a constant threat. But this sensual threat from John Severne was new. The song ended, and he led her back to the alcove. He turned her toward the other passengers. They stood with the wrought iron rail at their back, and she perused the crowd.

She could sense only Severne, but she'd been hunted her whole life. It wasn't her affinity but simple instinct that would help her to see the faces in the crowd that were most often turned toward her. She picked them out, one, two, three. Seemingly ordinary men and women whose body language gave them away. Four, five, six. Her pulse roared in her ears, competing with the mellow jazz piano as its player began another song.

There were plenty of tourists who glanced their way because of their exclusive positioning in the alcove, or maybe because of Severne's eye-catching appearance.

But the daemons looked at her.

Nightglow eyes occasionally glinted with refracted light. You had to look hard to see it—a flash and it was gone.

Ten, eleven, twelve.

Possibly thirteen, but the piano player wore sunglasses, and she couldn't tell if his focus was on her or the music he played.

Severne waited for the daemons to come into her focus.

"I want to help you find your sister, but you are in danger from more than your Order of Samuel. There are daemons that watch to see which side you'll take in an ancient revolution," Severne said. "A Council of daemons led a rogue sect that overthrew Lucifer. They have their sights set on a war with Heaven, but they have to defeat the Loyalists first. Lucifer's Army serves the Loyalists, who want to continue what was begun with the fall, when ancient daemons chose to leave Heaven and forge their own society in hell."

She began to gauge the daemons' allegiance. Six circled warily around the room. She could see minute indications that they coordinated their movements. There were seven more seated at various tables. She stopped counting. She'd identified more than enough. And all the poor humans inadvertently sat on a powder keg that could explode at any time. Real danger rode the glittering riverboat while she had indulged in her fascination with Severne.

"Did Victoria stumble into their sights? Did she take the wrong side?" Kat asked.

She no longer enjoyed toying with the attraction she and Severne felt for each other. Playfulness disappeared, replaced by fear.

"There is no wrong or right when every side is damned," Severne said.

He turned her away from the crowd. He filled her vision. Severne was a tall, dark, unreadable being who probably held her sister's life in his hands. She faced away from Severne, toward the river.

"You aren't here to bother them. You're here to enjoy yourself with me. Laugh. Smile. Prepare to be kissed," he said. "If you won't do it to protect yourself, you need to do it for the other human passengers. The only way to protect the people on this boat is to be harmlessly infatuated with me. I'm not sure how or why, but you're in the middle of this daemon war now, and I'd like to leave with you alive tonight."

Kat's eyes widened. She forced a smile, but her knees had gone weak. He pretended to be all business. Detached. But she'd seen the green in his eyes. He might think permission to kiss him for noble reasons would save her, but it wouldn't. Not at all.

He stood facing her, close at her side. Nothing but scrolled wrought iron protected her from the churning paddlewheels below. The roar of the water disguised their words.

"I'm going to kiss you and it's for their benefit, but I was always going to kiss you again. Whether they needed to see it or not. I need to taste you even if it will damn me with more sleepless nights," he said.

He reached to turn her face toward him, and he leaned to claim her mouth with no more warning. She wasn't prepared. Even with the heads-up, she wasn't ready. Because this time he wasn't holding back. She could only try to keep up. His hunger was a scorching, all-consuming thing.

She held the balcony rail. His calloused fingers were both hard and warm as they cupped her jaw. He used the slightest pressure to nudge her chin down with his thumbs. She didn't resist. She cooperated. She opened her mouth so that his tongue, rough and sweet, could claim the interior of her mouth.

Response coiled tight in her abdomen, chasing her fear away. There was no room for frightened butterflies, only ferocious desire.

Her tense yet willing and passionate response made Severne growl into the depths of her mouth. Her body still faced the river, but every part of her yearned to embrace him fully in spite of the other passengers and the daemon threat.

She eagerly tasted him with her tongue. She savored the full swell of his lower lip as if it was her secret discovery of his vulnerability made a hundred years ago only for her. Their deadly audience didn't fade away, but the real reason for the kiss was in the pounding of her heart, the heat in her belly and the hardness of his response to her tongue. She could feel his erection pressed to her hip. Another secret just for her in the dazzling fairy-lit night.

She finally turned from the rail to hold him, letting go of its support to exchange the cold iron rail for the heated iron of his shoulders and chest. Her move broke their kiss, but he only wrapped her close to his chest.

The embrace was a pause for both of them. A chance to breathe and control the fiery reaction they'd both experienced to the necessary performance of their supposed relationship. She could feel the breaths he took to calm himself. She could feel the unsteady pulse of his heart. The act was an act in name only. Their attraction was very real.

Kat tried to speak in hushed tones to ask more about Michael and her sister, but he quieted her with his lips.

So much for regaining control. If the alcove had been any less private, the stalking daemons would have had a very thorough show.

He'd distracted her from her questions, and it had almost killed him. He burned from her lips and the soft press of her body against his. Worse than Brimstone in his veins. Far worse. Far better. But she hadn't asked him more questions about Michael and her sister after a voyage that was all tastes and sighs.

He'd seen the Council's daemons and the daemons from Lucifer's Army ease back and melt away in the crowd. Though he'd prevented collateral human deaths, he still hated that he'd used the desire between him and Katherine to distract her from the truth. He'd saved her and deceived her at the same time. His deal with the Council protected Kat from that faction as soon as he showed she was with him.

He didn't know why Lucifer's Army hadn't attacked. He had hoped they would fear his reprisal. But he wasn't sure that had been enough to keep them from harming Katherine. He wondered what else might have influenced their decision to back off.

Her sister's association with Michael might have been more serious than he'd assumed. As an ancient one, Michael was a prince to them. Had his loose ties to Katherine through her sister helped to protect her tonight?

There were secrets here that even he didn't know. Unknown variables he couldn't plan for or predict. But Katherine was back at l'Opéra Severne. Her venture into the city had proved that she was more than a magnet for daemons. She was at the heart of the daemon political division, somehow in the middle, while being completely in the dark. She was an innocent bystander caught up in the revolution. Both factions, Lucifer's Army and the Council's rogues, were haunting her footsteps. The river cruise standoff had been a quiet prelude to slaughter that he'd manipulated so that it turned into a daemon retreat. From now on, he had to keep Kat protected within l'Opéra Severne's shadowed halls. He wished she could remain safe and unharmed. It wasn't an option. For now, he was her protector. But soon he would be the one who hurt her.

He couldn't run from that. He could only retreat to his gym and punish himself for what he was prepared to do to Katherine to save his father's soul. His soul would be damned forever now. He knew that. Even when the contract was fulfilled, he would burn for what he had done to Kat for as long as he lived.

Kat's lips were swollen and sensitive. Her fingers brushed her mouth again and again. She suspected Severne had been more thorough than he'd had to be. He'd helped her, but there had been deeper undercurrents to his fierce, passionate kisses. They hadn't been for show. She undressed for bed, taking care to shove the moss-green shawl into the back of a drawer.

She'd learned several things tonight.

There were political tangles between daemon factions she hadn't known about before. The hell dimension was embroiled in revolution. But most importantly, she'd learned that Michael was important and Severne didn't want her to know it. She hadn't been fooled by his kisses. She'd enjoyed them. Every single one would replay in her heated memories forever, but she'd known all along that he kissed her to silence her curiosity without realizing he only confirmed her greatest fear.

The daemon she most wanted couldn't be trusted.

Chapter 15

"Father Reynard, the arena has been prepared to your specifications," his new favorite novitiate said.

"Thank you, Peter. Please sound the call for assembly. The whole Order needs to witness this sacrifice," Reynard said. Joshua had displeased him. Peter had risen to the top. It was an endless procession he no longer even tried to recall.

"Sacrifice, Father?" Peter asked. His hand paused near the tasseled pull that would alert the monk in the bell tower to perform his duty.

"Few will survive. If any. But we must ensure that Samuel's gift is passed only to children who have been fathered by the strongest and most devout of us all," Reynard said.

"You are the Most Devout, Father," the young boy loyally said, ensuring his status of favorite for another day.

It was a title he was frequently called. A fact he had given a nod to in his words. He must begin to build expectation among the Order. A man could not lead warriors without ensuring that he owned their hearts.

"Yes. I am," Reynard agreed. "Ring the bell."

He'd been recovering for weeks with no opportunity to hunt. He'd been tormented in his dreams with visions of heated violence that often involved the D'Arcy sisters and their daemon champions he couldn't seem to defeat.

He needed release.

He needed at least to go through the motions of choosing the best of the best.

The coliseum-like courtyard of the enclave had been filled with cages. In each cage, a daemon had been placed. Above the courtyard, hundreds of monks sat in rows of seats arranged in circles around and around the open court below.

First they would release the children. Then the females. Then the males in order from weakest to strongest. He barely noticed the tears of the creatures inside the cages. The weeping of the daemon children and the screaming of their mothers was white noise for darker visions dominating his mind.

The Potentials were to be his gladiators. The daemons were the fodder for their blades.

Or vice versa.

"Release the first daemon," he boomed, and the crowd of bloodthirsty monks howled.

Three of his best men had survived. Even he had been shocked by their ferocity. Burned by Brimstone and slashed by daemon tooth and claw, they stood before him now, triumphant.

He greeted them in private audience, torn between duty to his cause and desire. They were obviously prime speci mens of manhood and devotion to the Order. Each knelt on bent knee to kiss the hilt of the blade in his hand.

Only one cried out when the blade sizzled on his lips.

Reynard whirled the blade and plunged it into the coward's bared neck. Blood flowed as he pulled the blade free and the dead monk fell to the side.

The other two remained silent, ignoring what secrets the heat of his blade might have revealed about its nature.

Saul and Simon were their names. He'd known them for years. Each had been a favorite of his for a time, specially trained to fight by his side. They had hunted with the D'Arcy sisters. Had they lusted for this opportunity? He didn't acknowledge the burn in his gut at the thought as jealousy.

"You have served Samuel well. He smiles at you from Heaven. One day he will welcome you home." The lies flowed easily from his lips. As easily as the blood he'd just spilled. That viscous fluid spread from the dead monk's body until he stood in a warm puddle of it, but he didn't edge away. He allowed it to soak into his shoes.

He could kill these two as easily. Even slowly, one at a time, and they would not fight. They would take his blade as willingly as the D'Arcy sisters would not. He had one moment of sweet hesitation in which he tasted their fear, and he weighed current pleasure against the more practical use of the warriors who would serve him so well.

The heat in his blood had caused him to have darker and darker visions of violence. Every time his blade tasted death, it only became hungrier for more. It was black with the dried blood of daemons and humans alike, so much so that even Brimstone didn't burn it away.

The men kneeling before him wore nothing but shredded robes. Their muscular physiques and disciplined demeanors shouldn't be wasted. In spite of his hungry blade, he needed to calm his shaking need and use the resources he'd been cultivating for years to help him reach his goal.

He chose to sheathe his blade and loose theirs.

For now.

"Rise and prepare to hunt. None of the rest of your brothers has found the D'Arcy women. This will be your final test," Reynard said.

He still needed recovery time. He grew stronger every day, but he wasn't ready, and it was imperative that Samuel's gift not be lost. Reynard's soul might depend on it.

"The one to find Katherine or Victoria D'Arcy will be the one to father the next generation of Seekers," Reynard said.

The two men rose slowly. They looked at each other. They looked at him. Only their blinking indicated their surprise.

Had they sensed how close he'd come to killing them with his daemon blade?

Chapter 16

He'd spent days avoiding Katherine while still trying to determine if she was drawing closer to his prey. It was a razor's edge that cut far too sweetly. Too often at the end of a long day or after a particularly brutal workout, he found himself near her. Her affinity for daemons and his Brimstone blood were the perfect excuse, but he'd been alive too long. He knew his motivations better than most mortal men.

Her music called him. Her hungry response to his touch and his kisses tormented him with physical needs he was usually able to deny. His gym was a cold release, a grueling punishment that didn't erase her taste.

Severne's tuxedo had been delivered. Sybil was an artist with needle and thread. She'd tailored his clothes as long as he could remember. But this time she'd outdone herself. He'd always insisted on black for the masquerade. He was repelled by the decadent swirl of color that never mirrored his heart on the one night a year when the opera house revealed its true nature to the world.

But this time, when he lifted the soft, clear plastic to glance at the formal suit, his gaze was held by the unexpected blend of shades and fabrics. The tuxedo was all black, no disobedience there; the elaborately stitched midnight brocade of the vest contrasted with the heavy cut of jet wool for the jacket and the obsidian shine of grosgrain cuffs and lapels. But at certain angles, the light brought out an emerald sheen in the brocade.

He lifted the domino mask from its place on the hanger and stared into its empty eyes.

Sybil saw more than she should. She was much older than he was. Wizened by age and circumstance. He would wear the tuxedo and it would be for Katherine, but no one would know. And when the time came, he would still do what needed to be done, the needs buried deep in his dark heart be damned.

Her cello stood in the corner, near the chair she used when she played it. Tonight it was in its case. She wouldn't hide behind it. In fact, even her mask was a slight frame of pavé gemstones for her eyes with only the sparkle of diamanté dust to hold its shape.

Her hair and eyes stood out. Chestnut curls and chocolate framed by black lashes showed darkly against the white, ivory and glitter of her costume. Everyone would know her. Which made the bodice of the gown that much more daring. It was a complement to the mask. A delicate network of crystal stones, the perfect, simple accompaniment to the layered opulence of her skirts.

But as the mask only framed her eyes and didn't hide her face, the bodice only framed her torso, allowing the honeyed expanse of her chest and the swell of her breasts to catch the eye. It was the possibility of catching a certain intense gaze that made her long to go back for her instrument. Severne's eyes would gleam green for her, only for her, in this dress.

She shouldn't crave that gleam.

The same young man who had initially welcomed her to l'Opéra Severne had delivered the *Cinderella* shoes to her door.

They sat on her bedside table while she dressed, a delectable challenge, before she finally decided to wear them. She wasn't sure if the idea of Severne requiring a payment for the gift weighed on the side of wearing them or not. She only knew they were perfect, and once she'd placed them on her feet there was no going back to the warehouse to return them.

She was walking on a cloud of anticipation as she wore them. The network of webbing that hugged her toes complimented the other textures and fabrics of the dress itself.

She didn't go back for her cello.

Even though she had not one ember of Brimstone, her blood was bolder than that.

It pumped hotly in her veins as she followed the flow of the crowd to the cluster of decorated salons that had been prepped for the fete.

She was braced for whatever this dark night would hold.

The sconces glowed. The murals seemed to moan—silently, eternally—and she walked on decadent feet, feeling at her most beautiful and her most vulnerable.

Her time with Severne on the riverboat had been unexpected. Tonight was different. She'd had time to regret the kisses they'd shared and pine for more. She'd anticipated and dreaded, planned and prepared.

For so many things.

Tonight she had to keep an eye out for monks from the

Order of Samuel. Worst case scenario, Reynard himself. She had to avoid shadows, watch for the patron named Michael who might have something to do with her sister's disappearance. She had to fear Sybil's mechanizations and the price of the dress she had yet to demand.

And John Severne.

She couldn't forget the man who was in the forefront of her fears.

It hadn't escaped her notice that he'd been around every corner and behind every turn in the last few days. Her affinity brought her to him, or his Brimstone blood brought him to her. Either way, they haunted each other's movements but avoided actual conversation and contact.

He was not being forthright with her in ways she couldn't ascertain, and yet she still tasted his kiss on her lips and longed for more.

But she wouldn't regret the shoes on her feet. Those she accepted freely. She might never truly know the side of the opera master he had shown her in the warehouse, but the shoes were a reminder he had a side that longed for something other than death and darkness. She couldn't refuse that part of him if he chose to share it with her. She wouldn't. Even if she couldn't trust him.

The salons were a crush of beautiful guests in an array of costumes, wigs, hats and masks. There were many in the Venetian style featuring long beaked noses in garish colors. The effect was edgy chaos just this side of madness.

Kat's heartbeat kicked up in response. The night would only get more chaotic as time passed and champagne flowed.

She made out several of her friends. Tess waved with a glass in her hand, the mask she'd worn as an older and wiser Juliet was already hanging from her wrist by its ribbons.

Music played in the background on discreet speakers. The orchestra had the night off. Instead of Tchaikovsky, an epic rock ballad played, surprisingly fitting with the decadent, theatrical mood.

There were many people she didn't recognize. So many people at the opera house were still new acquaintances. There were also former players, city officials and wealthy patrons. She would never be able to pick out anyone dangerous in the crowd.

But that lie held for only moments before a tall, lean figure dressed all in black parted the crush of partygoers gracefully, easily, with a masculine authority unmistakable, unmatched by anyone else.

He moved toward her slowly, but his approach was as inevitable as a bolt released from a crossbow. She was the target. He hit home with the intensity of his eyes while he was still half a room away.

They'd been drawn to each other for days. Tonight, behind the masks and in the middle of the crowd, could they indulge the impulse to come together?

The stiff black domino was perfectly molded to his face and seemed soft in comparison to his set jaw. A shimmer of starched silk over chiseled stone. When he was steps away, she noticed what Sybil had done.

Severne's formal tuxedo with all its textural fabrics in varying shades of black was the perfect foil to her own snowy ensemble with its shades of ivory and white.

They were a pair.

No one here would doubt it.

She was the Gothic angel to his heavenly daemon, and he took her breath away when she saw his eyes widen as he noted the costume magic, too. She could already see a hint of green glimmering from the shadowed holes of his mask.

"I've been to this masquerade a thousand times," he said.

He stopped in front of her only when they were toe to toe, only when he could tilt down to speak for her ears alone. "I've never wanted to dance before now."

She pressed willingly into his darkness, the white of her skirts crushed against his hard, straight form, the swell of her barely covered breasts full against his midnight brocade.

Contrast. And both costumes even more beautiful than before because of it.

He pulled her onto the dance floor, and she tried to keep up. He waltzed in spite of the modern music. No one cared. Many tried to emulate him without the practiced immortal moves of a man who'd been on the floor many times before. The short moments they'd been on the dance floor of the riverboat had been only a preview of what she experienced now.

"This isn't your first waltz," Kat said midwhirl.

"I've danced a thousand times before. Out of duty, obligation and boredom. Never need. Never hold my dance partner or die. Never hold her *and* die," Severne said.

She'd been approached with smooth, practiced lines before. But never such a raw emotion. She didn't reply in kind. Her need to be in his arms was a confession that stuck in her throat and warmed her cheeks to what must have been scarlet against the crystal gems below.

"I've known Sybil since I was a boy. She practically raised me. In this, she plays a dangerous game. Take care you aren't caught up in it," Severne said into the soft curls above her ear.

"She seems too serious for matchmaking," Katherine said.

"Never doubt it. She is," Severne said.

"Then she didn't mean for us to be seen as a couple tonight?" Kat asked.

"We are a pair, Katherine. But there are many pairs who

are destined to remain apart. Sybil's artistic needles and thread bewitch, but they are cruel. This night only shows us what we can't have," Severne said.

"Only this, then. The dance. Now," Kat said, fully surrendering to the dizzy thrill of circling the room in his arms.

"Yes. We have this dance and, for now, it can be everything," Severne replied. "Forget about all else."

Including promises and lies.

She didn't say it out loud. She danced. Until her head was light, until when he finally left her to stand alone by the dance floor, it took her long moments to catch her breath and calm her heart. Did he mean for the dance to be a finality between them? No more kisses. No more contact. No more desire.

As her pulse slowed, she took careful, steady inhalations until she could draw oxygen in and release it without the air fluttering from her lungs like butterflies shaken from a bush.

She planted her feet firmly on the ground. She forced her head to clear. She cursed the warm sensation he'd left on her body where his hands had been, on the small of her back and on her hand. She might want to follow him and the music through the crowd to discover wherever he'd gone, but she didn't.

Kat turned down several other partners.

She wished she had recovered sooner. It took too long to banish the dance. It was dangerous to fall under the heat of his eyes, his voice and his touch. His reaction to her was as heady as hers to him. She'd seen his cheeks darken. She'd felt the restraint he'd practiced not to hold her closer than the dance required. She'd seen the glitter of her bodice reflected in his eyes.

Her perceptions couldn't be clouded tonight.

She willed his effect on her away.

She tried to pick out individuals in the colorful mass around her.

Severne played havoc with her senses. His proximity had hidden Sybil's true nature from her detection. She hadn't discovered the daemons on the riverboat by their magnetic pull. She'd had to pick them out with only her eyes. The room could be full of daemons and Severne's monopoly on her affinity would hide them from her view. It was new, this feeling of uncertainty. She'd always rejected her ability to detect daemons, but now that it was hampered, she was frightened by her inability to sense their presence.

As she stood resolute and determined to recover from his touch, it was precisely the senses Severne had overwhelmed that pinpointed an anomaly.

She sipped a lemonade cocktail she'd taken from a server's tray, and the crowd whirled and laughed and sang and talked and argued. But one figure in a crimson cloak moved with steady purpose at the edges of her blurred perceptions. Closer and closer still the figure crept. Not dancing. Not pausing. Not accepting champagne. A porcelain mask painted in the French style of the pantomime clown, Pierrot, covered the figure's face. The stark white facade glowed brightly within the hood of the crimson cloak, its hard, pursed lips red and a single black teardrop painted on its cheek.

Kat forced herself to sip casually while she focused on the figure, but her attention didn't go unnoticed. Crimson-cloaked clown stopped. The swirl of the blood-colored fabric wrapped around its legs. Feminine hands reached from the cloak's folds to keep it from tangling in legs encased in black leggings and tall, shiny boots.

A woman.

And something about her hands…

It had to be wishful thinking, but as she watched the woman pause with one foot placed toward her, it was as if the cloaked figure would rather run to her side than run away.

Kat stepped toward the woman in red. She allowed the empty glass in her hand to drop and roll on the heavy rug behind her.

"Vic?" she asked.

The woman was too far away. Kat couldn't tell what color eyes shone behind the black holes of the clown mask. But when the woman in red heard the utterance of her sister's name, she backed away. Urgently. She bumped several other partygoers but didn't pause to apologize.

"Victoria?" Kat said, louder and more desperate now that the woman in the crimson cloak had reacted to her first cry.

Several revelers near her turned to see why she had called out.

The crimson-cloaked figure also turned and pushed her way into the crowd away from Katherine.

Kat followed. Her progress was slow. The crowd of people had tripled in seconds. They pressed in around her on all sides. She pushed. She apologized. She excused herself through dozens of dancers.

But she couldn't hurry. She could only propel herself desperately at a slow slog through people determined to ignore her pleas.

She reached the hallway as the crowd thinned. It branched in two different directions. The way toward the exit was the most crowded. The opposite way led into the heart of l'Opéra Severne. It was darker. The sconces had been turned low to discourage partygoers from areas that weren't part of the event. But it was the flickering sconces that lit the vanishing flash of crimson around a distant corner.

Kat bit back another cry of her sister's name. The woman had run from her when she'd called out. It was doubtful she'd get a different result now. She could only hurry after the woman in the crimson cloak and hope that her instincts were right.

Victoria was still in the opera house. And she'd come out of hiding to find Katherine tonight.

Chapter 17

Her footsteps were muted by the party noise at first, but as she chased Victoria farther and farther from the crowd, the music and roar dimmed and her steps grew louder. She could hear a hint of movement ahead of her, down each corridor, around each bend—a scuff of a tread, a sharper sound as a boot heel connected with the ground—but those noises, too, began to fade.

She found herself alone in an unfamiliar part of the sprawling building with only her own footsteps and her own quickened breathing making any sound.

Kat slowed at the intersection of the hallway she hurried down and a larger corridor that had no sconces glowing. The whole length of it, this way and that, was devoid of light. She stood, undecided, straining her ears to pick up any hint of sound. Both directions were black as pitch with darkness so thick it seemed impenetrable.

How had Victoria found her way, and why had she run from a sister desperate to find her?

There.

Was that a sound?

Kat stepped toward the left, but stopped when the sound of a footstep approached instead of retreated. Closer and closer someone came. Instinct urged her to back away. But her desire to see Victoria and make sure she was okay warred with self-preservation.

And won.

She stood her ground. The steps came closer still.

"A strange place to hunt for daemons, I must confess. Yet there are so many at this fete that my problem is choosing where to strike first." The voice was unfamiliar to her, but not so the robes that revealed themselves around the ruddy shine of a monk's face that at first seemed to float toward her from the shadows.

One of Reynard's men had found her, or else his stalking of l'Opéra Severne was a chance hunting foray that had proved crazily fortuitous to his master.

"Leave me and my sister alone," Kat said.

He came toward her with his pale hands stretched to the sides as if in supplication. His gesture said he had no weapons and meant her no harm. She knew better. Even if he hadn't been tall and broad and obviously scarred from his warrior training, his intent to harm was inherent in his quest to use her to harm others. She would never know peace or freedom as long as the Order hounded her footsteps.

And what of Victoria?

Her disappearance. The charred bracelet. Her almost haunting appearance near Katherine tonight, and now this sudden showing of their worst nightmare. Stalking, stalking, never stopping. Had Victoria been harmed, or had she finally decided to hide deeper than they ever had before?

"I'm no longer the Order's bloodhound. Tell Reynard

that. Tell him I'm finished. I won't be his servant anymore. I want no part of his obsession," Kat said.

The monk's face hardened. His hands, still held out at his sides, fisted. His hands were a truer indication of his intentions than his words.

"His obsession. His? We all have a divine mission entrusted to us by Samuel himself. Your family was blessed by his kiss. Specially selected by him to lead us to our prey," the monk said. He spat out each word as if it was a curse.

"Well, I refuse. You can tell Reynard. No more," Kat said.

She couldn't stop the tremor in her voice. The crowd from the party was so far away, there was no longer even a murmur from them. She and the monk stood completely alone. Isolated. Even the low hum she usually heard from the walls was silent.

"Where's your hellhound when I need him, Severne?" Kat muttered, but only the walls could hear her.

She was alone with a trained killer. A man used to dispatching daemons easily. He was not so proficient as his master, perhaps, but still formidable. And deadly.

"You can tell him yourself. I'm sure he'll be eager to see you again," the monk said. "It is your duty to come with me. It will be my duty to father the next generation of daemon Seekers. I've beaten Simon to the prize."

His anger had turned snaky and triumphant. His grimace turned up into a thin smile. He'd seen her glance around for help or a weapon. He'd seen her eyes go hollow when there was no help to be found. No witness for whatever he was about to do.

The monk stepped forward. Kat's heart jumped, and she stutter-stepped back. In the heavy skirts of the ball gown, she could never outrun him. All the Order's monks were as physically fit as soldiers, but this man was the largest she'd ever seen.

She wasn't expecting the harsh laughter that erupted from the monk's mouth or the wide grin that split his face. He was a serious hunter who rarely had the luxury of toying with his daemon prey. She, on the other hand, amused him. He thought she presented him with an opportunity to play.

Katherine stilled. Ball gown or not, she would make him regret that laugh. She could at least spoil his game.

She was a cellist.

Not a hunter.

Not a daemon.

But she was a fighter. She'd been fighting this battle her whole life.

When he saw her serious stance, his grin faded. "Come with me quietly and no one needs to get hurt," he said.

His cajoling tone upped her anger exponentially.

"I won't go quietly. You need to hurt," Kat said. "You need to bleed."

This time when he moved, he closed the gap between them without laughter. As he reached her, she dropped back in a defensive stance. She braced her body. She lifted her fists.

But a growl erupted from the shadows.

Unlike when the monk had stepped forward out of the shadows like a pale apparition, Grim brought the inky black of the corridor with him. Shadows clung to his fur so even when he leaped between them, it was hard to see where darkness ended and hellhound began.

"Samuel's kiss," the monk cursed. He fell backward in retreat, clumsily shuffling several paces away from the huge hound.

Grim bared his teeth. The white of his gaping maw startled, his giant teeth easily distinguished from the less distinct animal that bared them.

Had those teeth lengthened and thickened since the last time she'd seen them?

It was only then that Kat realized Grim had never truly threatened her. His ferocity had always been in check, muted for her benefit. He gave no such quarter to the Order of Samuel.

"Call him off. Tell him we'll be married. We will work together to fulfill Samuel's gift," the monk ordered.

This time it was Katherine's turn to smile. She did it sweetly. It turned out a cellist had no need for teeth and claws when such lovely ones were hers to borrow.

"I told you. I quit," Kat said. "Grim."

She didn't have to say more. The monk had already turned to run. Grim disappeared after the panicked sprint of the man who would have gladly dragged Katherine back to his master...once he'd finished with her himself.

A waft of cold, crisp, forest-scented air washed back over her face. The atmosphere contracted as if the pressure had changed. Her ears popped. Then the dusty, close corridor returned to the way it had been.

Grim was now chasing the monk over pathways she couldn't follow.

Instead, Kat turned and hurried in the other direction. She would try to find her sister all night long if she had to while Grim kept her stalker occupied elsewhere. A greater urgency now drove her search. If Reynard's men were here, he wouldn't be far behind. He'd sent his minions into the opera world to find her. Her time at l'Opéra Severne was running out.

Chapter 18

When she finally slowed to a stop, she was all alone and far from the distant crowded salons. There wasn't a hint of the crowd's murmur. Or of Grim's growls. There was only her, the carvings on the walls around her and her sister's dressing room. The key was tied beneath the folds of her dress, but she didn't retrieve it.

Severne's Brimstone heat had been the only thing to save her the night the shadow's touch had almost frozen her to death.

The dance had been a goodbye between them. She was sure of it.

Some pairs are destined to remain apart. But she couldn't confront the shadow without Severne's fire.

Kat clenched fingers gone suddenly icy. From fear. That was all. There was no preternatural chill in the air.

But there was a murmur.

He'd said not to focus on the murals. Not to look too closely. But it was impossible to ignore them completely.

From the corner of her eye she could see a woman embraced by a man brought to his knees with disappointment or pain. Even closer to her than that was the tragically rendered figure of an angelic form whose wings were being shorn from his body with a merciless sword.

Once seen, she had to turn. She couldn't look away. The angel's head was bowed. Chains bound him. She could see the profile of his beautiful face. As she focused, she noticed his downcast gaze and his sculpted lips.

Kat backed away.

The carving had moved.

She saw it then. On the angelic carving, she saw a brooch with the stylized *L* like the one she'd found in her sister's room. It was carved at the figure's neck as if pinned to stiff folds of a snood around its regal throat. Veins stood out in the wooden figure's neck as the angel resisted whatever unseen forces held it in place.

Wait.

There. There. And there. The walls were filled with figures that wore similar brooches. They'd been hidden to her conscious perceptions only by their number and by the chaos of the murals' frenzied composition.

But when she'd found the brooch, it had been familiar because she'd seen it hundreds of times.

The dimly lit hall made the revelation of the brooches a startling horror, but as her eyes focused, the flickering lights revealed a worse observation...

The figure still moved. And it moved to look with staring, wooden eyes directly at her.

She didn't recognize the danger soon enough.

Though the carving's wings were shorn, the shadow that rose from the wall fully outstretched its wings as it had before. Those wings reached for her. She was already too cold to move. She could feel the icy feathers as their tips approached her damp cheeks.

"Katherine," Severne said. He came up behind her. He placed Brimstone-heated hands on her shoulders and pulled her away from the wall. The shadow suddenly retreated as if sucked back into the carving that couldn't possibly have caused it.

"I thought I saw my sister. There was a monk from the Order of Samuel. I called Grim and he chased him away," Kat said. "And the shadow was here again. Right here."

"You're cold. I told you to be wary of the murals," Severne said. "And Kat, Grim only answers to me."

She didn't protest when he picked her up. She didn't argue. Her previous words had been expelled in puffs of white. Her jaw felt too cold to move.

It wasn't only his warmth she desired. It was the negation of his former proclamation. He thought they couldn't be together. He'd said she was alone.

She wanted to prove him wrong.

There was little to no light in the passages they took to her room. When she looked around, she couldn't see Grim. The hellhound was nowhere to be found. Had the poor monstrous beast been hurt by the priest he chased? The Order of Samuel was deadly. They trained from birth to defeat their enemies.

Poor, poor Grim. She'd feared him, but he had helped her when she needed him most. She could only hope he wasn't harmed.

Severne had been the master of l'Opéra Severne for a very long time. He must know it. Every passage. Every room. Every closet. Every face on its walls? He took her unerringly to her rooms. What must it be like for him to endure the stares of creatures like him, doomed to dwell in the opera house forever, but trapped in a never-ending purgatory of its walls?

She'd been distracted by her preparations for the ball and had left her room unlocked. He turned the antique knob and pushed the door open to carry her inside. Only then did she extricate herself from his protective embrace. She pressed against his hard chest and dropped to the floor when he released her. She moved several steps away. Then, when that didn't seem far enough removed from temptation, she moved several more.

The large suite was suddenly small.

The rumpled bed was an embarrassment. Not because it wasn't perfectly made, but because she could too easily picture herself on it, spread with him in passionate disarray.

She had edged toward the cello's corner without realizing it, but Severne noticed.

"Your music doesn't hide you from me. It doesn't protect you. It calls me. The siren song of your soul echoes the Brimstone in my blood. They sing together. They burn together." He watched her for her reaction. She felt her color rise and hoped he thought it was a blush. She knew better. It was desire. She wanted to burn with him. No matter the consequences.

Playing had never banished him from her thoughts. Not like it banished Reynard. It had never been a screen or a shield with Severne. It had been a display. A revelation.

Then why had her hand wrapped around the neck of her beloved instrument now? Why did she find herself reaching for it when it wouldn't protect her against him?

"Do you want to call me to you? You play with fire," Severne warned.

His voice had dropped, sweet and low. Threatening, but with the most delicious punishment she could imagine. His heat. His touch. Him drawn to her side. He had

allowed himself a stride in her direction. She could see
only a glimmer of his green eyes beneath the mask, a suggestion of sooty lashes. But he had stopped. He was holding himself back.

Katherine decided for him. They were a pair. Destiny
be damned.

She rubbed a thoughtful thumb across the cello's strings.
Her fingers detected the nonaudible vibration. Yet John
Severne heard it somehow. He closed his eyes. He clenched
his chiseled jaw. His flush deepened. He swallowed.

And held himself perfectly still rather than respond to
the instrument.

Katherine sat. She embraced the well-loved maple between her knees. She brought the bow across its strings.
This time the sound was loud enough for human ears. This
time Severne's eyes flew open, and she was impaled by
his vivid glare.

"You would torture me?" he said.

She paused. The last note swelled out, then faded, falling from the air like invisible rain. Only they could feel
the pulsations of atmosphere disturbed and then settling
on their skin. Severne turned his face to the sound as if
his hard visage could feel the kiss of its diminishment.

Then silence.

The hollow potential for seductive music held in her hands.

"Not to torture. No," Katherine said. She allowed her
yearning to glow on her face. She showed him the ache in
her eyes. Then she played again and watched him draw in
a gasp of reaction as if the notes she played touched him
physically, intimately. As if she wrapped her hand around
him when she wrapped her hand around the cello to play.

She paused again. The sound faded around them.

He opened his eyes.

"But it is torturous," Severne said. "Bliss and pain... there seems to be no in-between for us."

"I don't want to hurt you. I only want to touch you. To reach you. To call you from whatever cold prison it is that holds you away from me," Kat said.

The words weren't enough. She could play for hours and it wouldn't express the longing she had for Severne. This immortal creature she should have feared. And did. But still desired.

"Cold?" Severne laughed. He brought both hands up and burrowed them into his hair. Then he withdrew them into fists and paced away from her until he was on the opposite side of the room. "You feel my Brimstone burn. More than most. You've tasted my kiss. Damnation like ash on my tongue and you so very sweet. Cold?" he asked.

"You say some pairs are destined to be apart, like a warning before we've even been together. Yet you hold me like you'll never let me go. You're drawn to my music. Yet you push me away," Kat said. "You kiss me to quiet my questions, yet your kiss answers so many, all by itself." She stood and placed her cello to the side. She had refused to hide behind it. Now that she knew the truth, she wouldn't use it to seduce him. He would come to her or not without its call. "Aren't you cold and hard and impossible to touch?"

He didn't rush to answer, to contradict or confirm. He only crossed the room toward her, one step by agonizing step at a time. So slow. Until his approach seemed a confession he wanted to linger over.

See what I do for you.

Watch me.

Wait for me.

Welcome me.

Kat was weak in the knees by the time they stood toe to

toe. Once again, the black of his tuxedo was pressed into the white of her voluminous skirts. She tilted her chin to look up at him. She didn't need the cello. It was a song in her veins. She didn't need music at all. Her affinity sang. The cello only allowed her to express it audibly for the world to hear. She heard it every day, every night, in every dream and waking moment.

"Not cold, Katherine. Never that. There's fire in me for you. Enough to immolate. I've sought to tamp it down. To bury it. To control it," he said.

"Don't," she replied.

Immolation.

Self-sacrifice by fire. She went there. Into the flames. But it wasn't a hurried conflagration.

He reached for her face with one hand. She took one quivering breath when his warm fingers shook on her skin. How could his touch be so soft when he was all hard muscle and stone? How could the daemon master of l'Opéra Severne be hesitant and sweet?

But the exploratory thumb he brushed across her lips wasn't sweet. Like the thumb she'd brushed across her cello's strings, his thumb played her, using her soft gasps as a guide for which note should come next. From one corner of her mouth to the full swell of her lower lip, he caressed, and then he paused. He looked from the vulnerable gasp of her reaction to her eyes, then back again.

Her tongue darted out of its own volition. To taste his salty skin. To moisten the lips he teased.

He watched her lick. His eyes grew deeper and more serious. He moved his hand to hold her chin, and he closed the distance between his face and hers. He captured her lower lip in his mouth. He sought her bold tongue with his.

She would have melted to the floor. Her legs gave out beneath her. But he quickly pressed her to the wall, holding her up, sandwiched between its cool surface and his hard heat.

Did he taste her tangy cocktail as he hadn't tasted his own? Did he taste lemon on her tongue?

She tasted wood smoke. Not ash. The flavors on his tongue were rich and sweet and evocative of the moment when a log first becomes the flame. She tasted the sweet salt from his skin. He buried his hand in her hair, fiercely, until pins flew and chestnut curls tumbled down, and still he showed her he was far from cold. Because of his reaction to everything she did. His gasps. His widened eyes. The rise and fall of his muscled chest as his breathing caught, as it released.

She reached for his mask, and he paused. He stilled as if caught in a bargain he couldn't escape. She loosened the silken ties behind his head, and the black domino fell from his face. When she was able to see him fully again, it was almost as if she was seeing him for the first time. Behind the mask, he'd allowed his expression to soften. He didn't firm it again when the mask dropped away.

She reached for the buttons on his vest. Then on his shirt. He gave her time. No rush. He didn't pull away. She still feared retreat. Feared the withdrawal that always came.

But his face remained a soft revelation. Even though he was lean and chiseled and perfect, his expression had softened as he gasped just for her.

She was the one who rushed to find his heated skin. She splayed her hands on his chest. He was touchable. He was affected. Not cold. Never that.

He fumbled less. Though his hand had shaken on her cheek, he had no trouble with her formal clothes. Hooks and eyes, strings and lacings, buttons and ties…they all parted easily for his long-lived skill.

He was damned. Different. Doomed to be hunted and

dispatched by men who used her like a divining rod to find their prey. Their deserving prey? Maybe. Possibly. She might be risking hell itself to hold him. But if so, why did he taste like paradise on her tongue and feel like salvation on her skin?

He pulled back from their kiss as the delicate bodice fell away from her breasts. Against the white crystals, her hardened nipples were dusky, dark and pink. The fairy Gothic dress had puddled into a tulle pool at her ankles. She stood before him in nothing but a sheer blush of stockings, a wisp of panties and her shoes.

And her mask.

Unlike his, hers was gossamer. It was nothing for him to reach up and brush it aside. It drifted to the ground like a glittering snowflake.

She hadn't been as practiced or quick with his clothes. His shirt was parted, his trousers loosened and low on his hips. He pulled her to him before she could loosen them more. He brought her down on top of him as he fell back on the bed.

She straddled him.

His hard beauty, unrelieved by any softness, was cupped between her thighs.

She could feel his need, and it was a natural extension of the steel she'd felt everywhere on him whenever they'd touched. She reached for his erection, the hardness she'd wrought rather than the hours of work in his torture chamber of a gym that had hardened him everywhere else. But he rolled her to the side. He pressed her to her back. Suddenly fast and completely in control.

"I've shown you I'm not cold," Severne said. "Have I frightened you yet? Or have you kindled, Katherine?"

His voice alone, deep and low, was an intimate hush across her skin. His Brimstone-heated exhalations were hotter than an ordinary man's breath. His whisper tickled and teased. Yes. She was kindled. Already hot and humming with need. But when he followed his query with a warm hand down her quivering stomach to the barely covered V of pink lace, she burned hotter still.

"Severne," she said. It was confession. It was a supplication. He wasn't only the opera's master. He was her body's master. And she called him by name. "John."

"I'm here, Kat. I'm here," he promised.

And he brushed the lace aside to find her.

She was a gifted musician. She'd seduced him with her song. But his gentle, questing fingers found her hidden heat so easily. After all the resistance, the edge was easy. Too easy. Too strong. They were a pair. And it was terrifying, because the universe was in their way.

"I burn. I've always burned. But you burn for me, Katherine. And that's a gift I've never received," Severne said.

He was an impossibly hard man, but his fingers were an artistic maestro's fingers on her tender flesh. They stroked, they played, and when he penetrated her intimate folds, her hips rose to meet his careful thrust.

Kat cried out. Her body clenched around the rhythm of his fingers. With his other hand, he reached for her ankle and lifted her leg. The move gave his questing fingers better access, but it also brought the shoe he'd given her up to his shoulder. He allowed her heel to rest there against his Brimstone-blushed skin. The fairy-tale shoe he'd placed on her foot in the warehouse was now a sexy part of their intimacy. He tilted his face to nuzzle her leg, and she lost all control, finding delicious release. Her body pulsed around his fingers, and he allowed her leg to fall. His kiss muted her cries. He pressed his hot body against her. And as she came down from the high peak where she'd finally flown without the safety of a parachute, she tasted tears on her tongue.

Chapter 19

He was off the bed before Grim scratched at the door. Without her cello, with eyes closed and replete from orgasm, she was irresistible.

He backed away, resisting only by distance and ruthless determination. What he wanted was to bury himself deep inside her, paired with her forever.

That wasn't an option.

This hadn't been, either, damn it. She opened her eyes and blinked. He backed farther away.

She knew. Had known before she'd allowed him to touch her. He wasn't cold, but he was disciplined. He'd been disciplined for decades.

Until now.

Grim scratched again and whined urgently at the door. Something was wrong. Severne had sent him in pursuit when he'd seen Kat leave the salon after the crimson figure in the porcelain mask.

He didn't pause to button his shirt. He didn't say goodbye. He went to the door. She watched him leave. Silent. With large, dark eyes. The *Cinderella* shoes he'd given her were still seductively on her feet, a reminder of all he wanted to give her, but couldn't, because he wasn't a free man.

They had failed him.

Every potential he might have trusted to father seekers with the D'Arcy sisters.

Reynard had the man bound with heavy ropes after he himself repelled the hellhound. He wasn't sure how badly he had injured the beast, but he'd seen the Brimstone flare. He'd heard the hound's cries. It had disappeared back onto the cursed pathways only it could traverse.

But Saul had cried out the truth of where he'd been and whom he'd seen there.

"I found her. I'm the father of the next generation," the monk cried.

His blood stained the ground in pools before he finally breathed his last.

"You found her, but you didn't deliver her to me," Reynard declared.

He didn't have to wield the whip. Saul's brothers completed the task, brutally punishing their fellow monk for leading a hellhound into their midst and for challenging their master with his final breaths. They whipped the robes from his back and then they flayed the skin from his bones.

Saul had failed.

The pride swelled in Reynard's chest and elsewhere as he acknowledged the proof of his favor. He was Father Reynard. He was fully recovered. His blood pulsed as powerfully as it had when he'd first claimed the leadership role meant to be his.

The journey couldn't be completed in an instant, but

he made the calls and arrangements while Saul's blood cooled. He had always structured the universe to his liking. He'd been too patient. Too kind. Nearly dying had changed that. He'd felt as if he had forever to complete his task. Now he knew better.

Katherine D'Arcy was his. And she would lead him to her sister. They'd both always belonged to him. The bracelets had been a gesture on his part. A mark of favor. But first their mother had spurned him, and now her daughters had betrayed him. They required stronger chains. He would bind them and he would use them, willing or not, to continue his mission.

It was time to bring his Katarina home.

Chapter 20

Grim sat back on his haunches when Severne came out of Katherine's rooms. But as soon as the door clicked shut, he jumped to his feet and padded away. Severne followed, distracted, but too used to his sidekick's ways to refuse to follow him now.

The walls watched man and daemon dog pass. In the distance, the party had become more raucous. It was well after midnight. Champagne had flowed for hours. There would be mischief. There always was. Guests who started here would wind up there. Time would be lost. The hours stretched indistinct. Lovers would find each other in the shadows. Then they would find someone else.

The masquerade wasn't the most coveted invitation in Baton Rouge because it was a tame event with safe parameters.

L'Opéra Severne had centuries of decadent practice.

The opera house had been betwixt and between for decades. A little too close to hell for comfort. People were drawn to its mystery, lured by its secrets, seduced by truth and lies. But no human being had ever disappeared in its shadows.

The patrons and guests tonight would enjoy their revelry and return to the real world at dawn without realizing how close they'd danced to the damned.

Grim came to a halt down a long, dark, doorless hallway Severne had rarely seen. Even on his Brimstone-warmed flesh, goose bumps rose as the temperature dropped. He kept a wary eye on shadows as he leaned down to poke the puddle of crimson velvet and silk Grim snuffled on the ground.

The pale white mask stared up at him blankly from the cloak's red folds.

A lesser man might have jumped in surprise.

"I should have known it would be the catacombs. I know every other damned inch of this place," Severne said.

Grim whined again. This time the sound he made was low and uncertain as if he was afraid of who or what might hear. He padded over to an archway barred by a heavy iron door. The door had been left partially open, and an icy tendril of catacomb air teased eerily across Severne's face.

Grim stepped toward the opening.

"No. Come. If you go down there, you might never return. Even you can get lost, and you know it," Severne said.

Baton Rouge was below sea level. What lay beneath the opera house was geographically impossible, but the danger of the twisted caverns and the unnatural labyrinth they formed was very real.

If Kat's sister was down there, she hadn't ventured into the depths alone. His quarry was close. The end of his quest to save his father was so close he could taste it. Trouble was, he could also taste Kat's lemonade cocktail on his tongue. The memory of her kiss had followed him into the shadows.

He couldn't go into the catacombs without preparations.

For now, he reached out and closed the iron door. The echo of its clanging reverberated for a long time.

He didn't hurry away. He stood. He waited. Like Grim, he was standing guard. Closing the door wasn't enough. But as he looked down at the dog, he noticed that one of Grim's legs was held at an unusual angle. He wasn't placing it firmly on the floor.

Severne ignored the crimson cloak and the mask. Instead, he dropped down beside the hellhound whose whine now had a deeper meaning. Grim whined again. And then again. In all the years they'd hunted together, the hellhound had never been injured.

Severne hissed when he saw the ugly wound on the dog's hind leg. A serrated blade had slashed and burned a streak across his hair and flesh. The hellhound's skin was charred. The wound on his leg was angry and red.

They'd never had a man-and-his-dog relationship. Grim was no one's pet. But in his own monstrous way he'd been Severne's faithful companion for far longer than most men lived.

Severne reached to pick up the giant hellhound as if he was a Labrador retriever. A warning growl rumbled deep in the animal's barrel chest, but he allowed Severne to carry him.

"She told me she saw one of the Order's priests and I didn't heed the warning, Grim. I left you to face that threat alone. But you protected her, didn't you? Did you give worse than you got? Is there anything left of him for me to find?" Severne asked.

He needed to get the hellhound to safe care, and then he needed to be sure that Katherine wasn't being stalked by the Order of Samuel under his roof. Brimstone flared in his blood as he imagined Reynard or his minions stalking his halls.

He was the master of l'Opéra Severne. They would be very sorry if they breached his walls again.

He'd been used to the burn of Brimstone when Grim came into his life. He'd held the giant puppy often, unafraid of his scorching tongue. He'd always considered the hellhound a gift from his father, but he'd known who had really called the pup to come and live with him at the labyrinthine opera house full of danger and deadly shadows.

Sybil.

She'd always been there. She'd always been different. A daemon he didn't have to fear completely or hunt.

Grim was much heavier than he'd been as a puppy, though even then he'd been the size of a full-grown dog. Now Severne was glad of the discipline that had trained his body to bear the burden of his injured companion. It shook him to the core to see the hellhound brought down. It seemed a foreshadowing of worse losses to come.

"I feared this might be what all the urgent whispering was about," Sybil said.

He came into her sewing room with the ease of familiarity. He hadn't given Eric to anyone less than his foster mother. A "woman" who had raised him and cared for him as if he'd been her own child.

"What could have done this to him?" Severne asked.

Grim growled when he laid him on a high table that Sybil used for completing alterations. She must have cleared it before they arrived. It was spread over with a clean, white swath of cotton cloth to protect it from Grim's dark blood.

She'd always known more than most people about what

went on at l'Opéra Severne. He'd been taught to ignore the walls. Sybil didn't ignore them. He opened his ears and heard them now. The urgent whispers she spoke of. They must have alerted Sybil to Grim's injury.

"No mortal blade could have done this," Sybil said. She ignored the hellhound's growl to lean close and examine the wound.

"Lucifer's Army?" Severne asked. He placed his hand on the hellhound's side. "Grim is better than that. Too fast for them. Too fierce. They can never get close enough to cut him."

More growls from Grim rumbled beneath his hand. Either in agreement or because the hellhound wasn't used to having his ferocious adult dignity infringed upon with so much contact. It had been decades since he'd bestowed fiery puppy kisses on a laughing boy immune to being burned.

"Not Lucifer's Army. This cut is corrupt. It festers already. That's why it isn't healing. Daemon blades would have cut clean. This was a darker blade. Welded by someone unnatural. Unclean. Evil," Sybil said.

"What's darker than the damned?" Severne asked.

"Daemons are different, not damned. It's the Council that corrupts. They want war and conquest. They aren't satisfied with ruling hell. They want to reclaim Heaven. They corrupt everything they touch," Sybil said.

"Including me?" Severne asked.

"You remain your own man. Like your father before you," Sybil said. "They cannot corrupt your heart even if they do have a hold on the Brimstone they've placed in your blood."

She tended Grim's wound without looking up. But Severne heard the truth in her voice. She loved him like

a mother. She had hope for him. Just as his father had before he'd forgotten.

"He is well. The hydrangeas are blooming," he said.

"Blue was always his favorite color," Sybil said.

Severne had seen the daemon beside him wear every
shade of blue during his lifetime. From cerulean to azure.
It had always been a chicken-or-the-egg curiosity for him.
Had she worn blue for his father, or had his father loved
blue because she always wore it?

He'd known. He'd always known. She loved him like a
son. She also loved his father. But she'd let Levi Severne
go. It was as if she had outlived him even though he was
still alive.

"We all live by our promises. By our love. By our wits
and our will. By our blood," Sybil said.

Severne jumped to stop her, but not in time. She had
taken a large pair of fabric shears from a jar on the table.
She'd opened them and pressed the blade against her wrist.
The move to cut had been hard and fast. There was a flare
and then a crimson flood onto Grim's leg.

"His own Brimstone wasn't enough. So I give him
mine," Sybil said.

The hound cried out but then stilled as if the lava-like
liquid soothed instead of burned. Sybil didn't allow herself to bleed out. She pressed a cloth to the wound, and
smoke curled up from it as the Brimstone was absorbed
back into her skin.

"If you had told me, we could have used my Brimstone,"
Severne said. He shook in reaction to the injury.

"You wouldn't survive the loss of what he needed,"
Sybil said. "You are human, Severne. Though you sometimes seem to forget it."

Severne moved to wrap the maternal daemon in his
arms. She allowed it for several seconds longer than she

would have if she hadn't been weakened. Daemons were not demonstrative with the humans they held in their affections. Or perhaps it was just Sybil who had lived and loved among human daemon hunters for so long that she protected her heart.

"I promised your father I would watch over you. At the last, when he still knew my name, I promised him I would help you," Sybil said.

He would never ask her to help him kill her own kind. But he was grateful that she had saved his oldest friend. And that she'd given him a companion in the first place to ease his lonely existence.

"Thank you," Severne said into hair that would never go gray.

"Different, not damned. Remember that. There may come a time when you need to recall it," Sybil said.

A long soak, a change into jeans and a T-shirt, and an angry eruption of shoving the white dress into the back corner of her closet helped Kat get a handle on her emotions. She had begged for his touch. He'd obliged. He'd never promised her forever. Or even tomorrow. It hurt, but it shouldn't have surprised.

Daemons couldn't be trusted.

His touch had been a gift. He'd taken her so easily to climax. But there's always a price to be paid. That was what terrified her. She'd given him nothing in return, and all she could think about was how badly she wanted to settle that debt.

Katherine tossed and turned in fitful sleep. When she woke feeling as if she'd had too much champagne even though she'd had only one glass of spiked lemonade, she retrieved her breakfast from the cart at her door and took it to her vanity table.

L'Opéra Severne was staffed like magic. So many hallways and corridors. Hundreds of people working to keep the singers and musicians at their best for performances. And yet, more often than not, their comings and goings went unremarked and unseen.

It was only when she lifted a cup of café au lait to her lips that she saw the letters. They sat on her table. The familiar satin sash had been retied into a tighter bow.

She remembered the unlocked door.

Who had brought the letters to her while she was at the masquerade?

Had it been only wishful thinking when she imagined the crimson-cloaked figure behind the crying mask had been her sister?

She had to look. Quickly she exited her room and checked next door. Nothing had been disturbed. The hint of her sister's perfume was fainter than before. There was more dust. No crimson cloak on the foot of the bed. No empty-eyed mask propped on the pillows. Kat went back to her own room.

The letters had been left for her to find, if not by the woman in the crimson cloak, then by someone else. Daemon. Or shadow. Lover or enemy. Or both. She went to the bundle and untied the sash. The satin slid through her fingers and trailed silkily to the floor.

She opened the first letter, loosening each fold with trembling fingers. What she saw was faded ink written by her mother's long-dead hand.

Chapter 21

My Dearest Daughters,
I have failed you in so many ways. I didn't know how much until Ezekiel came into my life. How frightened I've been. How failed by my own mother. This is not the legacy I would bequeath to you. I know that now. I know what I must do. Reynard has found me for the last time. He intends to destroy Ezekiel. I must seek help from a man I don't fully trust. But I do trust Ezekiel in spite of his daemonic nature. We've been so wrong. So misled. Daemons aren't damned. They're different from us. More different than our human beliefs can describe.

I can only assure you that Ezekiel loves me as I love him, and he loves both of you although you were fathered by one of the monks who mercilessly hunt his people. No beings that love as fiercely as daemons love can be damned. I won't believe it.

Your biological father was as misled as we have been. He cared for us as much as he was able to care once the Order had corrupted his heart.

Please remember that when you think of him. He was not an evil man, but he followed an evil man, and for that reason and that reason alone he had to die. I will stop Reynard once and for all without help if I have to. Ezekiel doesn't know what I intend to do. If he did, he would try to stop me and the Order would have him. I can't distract him from his duty to his people. He's their leader now. I know it seems a horror for me to be in love with the Prince of Darkness, but I promise you that it isn't horrible. I've seen true darkness in my life. I've seen it always in Reynard's mad eyes.

Please know, if I fail you yet again, that I also do this for you. I can no longer justify running and hiding. I must make a stand.

My only consolation in this long, dark life has been my love for you both. You and the music have saved me. When we sing and play, I feel the love of Ezekiel around us. That sustained me for many years.

But now, I must step boldly into the shadows and meet my fate. If I succeed, we will be free. If I fail, you must continue the fight without me.

Love always,

Mother

Going back in time was messy. Especially when it revealed how others perceived you. Kat read all the letters, not only the final letter meant for her eyes. Her mother's words to Ezekiel, the daemon she'd loved, described her daughter as quiet, withdrawn, guarded and always alone. Her cello was her only friend.

It hurt.

But she'd come to l'Opéra Severne to help Victoria in spite of those things. She was stronger than her mother had known. The true revelation was about her mother's tragic past.

She'd loved a daemon, and she'd been forced to let him go. Their father had been one of the monks in the Order of Samuel, but their mother had never loved him. She'd been forced to marry him. Forced to have children the Order could use. She worried that one day they'd be forced to do the same. Ezekiel, in his letters, had promised to rain hell's fire on the Order's heads if they tried to hurt them.

They'd been loved.

In the great darkness of Anne's life, having children to resist the Order by her side had been a comfort to her. Time and again she spoke of her love for them in spite of everything.

They had never known.

They'd been told their father had died fighting a daemon to protect their mother. She told a different tale. About how her true love had tried to save her and how he'd killed their father when he wouldn't let them go.

Reynard had told them the same daemon had killed their mother, but her last letter revealed that she was going to try to save the love of her life from Reynard and that the obsessed priest might kill her if she got in his way.

What had Victoria thought of the letters? Had discovering Reynard's betrayal frightened her into hiding? Had their mother succeeded in saving the daemon she loved?

The letters raised more questions than they answered, but they also revealed that Anne D'Arcy was braver than Katherine had ever imagined. She prayed that they had that in common.

Chapter 22

L'Opéra Severne was muted the next day. Any loud noise drew dark looks from a multitude of people who had over-indulged the night before.

"You understand the twenty-four-hour recovery window now," Tess said. The cooling gel mask she wore over her eyes was an ironic commentary on the masquerade masks from the night before.

Kat had joined Tess in the quiet dressing rooms for pedicures. She needed the company, and the mundane beauty ritual was soothing. She'd opted for a deep crimson on her toenails as a shout of hope to a universe determined to throw her one tumultuous twist after another.

"I saw you dancing with Severne, by the way," Tess said. Her eyes were closed beneath her mask, but her tone was arch.

"We did dance. There was…dancing," Kat said.

Tess opened her eyes and glanced at Kat sideways. "He

terrifies me. I mean, in the most delicious way. But I'm still scared. Be careful there," she said.

Kat had a nailbrush full of Scarlet Temptation in her hand, but she knew her friend wasn't talking about being careful with the bold color.

"Have you ever known him to…date…performers?" she asked.

"He doesn't talk with us, Kat. Much less date. He's like the moon. Who dates a planet?" Tess asked.

"The moon isn't a—" Kat began.

"You know what I mean. He's above us all. Untouchable. Not that he hasn't been wanted. Most wanted," Tess said. Her soft words resulted in a chorus of shushes from women across the room who were also half-heartedly prepping for tomorrow night.

Quiet. Withdrawn. Guarded. Her cello was her only friend. Alone.

She had a lot in common with a daemon opera master.

Kat smiled at Tess though the other woman had lain back to close her eyes again.

"I guess I have nothing to fear, then," Kat said. "If he's untouchable, I can want him without being in any danger."

She knew better. She was in terrible danger. But she could seem to heed the older woman's advice without sharing her secrets.

Chapter 23

Opening night actually began long before dawn. Props were finalized and wheeled into place. Technicians spent hours troubleshooting last-minute problems with ancient wiring and lights. By the time the first of the audience arrived, the air was electric with tension and expectation. Traffic was blocked on Severne Row, and a long stream of limousines and town cars and giant SUVs with tinted glass began to dispense glittering passengers in designer dresses and tuxedos on the red-carpeted curb in front of the Théâtre de l'Opéra Severne.

Severne greeted the most important of the night's guests in person. He hosted preshow champagne in salons only slightly less crowded than they'd been the night of the masquerade.

And all the while, only one woman and her cello were on his mind.

When the tones sounded to alert the guests to find their seats half an hour before the overture, the heat in his blood was already high in expectation of what was to come. He stepped outside. Spotlights shone their beams high into the sky above the opera house, arching high above his head in shafts that crisscrossed each other as technicians manned the mechanical housing for the giant bulbs. The spotlights were also antiques. They'd been wheeled out once a year for decades only for the opening of the summer's *Faust*.

The Baton Rouge night didn't cool his skin. Nor did his temporary reprieve fool him. He was going to attend the show. He was going to listen to Katherine play. And even though she played for an audience, her true performance, that of the affinity in her blood and the music in her soul, would be only for him.

The house was full. The lights dimmed low. Voices swelled to fill the great performance hall. But it wasn't voices Severne heard. It wasn't voices that caused his eyes to burn and his chest to squeeze so tight he could hardly breathe.

It was Katherine.

The echo of her heart reverberated from the cello in her arms.

Every resolution he'd made in the past twenty-four hours burned away.

He found his place in the private box that was kept empty for the family. Once it had been occupied often. For decades it had been empty and still. He disturbed it now. He pushed aside the draperies and sat in the shadows. He watched her, secretly, while tears ran down her cheeks.

Did she cry for Marguerite, for Faust, or were her tears for other beings more real and tragic?

If even one salty droplet was for him, her pain pierced his damned soul.

The whole orchestra was dressed in gray, a soft dove gray that blended with dusky shadows. But to his eyes, Katherine's silk gown was iridescent. It hugged her subtle curves and shimmered with her every movement. In its simplicity, it allowed her to shine. Her fervor for the music was accented because there was nothing to distract, only the seductive compliment of unadorned fabric. So different from the masquerade. That night had been about masks and secrecy.

This night was about raw emotion laid bare.

He clenched his fists on the tops of his thighs. Grim whined from behind him, not quite materialized in this time and place. The hellhound was recovered. Sybil had healed him with Brimstone from her own blood. The dog was eager to stretch his legs.

Perhaps he should run. Run away until nothing was left but the burn in his blood, until his ache for Katherine D'Arcy had mercilessly cooled to ash.

He didn't.

He stayed.

There was nowhere far enough he could go. No amount of time or distance between them would change his need for her. Staying was a mistake, but a sweet one. Her heartfelt playing mingled with memories. She had cried out his name during her release. He had touched her intimate heat, and he could still feel her on his fingers. He recalled perfectly the look in her eyes when she'd said "seduction." So brave. So bold.

He was damned.

Even now, he and his father were lost. His grandfather had made the Severne blood in their veins a curse. Katherine's music didn't care that he was damned. Her playing didn't save him, but it seemed to understand and desire him anyway.

Her music came to him, mingling with his head, his heart and his blood. Meeting and matching the Brimstone burn. Each poignant note wasn't a reprieve, but it was a brief pardon. If not a salvation, a respite from what he'd done.

And what was still left to do.

He didn't make a conscious decision to go to her after the performance. It was inevitable.

He was already damned; he might as well enjoy the burn.

The first performance was a success. Her whole body—arms, back, core and thighs—ached to prove what the company had accomplished. Music extracted a price that was physical as well as emotional, but this night it hadn't been *Faust* that drained her.

She'd wept for her mother, her sister, her frustration with Severne as the music claimed all her inhibitions. She hadn't been able to focus on control when the cello required her concentration. And she hadn't wanted to. For the first time in her life, she'd let go.

Amid the blood, sweat and tears backstage, her damp cheeks went unnoticed. Or so she thought while she placed her cello in its case. She should have known nothing escaped Severne's attention, least of all her distress or pain. He'd seen straight to the hidden heart of her from the first time he'd approached her and Eric in the alley as they cowered from Reynard. John Severne was tuned to her need even as she sought to deny it.

The remaining stragglers were departing the joint dressing room of the orchestra and chorus when the opera's master filled the doorway. She was overwhelmed to see him, but not surprised. She didn't turn away. She wouldn't be ashamed of her human emotions. Whether he allowed himself to share them or not.

"You are so lovely. Even surrounded by stage opulence and all the beauty calculated to dazzle an audience, you glow. I thought it was your music. I thought the Brimstone burn in my heart was seduced by its accompaniment in the air. But it's you. You draw me. Your cello is closed

away in its case, but I stand here, unable to stay away,"
Severne said.

She should tell him to go. She tried to recall the chill
of his withdrawal the night of the masquerade, but her
strength was gone, spent over the long hours of performance. She was vulnerable. Unable to muster resistance
when capitulation was her heart's desire.

He was a daemon.

She was a tool for daemon hunters.

But for a little while, for tonight, maybe they could accept that her soul and whatever was left of his were in tune.

He crossed to her when she didn't protest. He reached to
touch her tear-stained cheek. His heat immediately soaked
into her body, finding and warming those places she hadn't
known were still chilled from the shadow's touch.

"I didn't play for you. I played for me. For the first time,
I played for me. Not to hide. Not to seduce. Not to impress
or endure. Just to feel," Kat said.

"And you can't stop feeling yet. You tremble beneath
my hand. Tears gather again in your eyes," he said.

"I'm tired of resisting Reynard, the Order of Samuel,
the winged shadow, the fear I might never see Victoria
again," Kat said. "You."

He leaned over her and pressed his forehead against
hers. She could feel his tension. She could feel how hard
he worked to hold himself in check.

"Don't resist me. Not anymore," he said. "I have to face
untold tomorrows alone. Be with me tonight."

Her gaze flew up to meet his when she heard the shaking need in his voice. She'd been averting her eyes to hide
what she could of what she felt, but as their gazes met, she
could see his need was fiercer and hotter than the damnation in his veins. He went against universal strictures
to touch her, to allow her to touch him. And she risked
everything to respond—her sister, her life and her soul.

His lips, when he swooped to claim her mouth, bespoke age-old secrets against her skin—fire and flight and shadows and song. Daemons were an ancient race. Their history was dark and tragic. They'd fallen from Heaven. They endured a revolution in hell where once-angelic beings fought lesser daemons that longed to conquer paradise. And Severne was somehow caught in between.

A hint of wood smoke flavored his tongue as he teased past her lips. And she boldly met him with hers, tasting, savoring, feeling the thrill of fear at his heat and obvious strength of the desire that shook his body against hers.

He encircled her with steel arms and she twined her arms around his neck to keep from falling, but also to feel how their twining tongues affected the strong being she wasn't supposed to be allowed to touch.

Daemons were hated. Hunted. Killed.

His muscular arms were living, heated stone, but she could feel the shiver, the tremble as he reacted to her taste and touch.

When he pulled his lips from hers to kiss her neck, her shoulder, and trail his mouth down to the swell of her breasts above the dove-gray silk gown, she cried out. His mouth was so hot and her skin had been so much colder than she'd known.

The winged shadow's chill evaporated off her skin like invisible steam everywhere Severne's lips caressed.

"Grim will lead us privately back to my rooms, but only if you desire it. I will walk away now if you don't ask me to stay," he said.

Her legs had buckled. He held her fully, with her back bowed and his face at her breasts. His words were a raw whisper that teased over nipples distended under clinging silk.

She answered by leaning to kiss his upturned face—forehead, cheek and then jaw as he rose with her once again in his arms. His skin was salty sweet against her tongue, his mouth slightly opened when she reached it. He moaned when she kissed him and paused at the door with the jamb at his back when she dipped her tongue inside his mouth, as if she weakened his knees. An impossible feat but one she gloried in. She felt empowered in his arms. Not like the quiet, hidden bloodhound for madmen. But like a woman with the world at her fingertips.

"Grim," Severne called hoarsely.

The hellhound materialized out of the shadows and led the way quietly, down dark, unoccupied passages filled with fog and impossible forest scents.

She'd never been to Severne's private apartments. She would never find them on her own. The way was long and far from every other part of the opera house. She wondered as the passages turned to carved stone if it was part of the world she knew at all.

Finally they came to a stone archway and a great wooden door. It looked more castle keep than opera house.

The door opened with a loud clang of rusty hinges and locks when Severne brushed it with his hand. Grim lay down in the hallway, and Severne stepped inside.

Just inside the threshold, Severne placed her on her feet and turned to shut the door. Her stomach plummeted as if she'd fallen from a great height. Fear, adrenaline rush and desire caught her. She firmed her spine and balled her fists. The door clanked multiple times as if locking itself even though Severne only pushed it closed.

He stood with his palm against the wood for a long time. She watched his broad shoulders rise and fall. His need for a pause cranked up the adrenaline flooding her veins. She wanted his kiss. She wanted to flee. She wanted...

"You fear me," he said as he turned to her.

The intensity in his face caused her heart to pound. She'd feared much in her life. Dark nights when she'd been stalked by killers using her to perpetuate their deadly cause. The loss of family. The loss of hope. She'd feared that one night she would stop resisting and become a willing slave to the Order of Samuel, negating years of the fight against darkness and death.

The tension in Severne's body caused her to ache to soften his shoulders and ease his constant muscular readiness for destruction.

"I fear what we are together," Kat said. "What we feel together scares me."

"I've denied myself for a long time. But I won't hurt you," Severne said.

"Not physically. I know. I trust your touch. You've shown me you can be gentle and responsive to my need. I fear how we might hurt each other tomorrow," Kat said.

"Grim is outside. You can leave. He'll lead you back to your room," Severne said. His stance between her and the door said other things. Darker, needier things.

And she didn't mind.

"I'm here. With you. I'm not going anywhere," Kat said.

It was a bigger confession than she'd intended to make. She didn't mean for tonight. She meant for as long as she drew breath. But he didn't have to know that.

He wanted to promise her the same. He clenched teeth against the impossible pledge. He wasn't a free man. He was bound. He could only pleasure her with all his might. Take some ease for the ache in his bartered soul. And then crush her promise to him tomorrow or the next day or the next.

For all his strength, he was weak in this. He couldn't send her away with Grim tonight. He had to accept her offer to stay. He couldn't draw another breath without her promised touch.

Chapter 24

She chose to be here. Always before, she'd obeyed her affinity for daemons, reluctantly, giving into the pull when she couldn't resist any longer. She stood across from Severne, and the pull of his Brimstone blood was so strong it vibrated every cell in her body.

Kat was more alive than she'd ever been. But not because of her affinity for daemons. She chose to be here.

Severne wasn't exerting any daemon influence. She wasn't a helpless bloodhound.

"I've never allowed myself to imagine you here," Severne confessed. His accented tones were liquid pleasure to her ears. His voice spilled over her body, already sensitized by her affinity, in waves. She trembled as the sound of it lapped her skin. "You. Here. In my rooms. It's a dream," he continued.

But when he moved to stand closer to her, the heat from his body was real. His tall, hard physique wasn't insubstantial at all.

"You're very real to me. As if everything that came before was the dream and I'm waking to you," Kat whispered.

He raised his hand to brush tendrils of hair back from her face. So soft. So light. As if he tested their theories of dream versus reality to see which of them was right. When he discovered solid hair and skin, he cupped the side of her face. Still hesitant. Still testing.

"I'm here," Kat assured him. Though his touch made her feel so light she might be less substantial than she should have been. It seemed she might be able to float away.

"I'm glad," Severne said.

His hand slid around to the nape of her neck and he gently urged her nearer to him. She obeyed, but only by a step because she wanted to look up into his shadowed face. He searched her expression, too, as if he still confirmed she was solid and not a figment of his imagination. Then he followed his gaze with his fingers. He trailed warm, calloused digits over her cheeks, jaw and neck until she drew in breath at the sensual tickle of his explorations.

This wasn't loss of control like the night of the masquerade. This was conscious capitulation to desire. For him as well as for her. His willingness to reach out made her knees weak. Suddenly she was terrified, and her heartbeat quickened. She tried to prevent her respiration from giving away her fears, but breathing normally while he touched her didn't seem to be an option.

His fingers soothed down to trace the edges of her collarbone exposed by the delicate silk bodice of her dress. His gaze moved from his fingers to her skin and to her face. He watched her reaction as her breath became shallow and quick, as her flush deepened, as her pulse raced in the concavity below her throat.

She swallowed.

And he noted the movement. He followed it by pressing one gentle finger on her pulse where it leaped beneath his gaze.

"You're right. You're here with me. This isn't a dream," he teased.

Then he dipped his head to press his lips to the pulse that betrayed her fear and desire.

His mouth overwhelmed the tingling of her affinity with a rush of hotter, more urgent reasons to get closer to this being who called her to him. This was age-old magic having nothing to do with Samuel's gift. It was Severne's kiss that was a much stronger draw than the affinity had ever been.

Kat cried out, and he responded by wrapping the steel of his arms around her sagging body. Her knees had finally succumbed to the sensations stealing their strength. It wasn't daemon influence. He used only wicked masculine seduction.

The move to hold her took his mouth from her skin, but he rectified the separation immediately by tasting the line of her jaw to the tender spot beneath her ear. His teeth nipped there as if a mere taste wasn't enough.

"Very real," he said in a low murmur against her neck.

Kat had reached for his shoulders when her knees gave out. Now she smoothed her hands to his neck, feeling his hardness and his strength, until she threaded her fingers into his dark hair. It was silky against her palms, a discovery of softness like the full lower lip that even now brushed her skin.

This wasn't rushed and reluctant. This wasn't a stolen moment like before. This was a slower exploration, a savoring of the attraction they'd resisted since the first night they met.

The difference frightened her because it was an intensification she wasn't sure she could face tomorrow.

But it also seduced.

Her body throbbed. Her heart pounded. Her head was light with possibilities because they were both here and neither of them planned to run away.

"With your simple gown and your hair tumbled down, I've never seen you more beautiful," he said. He had buried both hands into her chignon and he held handfuls of her hair in his fists. He tightened his fingers, and she gasped as he held her in place. Her head was tilted back by the pressure to give him the best access to her mouth.

But he didn't swoop. He didn't rush. He looked his fill first. From her eyes to her lips to see how she gasped for him, to see how she held her breath when the moment was prolonged.

Her nipples hardened.

Her hands tightened.

She did hold her breath until the tightness and expectation seemed prepared to burst.

And then he leaned slowly to press his mouth to hers.

Their lips clung. Their mouths opened. Tongues slid hungrily together. And pleasure arched from that rough, velvet contact to the tender core of her body that still hummed from the physicality of her performance and the affinity between them that danced to the music she'd made.

Kissing Severne was a full-body experience just as playing her cello was.

Tension stretched in her stomach and lower as if strings of her soul had been tightened until taut.

As his smoky tongue teased and tasted deeply of her gasps, he plucked those taut strings again and again. He might as well have touched her in the same intimate ways as he'd touched her before.

She used his body for support. She couldn't stand. But when his hands moved from her hair, down her silk-covered back to her hips, she melted even more.

He lifted her into his strength, curving his back so she was pressed against his iron body. He cupped and held her bottom, and she moaned because her long dress hindered her legs. She whimpered her need and he responded with masculine murmurs.

"Of all the things that have been in our way, this is nothing," he said.

He slid the gray silk up and up. He bunched the fabric as they kissed. Slowly, until after what seemed an age, she was able to wrap her legs around his waist. The affinity had become such a part of her physical reaction to Severne, she could no longer separate the two. She thrummed with need.

And only he could play her.

She reached for his shirt. She released his buttons— one, two, three—until the shirt and his tuxedo jacket were pressed off his shoulders. The clothing caught at his bent elbows when he didn't straighten his arms.

Kat hissed as her hand came into contact with his scorched tattoo. His marks were almost painfully hot.

"Careful. You might burn," he warned.

She'd already ignored that warning to be here tonight.

The heat was not quite pain. She explored each mark with her fingers. Then she risked leaning down to kiss each one in turn as if she could heal them and erase them by not being afraid. She didn't know what they meant, but he covered them whenever he was in public. They weren't marks he was proud to carry.

"Katherine, no," he said.

But she ignored him.

He let her slide to her feet and he tried to back away,

but their bodies still clung together. His moved. Hers followed. It only took a few steps for them to make it to the bed. He stopped with its edge against the backs of his legs.

She pressed his jacket and his shirt the rest of the way from his arms so he stood bared from the waist up. He'd chosen to be with her. He'd decided to explore the desire they couldn't deny. But he hadn't realized the exploration would go both ways.

"Severne, *yes*," Kat said.

She wouldn't be denied.

Her hands moved of their own volition, drawn by desire, but also by tenderness and sensual curiosity. She traced the marble-hard perfection of his chest, over the swell of his pectoral muscles, down to his abdomen. She could feel his Brimstone heat, his heartbeat and his held breath when his chest swelled beneath her fingers.

He released that breath in a long, quavering exhalation as her hands found his belt.

But he didn't say no again.

She unbuckled his belt. She unbuttoned and unzipped his pants. He watched her movements with glittering, dark eyes. She was only so bold. She couldn't look closely into his eyes to see if there was any green.

Unlike the rest of him, his erection was hard because of hunger, not because of denial. She had caused the heated iron that filled her hand. She gripped. She stroked. Reveling in what she had wrought. His head fell back, and the moment was the opposite of all the hours he'd spent in the gym honing away his heart and his desires.

His body was starved of all but muscled necessity.

His erection was hunger that couldn't be denied.

Katherine didn't hesitate. She dropped to her knees to worship the evidence of his vulnerability and his need for her. He was powerful and weak when her mouth closed over his heated skin. He cried out. But he didn't shout denials or rejection. He called her name.

His hands threaded back into her hair as she took him deeply, as she pleasured him decadently, when he was more used to stoic sacrifice and pain.

His hips jerked.

He grew harder in her mouth.

She gave him the beauty and ease he'd professed to have no time to enjoy. And he lay back to accept, to enjoy. He continued to repeat the mantra of her name, again and again.

But he stopped her before he allowed his release. He pulled her to her feet. Her breath caught. The warmth in her belly threatened to go cold. Until he stepped from his loosened pants and kicked them aside. Nude, he watched her reaction as he slowly lifted the silk dress from her body. The slide of it was like torture against her sensitized skin.

She wanted to wrap her legs around him again, to impale herself on him, a willing sacrifice, but he held her away.

Instead he fell to his knees in front of her and pressed his mouth to her skin.

The moist heat on her stomach made her moan. But it was nothing compared to what came after. He stripped her underwear away, tearing the scrap of lace. She didn't care. Not when it gave his tongue access to her throbbing heat.

He urged her back with a nudge, and she found the bed behind her. The room had fallen away in her mind. She didn't know up or down. She couldn't remember left or right. Nothing mattered but the hot connection he forged between them with his mouth.

He'd pleasured her before with his hands, but he hadn't allowed his own pleasure, and he had stopped before their bodies could come together. This was slower, deeper and the bravest thing she'd ever allowed. She couldn't hide beneath his mouth. He explored every secret sigh and soft cry. She was most definitely here with him, and there was no place else she could be.

Her hands found his arms. She placed one palm over his marks, taking their heat along with her pleasure. It was an augmentation, not a hardship. Knowing him while he knew her. Finding each other together, maybe for the first time.

The heat flushed over her body until her bare breasts grew wet with perspiration. Her orgasm caused the droplets to run down her skin in quivering streams.

"So much better than any dream," Severne confessed.

He rose over her, but again he paused and looked into her eyes. She easily found the green in his irises. She didn't think it would ever be hidden from her again. Then and only then did he bury himself in her still convulsing flesh. Her body gripped him in spite of the extreme heat. She wrapped her arms around him as her perspiration evaporated away from her body in a barely perceptible cloud of translucent steam.

"Promise you'll always play for me, Kat," Severne demanded.

"I've always played for you. From the first day I drew the bow across the strings," Kat confessed.

She hadn't met him on that long-ago day when she'd discovered the cello at l'Opéra Severne, but the opera house and its master were too closely blended to separate one from the other.

He tensed in her arms so hard, she cried out for fear he would shatter like metal that hadn't been tempered, but then the heat of his orgasm brought her to completion again. They both survived the ultimate rejection of their damned legacies together.

For the first time since the shadow had touched her, she was warm all the way to her soul.

Chapter 25

John Severne slept.

He was gentled somehow. He'd shared his intensity, his fire and his fully hardened flesh. Her touch had softened him in every way. His brow was relaxed. His jaw unclenched. His arms relaxed on the bed. His powerful legs were coiled in the sheets.

But as he slept and the call of his Brimstone blood quieted in her head, Katherine heard another call. This one was louder and hotter than any she'd ever experienced. Her head throbbed with pressure and pain. She crept from the bed as if pulled by a powerful magnet. She bit her lip until it bled against the whimper that tried to erupt from her lips.

She walked step by reluctant step into the next room.

A trance of purpose had claimed her, and she couldn't resist.

Beneath the glow of flickering gaslight sconces, an old, scarred trunk sat, worn from use and abuse. Made of some unknown wood blackened with age, the trunk seemed as if it had petrified to stone. There was no key. It opened to her touch. But held in its dark cavity was an iron cask that was obviously too hot for her hands. She drew back and squinted against its heat.

The magnet that drew her wouldn't be denied. There was Brimstone fire in that iron cask, and it wanted her to find it. She went in search of something to help her without thinking about what her prying might mean or what opening the cask might reveal. The call she'd always felt from daemons seared her brain, more demanding than ever before.

In Severne's spartan bedroom, there were only a few drawers and cabinets to search. She found clothes. Mundane toiletries. And a drawer full of rusty iron brooches that caused her to gasp.

Like the one she'd found in Vic's room. Like the one she'd seen on the carved angel's neck before the winged shadow had touched her. The iron brooches were heavy and marked with an ornate *L*.

There were hundreds in the drawer.

Her heart slowed to a sluggish stall. Her ears rang. Her mouth, still tasting of Severne's wood smoke, went dry.

Hundreds.

How many souls were trapped forever in l'Opéra Severne's walls?

She'd thought it a strange purgatory in a place plagued by curses. But now her heart whispered uglier revelations. About Severne. About what he had done.

She reached to pick up one of the brooches. All feeling left her fingers from its chill, like an echo of the winged shadow's touch. All feeling returned with a scorched sting when she used the brooch to flip back the iron cask's lid.

A scroll rested inside, and smoke rose as it unfurled

beneath her gaze. With a snaky hiss, the paper sizzled as the air hit the words emblazoned upon it.

The name Michael glowed in red.

Above it, she saw other names slashed through with burned black lines…just like the tally marks on Severne's beautiful arm. The marks she'd kissed to impart imagined healing.

The name most recently marked through was Lavinia. Eric's mother's name.

"You shouldn't be here. You shouldn't be anywhere near that," Severne said. "You'll burn yourself to the bone."

He came into the room and moved quickly to roll the scroll and shut the iron casket. He placed it back inside the trunk. Practiced moves. Ones he'd completed hundreds of times?

Smoke curled from his fingers, but he didn't cry out, protected by his Brimstone blood.

She'd felt those calluses intimately. The ones caused by being burned again and again.

"You weren't there to help. You were there for the same reason as Reynard. You were there to kill Eric's mother," Kat said. "You are a daemon hunter."

"Reynard completed the task set for me. But I wound up with much more to worry about. You. Eric. This," Severne said. He was naked, with nothing but the sheet wound around his waist. But he no longer looked relaxed. He looked as ready to fight as ever.

"Michael. I've asked you about that name. He was the patron dating my sister. He's the next name on your list. Did they run away to prevent his being a future tally mark on your arm? All those marks, all those iron brooches in your drawer," Kat said. She backed away from Severne. As she did, her bracelet made an unusual sound unlike its normal chime. She brought her wrist up and saw the silver had blackened as if it had been scorched.

She hadn't touched the iron cask. The *L* brooch had been ice in her hand. The only time she'd touched Brimstone's heat... Her eyes darted to the bed where she'd experienced the full burn of Severne's orgasm.

The blackened bracelet she'd found in her sister's room hadn't meant that Michael was a threat to Victoria. The threat to her sister was in this room because Vic had taken a daemon lover. She must have removed the bracelet as a rejection of the Order of Samuel. Something they'd always longed to do.

Kat reached for her own bracelet's clasp. It was still warm to her touch. It took longer than it should have because she'd never removed it and because the metal was stuck together, damaged by Severne's heat. Finally it loosened, and she was able to allow it to drop to the floor. Not just a rejection of Reynard, but of all she'd felt for John Severne.

Another mad daemon hunter who'd only wanted to use her to get to her sister's lover.

"Why would you murder your own kind?" she asked to buy time. She needed to get to the door. Would Grim let her pass? Could she find her way back to her room and out of the opera house without the hellhound's help?

"Katherine, I'm not a daemon. I never corrected your assumption because I'm no better than the daemons I hunt or the daemons I'm forced to serve. My grandfather made a deal with devils for financial gain. He sold our Severne souls. The only way anyone with a drop of Severne blood will ever be free is if I deliver Michael to the Council that rules hell since Lucifer was overthrown," Severne said.

"You've filled the walls of l'Opéra Severne for the

Council," Kat said. She saw the wooden faces in her memory. So many doomed by Severne's hand.

"A purgatory. A prison. A place where immortal daemons who still rebel for their lost king are trapped and kept from fighting the Council," Severne said.

"They haunt you. You're buried under the weight of all the daemons you've been ordered to kill," Kat said.

"They are the Fallen. Older than the Council. Old enough to remember leaving Heaven to rule their own realm. Lucifer and his fellows ruled a hell dimension. But other daemons resented being Lesser because they'd never flown in paradise. They intend to reclaim a paradise they never knew. They want to claim the hell dimension fully and then turn their attention to an invasion of Heaven. They hold my contract. Lucifer's Army is my enemy by the Council's order. My father doesn't even remember that he's damned. I fight for him. I go on day after day. Night after night. For him," Severne said. "He deserves to die in peace. Michael is the last name on the list. Once he's banished to the walls, we'll be free."

"Free to suffer for what you've done," Kat whispered, horrified. "Eric is innocent. You were going to kill his mother. You didn't stop Reynard from killing her."

"I can't save them. They are part of Lucifer's Army, and they doom themselves by rebelling against the Council," Severne said.

"Not Eric. He's a boy. He's not an army," Kat said.

"He's a daemon. Damned no matter what I do," Severne said.

"The daemons trapped in the wall can't fight the Council. They are forever paused. You've taken away their hope. And you risk being a part of the daemon faction that would try to invade Heaven. More war. More destruction," Kat said. "I thought we couldn't be together because you were a daemon, but now I discover it's because you're an obsessed man, a soulless hunter no better than Reynard."

She had no tears left. They'd all been burned away.

"Do not interfere. Do not get in the way," Severne warned.

"You were going to use me to get to Michael, weren't you? You thought I could find my sister and in turn, you could find her lover. You were using me as Reynard has used my family for decades. Know this, John Severne. Your family is damned, but my family is love—my mother, my sister and even me, Heaven help me. We've loved and lost. I will do everything in my power to help Victoria. To prevent her pain. Even if it means damning you to hell."

"Grim," Severne said.

Kat didn't know if the hellhound would leap from the shadows to find her throat or if he would keep her from entering the passageway. She braced herself for teeth or threatening growls.

"Take her to her room and keep her there," Severne ordered.

The giant dog came forward and waited for her to move.

Kat turned away from the man she couldn't allow herself to love. He didn't stop her. He let her walk away.

She needed to warn her sister about Michael's name on Severne's list. She needed to find Eric and get him away from l'Opéra Severne. But there was a hellhound at her heels shepherding her through space and time, and she didn't have so much as a single bone in her pocket.

"I need to see Sybil," Kat said. She whispered the entreaty over and over again as they walked down the halls. They'd come back into the part of the opera house where the walls had ears. Hundred of them. And lips to whisper and cry.

Was it her imagination or wishful thinking that Sybil's name was taken up in a sibilant chant across stiff wooden faces, hundreds of them, calling her name softly? Sybil. Sybil. Sybil.

She wasn't sure if she could trust the daemon that had cared for Severne like a mother for centuries, but she had no one else to turn to. She already owed Sybil a favor, but perhaps she could bargain another for her help. Sybil would know how to handle Grim. She would know where Eric could be found. She might even be able to get a message to Victoria.

Again and again, Kat spoke the daemon's name.

She wasn't paying attention to the walls or shadows. She blindly allowed Grim to herd her along like the German shepherd he vaguely resembled. She stopped in surprise when she rounded a corner to almost bump into Eric where he crouched at the side of the hall.

"I found my mom. It took me a long time because they move. That scared me at first. But I'm glad now. It would be bad to be stuck on the same wall forever. I couldn't memorize the halls. I just had to keep looking," he said. He finished chewing on a hard roll from his pocket and dusted the crumbs from his fingers.

Grim had stopped, too. He watched them. She didn't have long, but she couldn't simply pass Eric by. She gave the hellhound a stern look and quickly turned her attention back to the daemon boy.

"That's why you fill your pockets with food," Kat said. "So you don't have to stop looking to eat."

"Yeah. I got pretty hungry a few times. Sybil told me to rest. She'd find me and carry me to bed at first, but I learned to hide after that." He looked up at the carving with tired eyes.

"I'm so sorry," Kat said.

She came to his side. Grim didn't protest, but she could tell he tracked her movements vigilantly with his burning coal eyes. Eric's mother was indeed carved onto the wall. She stood with one hand stretched toward her son as if she would hold his hand. Her curved fingers extended from the wall, and Kat had to look away. Her stomach ached as if she'd been punched.

"It's not your fault. They've told me that. You were trapped like them. But you're going to get away. We all are," Eric said.

He reached up to touch Kat's face as she leaned down, and he hugged her more fiercely than he had before. Grim stepped closer. Katherine tried to ignore the giant dog. In this moment, her safety didn't matter, and neither did Severne's agenda. Only Eric and his mother mattered, and the fact that she hadn't been able to save him yet.

"I'll save him. I'll get him out of here," she told the carved representation of his mother's soul. Lavinia didn't move, but Kat reached out and touched her wooden hand. The wooden fingers weren't as cold as the shadow's touch, but they did feel like ice. She began to lose feeling in her hand, but she didn't pull it away. She endured the pain and tried to look into the daemon woman's wooden eyes. They were blank. There were no pupils or irises. Only an empty stare. But she met them and tried to reach the soul they contained. "I won't give up. I won't run away."

The cold crept from her hand halfway up her arm.

Grim growled deep and low in his barrel chest as if concerned that the cold might penetrate to her heart.

"I've been hiding for a long time, but I know it's time to take a stand," Kat promised.

The cold seeped through skin and muscle and bone. She began to shiver. Her teeth clicked together. And still she tried to communicate to whatever was left of Lavinia in the cherrywood. Had the fingers tightened on hers, or was that only ice and imagination?

She was no longer sure she could pull her hand away.

Eric tugged at her other hand as if to get her attention.

Grim was now at her side. He pressed against her legs, urging her to release the daemon's wooden hand. His heat startled her to action, and she pulled. It took more effort than she expected to break her hand free. The fingers of the wooden hand curled back on the palm as her fingers came away. The eerie reflexive action made her gasp and stumble away from the wall.

She cradled her cold hand against her chest, but the woman in the carving didn't leap from the wall to extract revenge. Whatever energy she had expended to hold Katherine's hand was gone…or saved for another time.

Eric saw her heavy breathing in response to being trapped by his mother's wooden hand.

"It's okay. She doesn't want to hurt you. She wants to help you just like you helped me," he said.

Unlike the ice of the shadow's touch, the cold from Lavinia's hand had already begun to fade away. As the cold faded, so did her fear.

"I haven't helped you yet, but I'm going to. I promise," Kat said. She reached to place her stiff fingers into the ruff of Grim's coat. He jumped as if startled by the cold, but he didn't growl or step away. He let her warm her fingers. It wasn't exactly like petting a dog. It was more like petting a dragon with fur. But she appreciated the movement it restored to her fingers.

Eric still held her other hand. He was warm, as well. Gradually she felt normal again, but she still cautiously stepped farther away from the wall.

"I'm going to save you both. I know what to do. Mom told me," Eric said.

"I've heard whispering from the walls, but I haven't been able to make out what they say," Kat told him. "I'm not sure they're actually communicating."

"They are. They're alive. Only trapped. It's up to me to set them free," Eric said.

Kat wasn't expecting the boy at her side to turn and run away. She called to him, but she couldn't follow. Grim had stepped between her and the boy's retreating figure. The hellhound's large body pressed against her legs, holding her in place. She was caught. Trapped by Severne's orders to his enormous and loyal beast.

"I thought we'd become friends," she complained to the hellhound.

He looked up at her with an inscrutable quirk of his head as if to say he had no friends. Only unbreakable ties to John Severne.

She had no choice. She could only hope the daemons trapped in the walls could communicate and that they would pass her message on to Sybil. Her mother had stood against Reynard and the Council with no help by her side. Kat needed to learn from her mother's mistake. She didn't intend for her stand to have the same outcome as her mother's.

When she made it to her room, Grim watched with his head down and his forelegs braced until she slipped inside.

To wait.

Chapter 26

Katherine paced the confines of her room. There was a hush around her. It settled against her skin. Expectation caused the fine hairs along her arms to quiver to attention. The walls didn't make a sound. The etched designs on her mirrors were still. Her colorful walls waited. The roses and their thorns. The birds and the petals were frozen in flight and fall.

Had her message reached Sybil? Would the daemon so long a denizen of l'Opéra Severne come to her aid, or did she see Kat as a flitting fancy, too soon gone for her concern?

Eric.

She had to find him.

He couldn't stay in the place. Not with the horror of its walls and its potential for malevolent shadows. And Severne's obsessive quest. His drive to save his father was as dangerous as Reynard at his pious worst.

Grim was outside her door. Severne had set him to guard. She didn't think the hellhound would hurt her, but he wouldn't let her pass. He was a massive physical obstacle even without teeth and jaw. The one time she'd turned the handle of her door to check on his position, he'd growled loud and low again, and this time it had been a more serious warning.

If Sybil didn't show up, Kat would risk it. She would force Grim to attack or move aside and let her free.

While she bolstered her nerve, she changed into jeans, T-shirt and a thick leather jacket. She'd bought the jacket because it was great with jeans on cool nights when practice ran late and dinner even later. Or for those times when Reynard stalked her until dawn before she could slip away. But the leather was also sturdy and protective. It covered her arms and fell to her thighs in a belted blazer cut. It would have provided cover and protection against a regular dog.

She thought it would probably melt like butter in Grim's mouth.

She pulled tall boots on even as she acknowledged a suit of armor wouldn't be enough. The hellhound outside her door had nightmare teeth that responded with size and ferocity in proportion to his needs. But she had to try.

The morning was only a few hours away. Crowds on the streets would mean more watching eyes and a greater possibility that she and Eric would be seen by someone who would alert the Order of Samuel or Severne to their whereabouts.

A light knock on the door interrupted her as she was wondering what she should use to cover her face and hands. She paused. The sense of relief that tried to rush through her was unjustified. Even if Sybil had responded, there was no guarantee her help wouldn't come with a price too high for Kat to pay.

Never trust a daemon.

And she was already in debt to the daemon she was preparing to ask for help.

Kat firmed her shoulders and tightened her belt. She walked to the door, taking a deep breath to prepare for negotiations. When she opened it, Sybil stood in the hallway. For the first time, she wasn't wearing a dress. She also wore a jacket and boots, though hers were vintage. And blue. She wore blue from head to toe including a white scarf with a blue floral design.

Hydrangeas.

The softness of the watercolor silk print didn't match her eyes.

"You called. I have come," Sybil said.

Her words sounded too formal. As if she was stating something for the record.

Grim stood behind her, still stiff, still at the ready. He looked as if he might jump on the daemon at Kat's door rather than let her come inside. Sybil ignored the massive beast as if he was of no concern.

Her nonchalance didn't matter. Kat was concerned enough for both of them.

"I'd invite you inside, but Grim might eat you before you cross the threshold," she said.

"I have known him since he was a tiny puppy no bigger than a German shepherd. I'm not afraid," Sybil said. "Cautious. But not afraid."

"Thank you for coming," Kat said, matching the daemon's formality.

She stepped back and held the door, ready to slam it in Grim's snout if he sprang. He would splinter the heavy wood into toothpicks, of course, but at least she might slow him down.

"He isn't going to harm us. He's only trying to impress upon us that his master is very serious about saving his father," Sybil said.

She walked into the bedroom. As she stepped forward, she began to remove her smooth blue velvet gloves by loosening one finger at a time. First from one hand and then the other.

"These were a gift to me, as was my scarf," she continued.

Gifts to daemons were more than thoughtful keepsakes. They represented bargains. Kat looked at the pretty scarf and soft gloves with more caution than she had seconds before.

"I made a promise in return. One I have kept for longer than you've been alive," Sybil said.

Kat backed away. She hoped it didn't look like a retreat, but the daemon was different than she'd been before. The wise, helpful costume matron was gone. Though her keys still hung at her waist, she was less maternal. Her face held a cold, inhuman expression.

"I owe you," Katherine said. "For the dress."

It seemed a more horrible debt than before, now that she needed another favor. Now that Sybil was harder to read. Who had given her the scarf and the gloves? Who owned her promises?

The daemon paused in the center of the room. Her blue reflections were all around them in the etched glass on the wall. She tucked her gloves into the belt at her waist where her keys hung on their iron ring. Her movements were distorted in the glass, broken into a thousand jagged pieces by the birds and thorny vines.

And that's when Kat saw it. Sybil was as hard as

Severne. She could have been perfectly carved of marble standing there. Untouched. Serene. But only because the long life she'd lived had chipped all else away.

"I'm extremely old by your standards, Katherine D'Arcy. I am old by John Severne's. In all that time, I've loved only once. Unwise to love a human, even a damned one. Especially a damned one. Too easy to grow too attached when their meager lives are extended by Brimstone. But it wasn't a choice any more than the wind chooses to blow or the rain to fall," Sybil said.

"Severne," Kat said. She'd fought her own feelings for the damned man she'd thought was a daemon.

"Yes, but not the one you're referring to. I care for John as anyone would care for a foundling. It was his father I loved. And even though I've lost him, I love him still," Sybil said.

The daemon was not here to help her.

Katherine's chest tightened. She was in more danger than she'd been before. Severne had feelings for her. They softened him. Just barely. Almost indiscernibly. But still… softened. His feelings lessened the threat of the hellhound outside her door. Grim wouldn't have harmed her. She was sure of it now.

Because she saw the real threat of harm burning in Sybil's eyes.

"Levi Severne is dying. He doesn't have much time. If he dies without full possession of his soul, he will experience an infinity of hideous burning pain, and then he'll cease to exist. That is damnation. Nothingness. The end," Sybil said.

She stepped toward Kat. There was nowhere left for her to retreat. Kat could only stand her ground.

"You can save him," Sybil said.

"How can I betray one man for another?" Kat asked.

"Not one man for another. One daemon for a mortal man. Michael will exist to fight another day. Levi will end. After tortuous pain, he will end. As if he had never lived. And so will John. If you love him, you can't let them come to that," Sybil said.

"I can't love him," Kat protested.

There was nothing in the room she could use as a weapon. Her cello was no defense against a daemon. Severne had shown her how the Brimstone responded to her playing. All the years when she'd thought she'd been hiding, she'd only been communing with the very creatures Reynard wanted her to hate.

"Severne's father is senile. He doesn't know me. He'll never know me again. To him now, I would be a monster with my marble skin and my nightglow eyes," Sybil said. "I can't love him. But I do. And I always will."

Kat could hardly breathe. She struggled to expand her lungs with every inhalation. Severne had done horrible things. He had imprisoned hundreds of daemons in a wooden purgatory for cruelly ambitious masters.

For his father. To save his father.

She couldn't love him. But she did. His torturously hard, lean body he had starved of ease for decades was now a revelation. His dependence on a monstrous daemon dog for companionship most would shun for gentler things had been a confession she had refused to see. His considerate touch had been almost worshipful of her softness, as if it was sacrosanct. Too holy for him to taste.

If Sybil cared for him because he had been lost, Kat loved him because, in her, he was found.

They were a pair destined to be apart. But that didn't make her love impossible. It only made it unbearably painful.

It wasn't safe. He couldn't be trusted. His obsession with saving his father and completing the bargain his grandfather had signed in Severne blood was absolute. It both revealed his heart and showed her that their love could never be.

He'd been driven by it to do horrible things. The contract he was determined to honor to save his father stood between them. Irrevocably. He had tried to use her in the same way Reynard had used her.

And just as she dealt with Reynard, she could only run away. Refuse. Reject. Abstain.

"The dress for Michael. Save our Severnes and in return I will help you save Eric and your sister. You can take them away from his haunted place," Sybil said.

Did her sister love the daemon Michael? Was that why she had run away? Was she protecting him or was he threatening her in some way? If she led Sybil to Michael, she would pay for the dress. That was one bargain. If she allowed Michael to be killed, banished to the walls of l'Opéra Severne, she would give John Severne and his father their souls back. The contract John Severne's grandfather had forged with the Council would be fulfilled. That was the second bargain. In return, Sybil would help her save Victoria and Eric.

Terrible and fair.

Her painful love for John Severne sat like a scorching knot in her chest, tightening around her heart.

Michael would be imprisoned. Not dead.

She and Victoria could take Eric into hiding with them. Somehow they could try to protect him from the Order of Samuel.

"And what will you do?" Kat asked.

"I made a promise to Levi Severne. It will be fulfilled. I could be free. But I will stay. I will watch over them. Until they die natural deaths. Until l'Opéra Severne crumbles to the ground and all the souls within it," Sybil said simply, honestly. "That's the price I pay for loving a human."

Silence was suddenly broken by thousands of whispers. The corridors and hallways of Severne echoed with the sound of voices too trapped in wood to be fully heard.

"The dress for Michael," Kat said. "John and his father's souls for Victoria and Eric's freedom."

Sybil nodded and stretched out her bared hand.

It was wrong. For the first time she'd be agreeing to lead a hunter to a daemon and sealing that daemon's fate. But for Victoria, for Eric and even for John Severne, she had no other choice.

She took Sybil's cold, hard, immortal hand and, palm to palm, it became suddenly so hot that she cried out. She swore she heard a sizzle before she could pull back her reddened palm.

She looked down to see the red fade, but not the feeling that she'd received a steam burn. Her flesh was tight and pink and painful to the touch.

Her promise to Sybil had marked her just as Severne was marked, time after time, in angry slashes of tally marks on his skin.

"Go home, Grim. Go home," Sybil commanded when she opened the door.

With a whining cry of protest, the great hellhound began to dissolve into the air. He rose like black mist from his back down to his paws with his bared teeth left for last, a ferocious Cheshire cat.

"No!" Kat said. She rushed to where the hellhound had been. There was nothing left but shadows and the scent of Brimstone. Tears rose up in her eyes. She'd fought them back so many times, but for the great ugly beast of a daemon dog, they fell.

He'd protected her from the Order of Samuel. He'd led her through pathways few mortals had traversed. He was a part of Severne. He was a hellish creature, but he had known the boy before he became the hardened man.

"Katherine, he isn't gone. He'll return. I only bought us some time to complete our business. He'll be back, and he'll hunt us down for John. Hurry. There isn't much time. You must be away with your sister and Eric before John comes to claim Michael," Sybil said.

She'd never seen Grim dematerialize. He'd always been out of sight. Sweet relief flooded her. It hadn't been a pleasant process for him to go through unwillingly, but if Sybil spoke the truth, the hellhound wasn't destroyed. He would be back at Severne's side. Probably sooner than she would wish!

She had to find Victoria, betray Michael and leave l'Opéra Severne with Eric and her sister before Grim was back to interfere.

"Your sister is hiding in the catacombs. You must go to her. Michael will be with her. Lead me to them and I'll allow you to take Eric when you flee," Sybil said.

She led the way with a determined stride to the familiar spiral stairway Kat had taken to go down beneath the opera house's main stage to the costume vault. But instead of turning toward the warehouse-like vault, Sybil led her to another staircase and then another.

They spiraled down, down, down until the air grew cool and damp. Drafts of dirt-scented air reached her nostrils, and goose bumps rose on her skin.

"Isn't Baton Rouge mostly below sea level?" Kat asked. Her imagination could almost hear the Mississippi flowing above their heads.

"Nothing at Severne is as it seems or as it should be. The line between your world and mine is a veil of illusion that flutters in breezes we cannot see or feel. L'Opéra Severne is a building in your world. But my world creates within its walls an infinite labyrinth, a beautiful prison, and beneath it all, catacombs of tunnels," Sybil warned. "It isn't safe. A human being could wander and grow old and die. But your affinity should lead you to Michael now that you're farther from Severne. Once I leave you here and go back to the main levels, you will find your way."

It was true. Kat could feel the pull of Sybil now. The unmistakable magnet of Brimstone blood that had been hidden beneath her rush of desire for Severne was obvious. Much farther away was a fainter call. It tingled along her skin as awareness, an inexorable pull.

"Go. I will ready Eric to leave with you. Don't fail. This is the only way," Sybil said. She placed the hand that still held the heat of their bargain on Kat's cold arm. "Our bargain is sealed, Katherine. To break it now will mean your death. My Brimstone has marked you. That daemon mark is connected to your heart."

Kat looked down at her burned palm. There was always a price to pay. Her life was on the line. It didn't feel like an escalation. Someone with Brimstone blood had already marked her heart.

Chapter 27

When she'd been a girl, she'd read a story about a labyrinth and a monster. In her child's mind, she'd imagined the sort of maze a mouse might be put into to test how well it could find a block of cheese.

The reality of a labyrinthine network of tunnels was much worse.

Sybil had given her a small flashlight, but its beam lit just a few yards in front of her. All else was echoing darkness.

Kat could only follow the faint call of daemon blood and hope that she'd find her sister. She couldn't imagine what else she'd find. If Michael was with her sister, was he friend or enemy? A lover could be either or both. She knew that now.

She missed her bracelet. It was crazy to long for its sound. To miss her pretty chains. She missed the chime of it when she moved. She missed the respite she and Victoria had managed to achieve whenever they'd escaped Reynard's detection. Rome, Paris, London, Austin, Tokyo, Sydney, San Francisco and Savannah…they'd fled around the globe many times.

Her fingers missed her cello's strings. It hadn't been long since she'd played. But it felt far longer. An age since the music had carried her away from fear.

She pressed on.

She might encounter Grim or his dark master around this corner or that. She longed to see Severne again and dreaded the possible confrontation. She tripped often on the uneven floor of impossible tunnels that seemed hewn from solid rock.

There were no sconces in the tunnels she traveled. She had left them behind in the main part of the opera house. The flashlight in her hand was the only light in the labyrinth. The shadows it created leaped and cavorted on the walls in dark mimicry of the murals elsewhere in l'Opéra Severne. Her cautious figure crept along, but all around the shadow her body made, less definable shapes flew, dipped and dived with the movements of the light in her hand.

She walked for what felt like days. With each turn she chose, the maze took her farther and farther away from sunlight and life. The night she'd spent on the river with Severne was eons ago. Could it have been only hours since she'd held him in her hand? Since she'd experienced the betrayal of his true nature and purpose?

When her flashlight flickered, she stopped midstep. Her breath caught in her throat. The light came back on, and she breathed again. But her heart was racing. If her batteries died, she would have to feel her way with only the rough-hewn walls to guide her.

Feel her way.

There were no faces carved in the catacombs. There were no murals here.

The reassurance didn't help.

She didn't want to run her hands along the sides of the maze in the dark. She too easily recalled the cold feel of Lavinia's wooden fingers.

Her steps were quicker after that. She hurried toward the faint call of Brimstone. It seemed to get no stronger, but she refused to give up.

Even when the flashlight began to flicker with every stride.

Where was Victoria?

Why had she deserted her only sister?

After the intimacy she'd allowed herself to share with Severne, the cold tunnel felt even more isolated and lonely.

Cold?

She stopped in the middle of the tunnel that had narrowed around her. The flickering light in her hand cast her shadow as a huge hulking shape on the wall.

But it was her shape.

She raised her other arm to be certain. Yes. The shadow moved with her. It was hers. Yet gooseflesh had risen on her skin in spite of the jacket she wore. She breathed out as a tentative test, and her quavering release of air was suddenly visible in the chilling air in clouds of white.

She'd walked a long way.

She was deep underground, but there was no logical reason for the cold creeping over her skin with insidious, icy fingers. She circled the light around her body. It wavered, off and on, off and on, in her hand. The tunnel in front of her was empty as far as she could see, but she'd just made a turn. The gaping mouth of the tunnel she'd left was black as pitch.

As black as a shadow she could feel but not see.

Kat edged away from the black hole.

She was too far from Severne to survive the shadow's touch. Her respiration betrayed her fear. It was fast and light, each breath revealing the cold that foreshadowed a worse freeze to come.

If the shadow was here...

If it touched her...

Her flashlight flickered again. This time it came back on dim and low. She felt relief, but that changed to despair as the light faded, faded, like invisible, malevolent fingers dialed it down.

The dark claimed her.

The light was gone.

Her fear was too great to shake the flashlight in her hand. But even if she could have moved, she wouldn't have, because instinct warned her to stay perfectly still as a greater cold approached. She felt its strong presence at her neck and back, and then the chill circled around to her face. She imagined the giant winged shadow crouching down to look into her wide, staring eyes that could see only endless dark.

She held herself quiet and still.

The cold was bad. To touch the shadow accidentally in the dark would be worse.

"I love you, Victoria," Kat said through chattering teeth. It was important. If she failed to find her sister, if she was frozen to death in this spot, buried beneath l'Opéra Severne, she wanted her sister to know she'd tried. She hadn't stayed hidden. She had come to help.

Another name was spoken by her slowed, thudding heart. She kept it secret. Her icy lips pressed against a truth no one needed to hear.

Her flashlight flickered to life at the same time the cold

faded back and away. She shivered, but her respiration was no longer apparent in white puffs from her lips.

There was no shadow. None that she could see. Only her movements showed on the wall. But she blinked and tested with a raised arm again because for several seconds she thought she'd seen vanishing wings.

Kat moved slower for several yards while feeling returned to her stiff legs. The light remained strong. She tried not to think about why it might have failed.

She heard the singing long before she saw a light. An old French lullaby lilted hauntingly down the passages around her. It came from far ahead but seemed to surround her. It was the daemon call she still followed because the direction of the singing was indistinct.

She stepped quietly, afraid that her sister would run away as she'd run before. There was no mistaking the beautiful voice. Even the echo couldn't disguise the lilting purity of tone so many treasured, including her. In spite of her determination, a part of her had been afraid she'd never hear her sister sing again.

The scene was unexpectedly peaceful when she finally rounded a last bend that brought her into a deep underground chamber. There were colorful Persian rugs on the walls as well as the floor and a fireplace where a small blaze burned, vented, no doubt, miles above their heads or into some other hellish dimension she hoped they'd never see.

A four-poster bed sat in an alcove off to the side, framed all around by overflowing bookshelves full of everything from magazines to antique tomes to art and bric-a-brac. She was certain she glimpsed the work of masters placed haphazardly beside plastic toys from fast food restaurants.

Near her sister's rocking chair was a table set with a silver tea service fit for a queen.

But it was the rocking chair, the singing, and the nearby cradle, which Victoria nudged with a gentle foot, penetrating the shocked fog that had threatened for several seconds to claim Kat's consciousness.

There was no one else in the room.

No dangerous daemon.

No solicitous lover.

"Victoria," Kat whispered. Horrible, wonderful knowledge exploded in her mind. The truth of why her sister had run even from a beloved sibling. She might even have begun to suspect when she'd first heard the lullaby their mother had sung to them so many times as they'd grown. Maybe her suspicions had caused her to approach slowly more than her fear of scaring her sister away.

A baby.

A precious, innocent baby.

What else would have caused Victoria to run and hide from the one other person on Earth who might have been able to lead daemon hunters to the father of her child?

An innocent half-daemon child caught up in a terrible war.

"You have to go," Victoria said. "I knew you'd find me eventually. And I wanted to see you. But you have to go." Kat could see tears of joy and fear on her sister's face. Joy at reunion. Fear that their reunion might endanger her child.

It wasn't a rejection. Together, their affinity would attract dangerous attention to the baby's location.

"You should have told me. You should have warned me away," Kat said.

Her throat burned. Her chest was tight. Her legs carried her numbly across the room. She had to see the baby. But she also knew she needed to run away. She endangered the baby by simply being in the room.

"It's okay. We're hidden well. His father saved him from Reynard," Victoria said. "He sacrificed himself for us. I've waited until he's strong enough to move. We're going to slip away. And you'll have to let us go, Kat. It's the only way. Bad enough that I have to be with him until he's older. He needs me. I can't let him go. But it would be worse for the both of us to be together. You know Reynard always finds us more easily when we're in the same place."

Katherine tiptoed to the cradle and looked down. *He.* Victoria had called the baby *he.* Kat's nephew was nestled in the cradle as it rocked. His sleepy eyes glinted in the soft light above cherubic cheeks and the bow of a tiny newborn mouth.

"Where is Michael?" Kat asked. Her mind was already formulating ways to fix this. To help them. To make the evil of the situation go away.

"You mean the baby's father? Reynard killed him, Kat. When we realized I had conceived after a night in one of the suites of *The Blues Queen*, we were going to run away together. He said it wasn't safe for the baby at l'Opéra Severne. He said we had to leave. But Reynard found us in Shreveport. He killed Michael." Tears coursed down Victoria's face, but her foot remained calm, carefully nudging the cradle so the baby wouldn't be startled. "I ran away and came back here. This alcove was Michael's secret. He said no one else knew about it. And no one has ever bothered us here."

She continued to rock the baby, but she looked up at Kat. How many times had Katherine seen this exact look on her sister's face after she had sung the role of Juliet? Perhaps her penchant for the part had been a dark premonition.

"We met during a rehearsal of *Roméo et Juliette*. The

university had borrowed the stage of the opera house, and teenage performers were taking instruction from some of the singers. I had slipped up to one of the private box seats to watch them. You know how much I love that role. He found me there. That was the start of it all," Victoria said.

No wonder her sister had fallen madly in love with a daemon. She'd been preparing for just such a star-crossed romance her whole life.

Michael was dead. But the name on the list hadn't been marked through. Severne didn't have another tally mark on his arm. His grandfather's contract hadn't been fulfilled. His father wasn't saved.

"I'm glad I came back. When I saw you, I knew it was wrong to leave without saying goodbye. I left the bracelet where you could find it. And Mom's letters. I put the ticket from our river cruise in your cello case. I left the opera glasses on my pillow. I wanted to talk to you, but Michael had said to avoid John Severne and his dog. He said they were dangerous. That they would hurt the baby."

"No. No, they wouldn't. Never," Kat said.

She looked down at the wiggling baby. He blinked up at her and fisted his hands.

"Sybil helped me when I went into labor. She promised she knew what to do. She'd delivered babies before. It was scary, but I didn't know what else to do. I was afraid to go to the hospital. Reynard might find us again," Victoria said.

"Sybil helped you," Kat said. The world dropped from beneath her body. She floated where she'd stood, trying to rediscover the feeling of firm ground beneath her feet. But there was nothing. No support. She was utterly abandoned by the universe.

"Her face was the first face Michael saw when he came into the world, but he didn't seem intimidated at all," Vic laughed through her tears. "Even though she's always frightened me a little."

"Michael," Kat said, repeating the name. Wishing it was any other name.

Because she suddenly knew.

"I named him after his father. I wish you could have met him, Kat. He told me such stories. Of a time before time. Of Heaven and hell. He was very old. Very, very old. He had scars on his back where he said he'd once had wings. We were wrong about daemons, Kat. Mom knew. That's why she risked her life to save the daemon she loved. They aren't damned," Vic said.

Only different. So different that a daemon woman would sacrifice an innocent baby to save someone she loved, but she'd need help to do it if she'd made a promise she had to keep. Sybil had promised Victoria that she would help her with the baby. That was why she needed Kat to deliver baby Michael to Severne.

Kat thought she might die the instant she decided to break her bargain with Sybil. Her hand did throb so hotly that she fell to her knees beside the cradle. But she didn't die. Not yet. She assumed her heart would stop in the next second or the next.

"Please. Please let there be enough time," she said under her breath so Vic wouldn't hear.

The little baby looked up at her with nightglow eyes. He would live.

And she would die.

That was a deadly promise she had to be brave enough to make.

"What is it, Kat? What's wrong?" Victoria asked.

Perhaps she'd felt the chill increasing around them, or maybe it was only the stark look of determination Kat could feel on her hardened face.

But as her sister stopped rocking the cradle, a shadow fell across the wiggling baby. Kat struggled to her feet, adrenaline flooding in to fill the hollow places where only shock had been. She vaguely heard Victoria call out a warning to stay away. The baby wasn't distressed. He laughed again. He reached up to touch the frigid darkness as if it had tickled his face.

He must have been protected from the shadow's ice by his father's daemon blood.

His father. The ancient daemon that once had wings.

Kat saw it then. Above their heads, there was a giant winged shadow on the wall. It hadn't been there when she'd hurried into the room. If it had been a normal shadow, thrown by the fire, it would have fallen across her sister's lap and onto Kat. Instead, the edges of it avoided them. It stopped where their bodies began and came into being again beyond them.

Had it followed her through the labyrinth, watching and waiting to see what she would do when she found the baby? Had whatever remained of the father weighed her life in his frigid inhuman mind and decided whether or not to let her pass in the dark passages of the catacombs?

She tasted mortality then, like cold, damp ashes in her mouth.

She'd been right to fear the shadows. But she was glad she'd been bold enough to pass through them.

"I won't betray them," Kat said.

The shadow responded. It swelled out bigger and bigger. Then, just as she feared it might attack her to be sure she didn't threaten the child, it diminished.

"Of course you won't," Victoria said. "I told him that."

Katherine looked at her sister. The other woman didn't cower from the cold shadow on the wall. She was used to its looming presence.

"It isn't him. Not really. But there's something of him left. Like a ghost, but more. I have to admit that's another reason we haven't left again. Michael is strong. Stronger than a human newborn would be. He can leave whenever I'm ready," Victoria said.

Victoria's clothing finally penetrated Kat's overwhelmed senses. She was bundled in a thick sweater, and woolen socks showed above heavy shoes. Across her lap was draped a heavy quilt.

The shadow watched and waited.

"You need to be ready. Now," Kat said.

"I know. I know it isn't safe. The cold is very bad. Even the fire doesn't warm me. Only Michael keeps it from stealing my breath," Vic admitted.

"That's not the only reason. He was right. It isn't safe here. I think the shadow has been trying to warn us all along," Kat said.

She didn't know how far she would get before her daemon mark killed her because of the broken bargain. She would do all she could. She'd hidden for years. She had to be braver than that now. She had to fight.

Victoria was already dressed practically in jeans along with her heavy sweater. Kat helped her add to a large diaper tote bag while the baby cooed at the shadow on the wall. When Kat moved to pick Michael up, the shadow once again grew, and its wings stretched out to span the room. The warm baby in her arms diminished the shadow's threat. His Brimstone heat was daemonic, but not monstrous at all. Only different. And adorable.

She would never hold a baby of her own.

Kat pushed that knowledge away.

"We'll have to separate once we're away. You can't try to contact me. Ever again," Katherine said. With luck, her sister would never discover that Kat had died so she and her baby could live.

She handed Michael to his mother. Victoria took him easily and cradled him close in her arms, already practiced at being exactly what her baby needed.

The shadow diminished in size again when the baby was placed back in his mother's hands.

Kat couldn't tell Vic about the daemon mark. Victoria feared enough for Michael. Kat didn't want her to have to fear for her sister, as well.

She would go. She would help. Until her heart stopped. She would give all to her nephew, as she would if he was her own son. As she wished someone had given for John Severne all those years ago. To save him before he became the tortured, bartered soul he was today.

She held her bad hand against her chest. Victoria didn't notice. She was focused on the baby in her arms. As she should be. Kat ignored the pain. They needed to find Eric and outsmart Sybil. She was certain the shadow would follow them as they made their escape. It had shrunk, but whatever was left of Michael still lurked on the wall. While they hurried from the last refuge they'd known, she pretended Grim and Severne wouldn't try to stop them.

She was wrong.

Chapter 28

Grim materialized beside him as he ran the levee toward Brightside. He'd thought to run all the way to New Orleans, but Grim's appearance interrupted him. The breeze off the river ruffled the massive hellhound's fur as it came into being, first as a mist and then separating into each individual hair. It was a slower process to witness than he was used to. Something was wrong.

The dog had to will himself into being.

He chuffed. He whined. He stretched and moaned.

The sun hadn't risen, but there was no fog. In the city lights, the sudden appearance of a giant dog that looked like an enormous mangy wolf might not go unnoticed.

Grim was always discreet. He shied away from curious eyes and often ran with Severne at the edges of his perception, unseen, amorphous.

It was terrible to see his old companion pained by this solid materialization. Severne stopped. Gravel flew in a spray that sprinkled down on the path.

"What's happened? Severne asked. The hellhound was finally fully formed. But he stood as if uncertain where to place his paws or if they would respond if he told them to move. "Where is she? Take me there," he ordered. There was no doubt Katherine was in danger. Otherwise, Grim would never have left her side.

He'd been running away from her, trusting that the hellhound could keep her safe. Now that Grim had come to find him, he knew he should have stayed with her. He'd kept his distance from her for too long. And now it might be too late.

The hellhound couldn't tell him what was wrong. All he could do was lead the way. Severne ran. For the first time he ran to his heart instead of away from it. Unfortunately, the discombobulated beast didn't lead him to Katherine. Grim led him to Sybil.

They came into the hallway outside Sybil's sewing room with an atmospheric pop. Sulfuric stink wafted around in place of the usual Brimstone burn. Severne stumbled as his nose protested, and Grim whined an apology.

What had happened to make the usually reliable hellhound so clumsy?

The door to Sybil's sewing room was open. She was inside. Her fingers flew as she busily picked at the seams of a pile of white fabric on her workbench.

"Sybil, what's wrong?" Severne asked. He'd run so hard even he was slightly breathless. His lungs sucked air as he watched her continue her work. She didn't even look up as Grim flopped down on the floor at his feet, spent.

"She said she would bring me Michael. I couldn't take him when he was born because I'd promised to help Victoria deliver him safely. I didn't know his name. I didn't know until she named him. I had to come up with another way to help you. Too many promises. Being an older daemon carries such a burden of promises. I'm sorry about the hound, too. I had to send him away. Forcefully." And still she didn't look up as her fingers continued to work.

Severne's lungs stopped. He had to force himself to take the next breath. If he could, he would have abstained. Because now he knew he might as well be dead already.

"Michael is Victoria's baby?" he asked. He'd lived a very long time. His life's purpose had never changed. Fulfill the contract. Save his father. Send all the daemons back to hell.

"She promised. Bargains can't be broken. You know there's always a price. She shook my hand," Sybil said. She continued to pop the seams of the garment she worked on with steady, practiced fingers.

"What have you done?" Severne asked.

The woman he'd always seen as a maternal figure now seemed a threat to all he'd tried not to hold dear.

"I'm trying to fix it. I'm trying. I know it will hurt you, and I promised your father I would watch over you. There's always a trick to every bargain. A trap. A release. I'm trying, but I might be too late," Sybil said. Her fingers flew. Pop. Pop. Pop. Perfect stitches in luxurious white fabric of a myriad of shades—white to ivory. And a sparkle. There. Beside a crumple of tulle.

Severne fisted his hands as Sybil stood. The beautiful ball gown Kat had worn to the masquerade was unmade. Thousands of pieces fluttered to the ground as Sybil moved. Tulle floated softly. Crystal beads fell like frozen rain.

"It might be too late," Sybil said. "She owes me less now. That might save her life."

"Grim," Severne shouted. If he couldn't save her, he would hold her where she fell, and then he would burn there, too. He wouldn't doom her nephew to the walls. Not an innocent baby. His father had been innocent. He had been innocent. The sacrifice of innocents had to stop. He would end it now.

His promise to Kat would be that. He hoped he would reach her in time to pledge it.

The baby's Brimstone call was faint. His tiny heart wasn't full-grown. And the heat in his blood would be diluted by his mother's mortality. She tried to feel Eric over Michael's Brimstone, to hear the call of his Brimstone blood. But as they left the catacombs, there were other daemons in the main part of the opera house. Sybil. Possibly even Tess and others. The monk had said there were many daemons at the party. Severne had hidden them all from her affinity. He had completely filled her world.

Him she could feel.

As they hurried through the corridors of l'Opéra Severne, she could feel the man she loved all around, and she felt the impending loss of him, too, squeezing her daemon-marked heart.

As they climbed one of the spiral stairways up to the main hall's level, Victoria suddenly stopped in front of her. Kat ran into her sister and then held onto her and the baby so none of them would fall. She urged her sister to step off the stairs.

"I smell smoke!" Victoria whispered urgently.

Her sister held Michael to her heart as if she could absorb the baby back into her body to protect him if she needed to.

Kat looked at Victoria and suddenly imagined her mother looking exactly the same. Fear was their legacy. She wanted to end that. To break the horrible chains that had held them to the Order for far too long.

"Kat, I definitely smell something burning," Victoria insisted.

Kat breathed in the musty, dusty smell of the opera house. She coughed as an acrid smell joined the nostalgic smell of powder and makeup, rosin and dust. They had climbed two flights of spiral stairs. As they exited the second, they ran into a smoky hallway.

"L'Opéra Severne is on fire," Victoria said.

"You have to get Michael out. I'll look for Eric," Katherine said.

Thick, rolling smoke came toward them, blocking the way. Katherine hesitated. She knew they had to get out of the building, but she couldn't envision a way that was safe for the baby even with the Brimstone in his blood. If the building was on fire, they might be crushed by falling debris, and even Brimstone wouldn't protect Michael from that.

As she frantically tried to think of the safest way to the nearest exit, Grim materialized out of the smoke. It clung to his fur as shadows always had, parting reluctantly, gray from black, until he was large and solid and impossible to pass in front of them.

"No, Grim, no! Don't hurt them," Kat ordered. The hellhound looked at her and then directed his full attention back to the baby in her sister's arms. His prey? "Please. Please. Don't," Kat said.

He was a hellhound, but he was also a guardian and a provider of pathways. If any creature could get Victoria and Michael out of the burning opera house, it would be Grim.

"Grim, take them to safety. Save the baby. Save him," she said.

She was no longer the timid cellist hiding behind her instrument. She was desperate. Smudged. Dirty. And determined.

* * *

Severne had never seen a mightier sight as he followed the hellhound into their path. And her strong heart might cease to beat at any time. In spite of what he understood about her past, he'd known her only as a ferocious protector and a woman brave enough to reach out to him through the fire of his damnation. Tonight she was even more amazing. With wild eyes and a mane of chestnut hair, she stood in front of a hellhound as if she would kill him with her bare hands if he threatened the baby her sister held. On top of that, she ordered the hound to protect the baby that he should have been prepared to attack.

He was almost sure in the seconds before he spoke that Grim would have obeyed this powerful woman. With her affinity for daemons that glowed like an aura of power around her, she was surrounded by Brimstone blood.

He didn't wait to find out.

"Do it, Grim. Protect. No matter what happens. Understand? Michael is your master now. Lead him. Guard him and his mother from *all harm*," Severne ordered.

He stepped from the smoke as he spoke, and he saw Katherine's face. Her joy and despair at seeing him. Her understanding as his words penetrated her stressed haze.

"No," Katherine said.

But the atmosphere had already stilled around them. Molecules of ash and dust that had swirled now hung suspended in midair.

"He will be your son's champion, Victoria. Forever," Severne said.

The bargain was sealed.

Severne's gift was one only she and he could understand. Victoria might learn in time what the Brimstone-kissed master of l'Opéra Severne had given her baby. It was reparation. It was apology. It ripped his heart from his chest and sacrificed all for her family, for her.

His sacrifice sent her to her knees.

"Go. Now. I have to find Eric," Kat shouted at her sister.

Victoria's instinctive drive to protect her baby overcame her hesitation.

"I love you Katherine," she said. Tears tracked down her face, already smudged by smoke. She was beautiful. She was a mother. And their mother would have been so proud.

"Love Michael. Love him and leave fear behind," Kat said.

Grim helped. He suddenly pressed against Victoria's legs, urging her to leave. Victoria shielded the baby's face with a corner of his blanket before allowing the hellhound to force her away. She looked back once, and Kat tried to memorize her sister's face before the smoke rolled closed, swallowing the vulnerable figure of mother and child. Grim looked back once, too. But he didn't pause. The glance he spared for Severne held all the devotion he would now give to his new charge on Severne's orders. Then he was gone.

Severne had come to her side and dropped down onto his knees to wrap her in his arms. She didn't even know how she had gotten on the ground. She didn't remember falling. But she would remember being held. She would remember this embrace after the fall.

"I'm sorry I didn't trust you. I'm sorry I was afraid," Kat said.

"No one has ever been bold enough to love me. I'm scarred. Hard. Damned," Severne said, as if she needed to be reminded why she should be afraid.

"I'm stronger than I look," Katherine said.

But her heart disagreed. Its beats were stuttered, strange, wrong.

"And I'm more vulnerable than I seem," Severne said.

"I know," Kat said. She reached for Severne's face as he leaned to kiss her. Smoke rolled, but it was Severne's wood smoke lips she tasted.

"I will never harm Michael. Grim is my promise," Severne said.

"I love you. I thought I couldn't, but I do. You're not like Reynard. You've been a hunter, but it was always for love. You tried to save your father," Kat said.

"And now my father and I will burn. But not yet. First I'll save you," he said. "Since you saved me first, it's the least I can do."

He picked her up. Flames wouldn't touch him with the Brimstone in his blood, but she was highly flammable. There was no way she would leave the opera alive. She would burn or her heart would stop when her bargain with Sybil was broken as the baby reached safety.

Either way, she would die in Severne's arms.

Chapter 29

They didn't have Grim to guide them. They had to press
through fire and smoke. Debris fell before and behind,
impeding their progress. Kat cried out several times as
blasts of heat hit her face, but her cries were lost in the
cacophony of destruction.

"We have to find Eric. We can't abandon him," Kat
shouted. "I won't leave without him."

"You have to get out now. I'll go back for him," Severn
insisted against her ear so that she could hear above the
din.

He loosened his arms and let her slide down his body
to find her feet. They were in the original corridor she
had traversed when she'd first come to Severne. He had
carried her far enough for her to make it out of the building alone. She nodded. She agreed. But when he no longer held her, she was suddenly bereft. It would be better
to burn together than die apart.

Severne looked at her for as long as he dared before he leaned to touch his mouth to hers. It was a desperate press of their ash-coated lips, but she ignored the ash and the smoke. All that mattered was feeling the connection they shared, perhaps for the last time. She let him go when he pulled away. He ran back into the heart of the burning building to search for Eric before he was crushed beneath its collapse. She'd wanted the kiss to go on forever in case they had no chance for future kisses, but there was no time to call him back.

He was gone.

And her heart was still beating.

Fear almost made it impossible for her to move, but she had to make it to the exit in case there was any chance that they might all make it out alive.

Before she could continue to make her way to safety, a dark figure stepped from the roiling smoke, directly blocking her escape.

No.

Not now.

She couldn't call Grim from the baby's side. Severne had to find Eric before it was too late. Somewhere deep within l'Opéra Severne, her precious cello burned. She had no defense left against the evil monk who approached through the fog of chaos.

"Katarina, how I have missed you. You don't look well. These last days have fatigued you. Consorting with the devil is never advisable. Bad for your health. There's always that pesky possibility of your blood turning to ash," Reynard quipped.

Kat could feel the tremendous heat at her back. But she couldn't escape it by running into Reynard's grasp. She wouldn't. She refused. Better to burn.

"He's gone back for the child? You must take me to

them. Allow me to finish what you so rudely interrupted before," Reynard said. He looked in the direction Severne had disappeared. He took several steps toward the damned man she loved and the poor daemon child she'd tried to save. "Once we've dispatched the daemon, you and I will return to the enclave to ensure that Samuel's gift is passed to the next generation."

The inference in his words made her stomach twist with nausea. Her mother had been forced to conceive and bear Katherine and Victoria, but at least her husband had been a young man who had cared for his wife in the end. Reynard was a monster. The idea of him as her husband sickened her to the core. She would never be his Katarina.

"How about one last game of hide-and-seek instead?" Kat muttered. She backed away from Reynard. Her movement caught his attention. He turned and followed.

Her only hope to help Severne and Eric was to lead her lifelong tormentor away from where they might be. Into the fire. Into the flames. What she'd most wanted her whole life was to escape Reynard, but now it was up to her to use his habitual dogging of her footsteps against him.

"Catch me. Catch me if you can," she said.

He actually laughed. A sound she remembered from her nightmares. She didn't pause even when crashing timber drowned out the sound.

Her mind quickly cataloged all the places she'd been in l'Opéra Severne. She couldn't risk going back down to the catacombs alone. She might get lost. She settled on the one other place she could think of that might provide the perfect place to lead Reynard on a fruitless chase.

The props warehouse.

She raced for the stairs and was relieved to find them intact.

Fire was a threat, coming close and closer, and smoke

hung in the atmosphere like tendrils of fog above a dismal swamp. Ribbons of gray crept in sparkling with dust motes in the flickering light. The ribbons penetrated, curling up into all the lofted naves and nooks of the opera house the human eye could hardly see.

She had one opportunity to lead Reynard away from where she thought Eric might be. But that didn't mean she wanted to be found by the murderous stalker she could never seem to escape. She hoped to avoid Reynard among the funhouse jumble of garish props.

Kat had left him behind, but she could hear his whistle in the distance.

He was a madman. How could he whistle a jaunty tune while the rest of the opera house was in a tumult of fear and evacuation? How could his unhurried footsteps echo behind her on the wrought iron spiral stairs as if he was only on a boring tour while a mother fled with her newborn child and Severne searched for Eric in the flames?

This time she hurried into the warehouse not even bothering to try to silence the massive doors. The rows of vintage costumes hung on their racks, indifferent to the fire that would soon consume them and uncaring of Kat's fate. They were ghostly vestiges of the opera house's past, forgotten and still while the living rushed for their lives several floors above.

Last time she'd been here, she'd laughed silently to herself because the dust motes in the ghost light's glow had been like the caterpillar's smoke from *Alice in Wonderland*. Now, she cringed at her earlier fancy.

Severne's fairy-tale memories would burn away.

She drew up short as she realized her mistake. Her rush to the warehouse had been instinctive, like a wild animal searching for a hideaway that had offered it safety before.

But there was no place safe to hide from Reynard. There never had been.

She was stuck with her choice now, a fairy tale that would become a nightmare when Reynard invaded it.

Kat plunged into the costume racks in order to get quickly to where the props loomed on the other side. Mothball-scented cloth of every kind clung to her body as if to prevent her passage. Scratchy starched lace and moldering velvet, musty furs and the cold brush of buttons, feathers from ostriches so long dead the quills were yellowed and cracked—Kat pushed through them all. She couldn't prevent the overburdened rack from shaking on the chains that suspended it from the vaulted ceiling.

Reynard would see where she'd passed.

There was no other way.

The obsessed monk was behind her. She could still hear his whistle in the distance even above the shuffle of movement she assumed was the evacuation.

She finally extricated herself from the costumes and came out on the other side where the strange arrangement of theater artifacts waited, a forgotten city of backdrops and scaffolding, statuary and artificial trees.

The huge head of Mephistopheles dominated the tableau. The hulking face of the figure used in the final act of *Faust* tilted to one side of the warehouse like a reclining evil emperor. The encroaching smoke swirled around the ram's horns and curled out from the holes of its empty eyes where red lights would gleam during the show.

Kat avoided the face, choosing instead to crouch behind a table of goblets, each blackened by the pyrotechnics used to make them flame when it was their turn to be a part of the show. The chorus always coughed and complained at the goblets' sulfur smell. It seemed a foreshadowing now of the fire that raged upstairs.

How many times had *Faust* been performed at l'Opéra Severne? It was the company's specialty. Fitting, but it made Kat shudder to think how the opera mirrored Severne's life, a constant reminder of the nothingness that threatened to consume his father and him when it was time.

Now it was Kat's turn to feel haunted and hounded by the devil. Reynard had manipulated them for his dark purpose their whole lives.

She had to stay lost while Eric was found. She believed in Severne. It was new, a blossoming in her chest she'd never felt before. He'd given Grim as a guardian to Michael. That heroic sacrifice stole her breath. No matter what happened to her tonight, that part of the fairy tale was real.

Or maybe that was the daemon mark expanding in her chest, crowding out the oxygen and her life.

Her hand was crippled and curled against her side, the opera house was on fire, Eric was missing and her greatest enemy stalked her in creepy shadows, but she hoped. She avoided Reynard to buy time for Severne, her sister and Eric, but she didn't hide.

She hoped.

Her heart rushed with the thrill of it.

But she was also afraid.

Some props around her were damaged. Ragged canvas fluttered in unseen wafts of air that might have been caused by the doors of the warehouse opening and closing when Reynard came inside. The movement drew Kat's eye. She tried not to see Reynard with every harmless shift of smoke or paper. She failed. She saw him everywhere. There, only it wasn't his robe but a playbill that drifted down from some disturbed place she couldn't quite see. Had Reynard brushed against it so that it fell? There, only it wasn't his steps—it was a settling of the rafters

far above as the opera house began to lose its structura
integrity to flame.

Kat could draw Reynard's attention for only so long be
fore she condemned herself to burn with him.

"You have run down the rabbit hole, Katarina. Such a
warren you've discovered for yourself. Has your daemon
loving sister left you to burn? And what of your lover'
Where is he while you cower here with me?" Reynard
called. His voice echoed. Kat couldn't see the monk him
self. "Oh, yes, I know you've been tempted by darkness
You'll be punished for that, but don't worry. In the end
your blood is too valuable to waste."

The props created the perfect place for both of them to
remain unseen if they wished.

Her gaze was drawn again and again to the wide-oper
grin of Mephistopheles's gaping mouth. She could hea
the same grin in Reynard's voice.

"My patience grows thin. As thin as the air in this place
Do you feel it? The way the oxygen leaves us? The tim
has come for you to leave with me and quit your games,
Reynard said. "You have a duty to perform, as do I."

He began to hum. Music from Gounod's *Faust*. N
doubt inspired by his surroundings. The hum came an
went—farther, then closer—as he searched for her. An
still she couldn't see him.

Had Severne found Eric? Had her sister and the bab
escaped with Grim?

"Your mother tried to stand against me, you know. Sh
died for her treachery. Her blood still colors my hungr
blade. Fitting that it should join with that of the daemon
I've sent back to hell," Reynard said.

Kat clenched her fists. She had known. Her heart ha
known even before she'd found her mother's letters. She'

Barbara J. Hancock   265

always feared Reynard for good reason. Her mother had lied trying to save the daemon she'd loved.

Victoria hadn't been able to save the father of her baby. Their mother had failed to save them. Kat wondered if her mother's daemon love was trapped in the walls of l'Opéra Severne. All because of Reynard. Poor baby Michael. He would never know his father.

Kat rose and stepped from behind the prop's table. Smoke rolled around her ankles. The air was thicker. Reynard had been right. There wasn't much time. Her movement wasn't immediately obvious to the stalker who hunted her. She waited in the open, unhidden, for Reynard to find her.

Severne, Eric, her sister and Michael. Even Sybil. They would all live. It was time for Reynard to be stopped. It didn't matter if she had to die to ensure it.

"You are very like her. More like her than your father. He was a weak man. Never able to control the wife he'd been given. I think he might have loved her in the end. He refused to kill her after she'd given birth to more biddable daemon detectors. He rebelled against the Order. Even suggested we not hunt and kill the daemon she loved," Reynard scoffed. "So he was punished, of course. He died from the lashing we gave him. Weak to the end. And the woman he'd tried to help didn't even mourn his death."

Kat knew he was wrong. Her mother had been in mourning her whole life. She'd only expressed it in song.

So he was responsible for her mother's death and her father's.

And he might kill her after she'd given him children to pass on Samuel's gift, but not before she tried to end his madness for good.

"My affinity is the greatest in my family. Victoria and my mother knew it. That's why we separated often. I was the one who was most often drawn to daemons," Kat said. Her eyes strained to find her tormentor in the darkness. His disembodied voice was impossible to track, but she looked at Mephistopheles again and again as he spoke.

"You betrayed them. It was you I was most often able to track. You are quite the magnet. I can attest to that," Reynard said.

When he stepped from the mouth of the devil in a revelation of parting smoke, she felt no surprise. His serrated blade was drawn. He held it up as if prepared to attack. Perhaps he wasn't as smoothly confident as he had seemed.

"Come with me before the whole building is engulfed. Stay with me. Be my willing instrument and my wife and I'll let your sister remain free," Reynard said.

Another bargain.

One that would have been tempting if it didn't include being in a partnership with her parents' murderer or allowing him to come anywhere near her.

"We should go now," Kat temporized.

She knew what she had to do. He approached her with his knife still drawn. She tried not to look at its stained blade.

"Then you agree to come with me?" he asked.

Kat had learned to be cautious in her dealings with the devil. Just because Reynard was a human didn't make the moment less treacherous. She chose her words carefully.

"Do I have any other choice?" she asked. "You always find me. I'm tired of running. I'm tired of hiding."

There were always choices. And being helpless never had to be one of them.

She led the way with Reynard's sharp knife close to the small of her back. He still didn't sheathe it. He was too used to her slipping away. He didn't know that this time she was determined to face him and fight him and put an end to it all.

Had Eric been found? Had Severne been able to help the small boy get away? The stairs and halls were deserted as they made their way toward an exit. Smoke became an impenetrable wall. It blocked their way, this way and that, but Reynard pushed her forward through it in spite of coughing and choking and streaming eyes.

He must not have noticed the change in the mural on the wall.

Katherine had assumed the great shuffling she'd heard above her head while she'd been in the warehouse had been people evacuating. But now she saw a different explanation,

Every figure on the walls had moved to face outward. They stood side by side by side. They lined every corridor in a great unending row of lost souls doomed to burn. Nothing could free them. They would be consumed by flames when the opera house burned.

As Reynard hurried her along, it wasn't only smoke that made Kat's eyes stream.

She hoped Eric had been right. She hoped Lucifer's Army didn't blame her for their imprisonment and their impending demise.

The opera house seemed to be fully evacuated. Every door they passed hung open. Every room was empty. There was no one running around them in the halls. Distantly Kat could hear sirens, but she could also see flame. It licked around the ceiling's edges. If she didn't get out soon, it would be too late.

"Hurry," Reynard urged. Even a madman could see they didn't have long before the building came down on their heads. Heat had joined the smoke. Tears evaporated off her face as they fell.

Finally Kat saw what she'd been straining to see. Hundreds of daemons were carved into the walls, but she saw Michael easily because he stood by Eric's mother, a face she would never forget. Lavinia looked at her. Michael was tall and beautiful beside her. Not as beautiful as Severne. Her human lover was all the more attractive because of the vulnerable edge to his hardness. The fact that he'd claimed his perfection with sweat and blood and determination in the face of fear made it even more striking, a human achievement of the most divine. But Kat could see why her sister had fallen in love with her baby's father. His angelic face was angular and sad. His long hair swept back from his cheeks. The absence of his wings was obvious in the scars on his shoulders. Michael stood as if the weight of his wings was still down his back.

Her sister had loved this daemon. And even though his ghostly shadow had almost chilled her soul to death, Kat thought he might help her now. He was Victoria's immortal Romeo. He had died for her. He had helped her beyond his death. Would he continue to help her now?

She stepped closer to Michael and Lavinia. Reynard followed. The monk was so used to stalking her, he didn't think to be cautious now. When they were close enough Kat pretended to stumble. She fell into Reynard, risking his blade to press his body against the figures on the wall. She didn't know what mighty manipulation of will they'd had to use to move, but she imagined they had waited for an opportunity like this.

Wooden hands closed around Reynard's neck and arms before he realized what had happened. She saw them move in the same way Lavinia had moved to grip her hand, but faster, as if they had stored their energy for this moment. Did Reynard immediately feel the cold begin to leach his life? His blade fell to the ground at Kat's feet.

"What are you doing? The Council will avenge me. I've been their instrument for decades," Reynard shouted.

Kat bent to pick up his blade, but Severne stopped her.

"Don't touch it. It's a daemon blade. He must be the one who injured Grim," Severne said.

"I tried to follow that beast after he delivered one of my men back to the Order half-dead from fleeing his evil jaws. He turned on me. I cut him, but he got away," Reynard said. He continued to struggle against his wooden captors. They held him without expression. Completely still and impossible to dislodge.

"He would have died without Sybil's blood. She saved him. I think she also saved you, Kat. She unmade the dress. I've never seen her so...emotional," Severne said.

Kat had been using her bad hand. It was no longer painful and useless. It no longer curled against her chest. Her heart beat quickly because of the circumstances, but it no longer pained her with every thump.

"Eric is waiting with Sybil outside. Everyone is out. The building is lost. It will fall," he said. "There isn't much time."

"We can't let him burn," Kat said.

Reynard cursed and shouted above the sound of crashing plaster. Deep beneath their feet, the catacombs moaned as air was compressed by the weight of the building preparing to fall.

"If what he says is true, if he's the Council's man, he sold his soul. Just like my grandfather. He will burn. No matter what. Just like me," Severne said.

"Samuel had the affinity. We used it for decades. But then he refused to help me any longer. He said we'd been wrong. I had to make a deal with the devil to continue our quest," Reynard said.

"Samuel refused to go along with your agreement," Kat said.

"He was my partner for years. We killed so many. Then he decided it was wrong. He went against all we believed," Reynard said.

"Against you," Kat said.

"We fought. I stabbed him," Reynard said.

"But he passed his gift to my grandmother before he died," Kat said.

"He betrayed me. I created the Order of Samuel to make things right."

"You retroactively made him a collaborator in your mad scheme," Severne said.

The opera master reached to pick up the daemon blade, but Kat moved to take it from him. Severne protested, but when her hand closed over the hilt, he grew suddenly silent. He released it to her fingers. She could feel its great heat in her hand, but it didn't burn her skin.

"I can't save you, Reynard. You'll still burn. But I won't leave you here to burn alive."

Katherine D'Arcy plunged the blade that Reynard had used to kill her mother into his Brimstone-tainted heart. As the knife entered his chest, a great winged shadow she'd seen before swept out from the carving of Michael on the wall to engulf Reynard's writhing body. She'd seen daemons consumed many times, but this was hotter and brighter. She fell back from the conflagration as her would-be rapist burned and Severne caught her to keep her from falling to her knees.

"My name is Katherine," Kat quietly said to the man who had respected that fact all along.

She would hear Reynard's screams for the rest of her life. It was a horrible sound, but a fitting end.

The intense burn as damnation claimed him to nothingness cleansed her mother's blood from the daemon blade

The winged shadow disappeared at the same instant that Reynard's ash disintegrated in the air.

Severne lifted her into his arms. She didn't protest. He could run faster, and the building was beginning to fall. She touched the carving of Michael's face. It had been blackened by the burning struggle with Reynard. She brushed Lavinia's hand. The chill in the wooden fingers was gone.

Severne pulled her away from the bas-relief mural. She could see the fire already flickering up the walls. Then she was enveloped in an explosion of lava-like flame that should have resulted in horrible scorching pain.

But didn't.

She was in Severne's arms. It was where she most wanted to be. He took her through the flames to the other side.

Chapter 30

Fire and rescue personnel had responded to the blaze on Severne Row, but no training could have prepared them for a conflagration of hellish proportions. When Kat's eyes fluttered open, ladder trucks were fully deployed and fountains of water fell on nearby buildings to keep them from going up in flames. The great light of l'Opéra Severne created thousands of leaping shadows everywhere she looked.

Later there would be speculation about the miraculous localization of the fire. Grizzled firefighters with enough experience under their belts to recognize the impossible would cross themselves years from now when the fire was mentioned. The habitual muttering of prayers whenever Severne Row had to be crossed would become a tradition for all department captains.

Tonight, as water fell like a soaking, soothing rain, Severne held her. His embrace was like an answer to her prayers that he would live.

L'Opéra Severne continued to burn.

It had been given up as lost. The roof had caved in, and flames blazed into the night sky.

Kat looked up at Severne. His black hair dripped. His white shirt was plastered to his muscular frame. He was altogether glorious. She suddenly remembered the others and looked around to see hundreds of performers, musicians and technicians milling around.

The conductor was tended by paramedics. He wore a blanket as if it was an evening cloak. Tess carried steaming cups to the artists she usually helped in other ways. Supportive as ever. When she looked Kat's way, her eyes glowed, but it was only the reflection of the fire. She was human even if her abilities as an experienced prompter were inhumanly brilliant.

Finally, as Kat had begun to lose hope, she saw Eric. The young daemon boy was cradled in Sybil's arms in the shadow of an ambulance. Kat extricated herself from Severne's hold. He had to loosen it to let her go. She rose and steadied her legs before she approached the daemon woman who had almost killed her. Severne rose to follow her, but he didn't interfere.

"You would help him now?" Kat asked.

"I've always tried to help him, even though I let him wander the halls more than I should have. I didn't know he planned to burn l'Opéra Severne. I would have tried to stop him. They should never have asked such a sacrifice from a child," Sybil said.

Eric had turned his sooty face toward Katherine. He'd been crying. The water from the firefighter's hoses didn't account for his reddened eyes.

"They?" Kat asked. She couldn't believe the daemon boy had started the fire that burned what was left of his mother.

She reached out and Eric took her hand, but he didn't release his hold on Sybil with the other.

"Lucifer's Army. They used Eric to burn the opera house so they could be freed," Sybil explained.

"Now they're nothing but smoke and ash," Severne said. "Why would they choose death over imprisonment?" His fists were clenched. His jaw was tight. He was helpless to save the daemons he'd captured.

"No," Eric said. He shook his head. To Katherine, he continued, "They aren't dead. Some of them will die in the fighting, though. They warned me I might not see my mother again."

"He freed Lucifer's Army to attack the Council. They were taken and imprisoned one at a time, but they were released all at once. They planned a surprise attack to take the Council unawares. It will be a horrible battle," Sybil explained. "He weeps because of that, not because of the fire."

Katherine let go of Eric and backed into Severne's arms. Here, a huge historic building burned. There, in the hell dimension, a daemon war would rage.

"You'll be safe with us," Kat said. She meant Eric would be safe, but she included Sybil, as well. She didn't trust the daemon woman, but she didn't want her to have to go to war.

A loud roar shook the air around them, and the ground trembled. A woman screamed and the whole crowd cried out together, their exclamations blending into a great sound of dismay, punctuated by embers of cherry ash falling from the sky.

L'Opéra Severne was gone. John Severne watched its final collapse, flames and shadows dancing on his stark, handsome face.

His eyes weren't red, but his face was wet. They were

all soaked from the fire hoses' rain. Still, water and tears ran together so no one could tell where one became another. Kat turned and buried her face in Severne's chest. He pulled her closer. Sybil hugged Eric, protecting him from the falling remnants of the building no one would ever know he'd burned.

It hadn't been arson. It had been a revolution. One even a small boy couldn't escape.

Sybil had never intended to endanger him. Her bargain had been a bluff. Kat could tell the daemon would have helped Eric no matter what she'd done.

"Katherine, you aren't burned. The building was engulfed in flame when I carried you out. I couldn't avoid the fire. You should have died. You aren't even injured," Severne said.

He ran his hands over her damp skin, checking for burns that didn't exist.

She remembered the heat. She remembered how he had been afraid for her to touch Reynard's blade. But neither his knife nor the fire had burned her.

"Brimstone protects you from flame. The danger to Eric wasn't from the fire, but from the building's collapse," Sybil said.

"Kat has no Brimstone in her blood," Severne said.

"But the baby she carries does," Sybil said. "Brimstone isn't always a curse. It can be a gift. Tonight, Brimstone helped protect you. The baby will be human as you're human, but the Brimstone will make her or him a little extraordinary, as well."

It should have been too soon to feel a stir, but at Sybil's words, Kat felt a quickening in her womb. It was a fluttering to life of warmth she and Severne had created. The early movement was proof that their baby would be special. Sybil was right.

"No. It isn't safe. I can't endanger a child with my cursed blood," Severne said.

But he held her closer.

He would never let her go. She trusted him completely. He'd come back for her. He'd let Michael go, safe and sound. He'd even given Grim to the baby to guard him and her sister.

He only needed time to discover the love he already held in his heart.

"Who knows whether the Council will be able to hold a contract over your head after tonight? They have their hands full facing Lucifer's Army," Kat said.

She put one hand over the place where she'd felt the baby move. She promised him or her that it wouldn't matter. She would protect the baby with all she had even if the Council wasn't defeated.

But her promise was interrupted.

Severne cried out and sagged against her. A blazing light flared from his arm. It burned through the wet material of his shirt. Steam rolled as if boiled away from the fabric. The man she loved fell to his knees. Had the contract claimed him? Had freeing Michael hurt him after all?

She couldn't watch him burn now. Not when their baby was just beginning to grow.

Kat sank down beside Severne.

"Get back. Get back," he warned.

His shirt was burning away. She couldn't hold him. Even with the protection of the baby's Brimstone, the heat was too great. They watched his shirt turn to ash and fall from his skin. But as the ash fell, the tally marks on his arm glowed. It was the marks that had flared, blazing to life and burning the shirt away.

Kat reached toward him, but he held her away.

Eric sobbed. Steam rolled. The rest of the crowd was

too busy gawking at the collapsed opera house to notice Severne burning.

But before his skin ignited, the tally marks changed from flame, to fierce ember, to charcoal, to pale gray lines she could hardly see.

Severne held his arm up in disbelief.

"Kat...they're fading," he said.

He didn't stop her this time when she reached to feel his rapidly cooling skin.

The daemon marks were gone.

Crews dug for hours for the chest that had been in Severne's rooms. When it was finally found, they brought it forward as if they were frightened to touch it. Everything else was gone. Only the chest remained.

Severne and Kat opened the chest in private. Inside, the cask still smoked, but when Severne lifted its lid, the contract inside was gone.

Only ash remained.

Chapter 31

The next day dawned before they were able to leave the wreckage of the burn site. She and Severne cleaned up the best they could with borrowed clothes so that Levi Severne wouldn't be frightened by their appearances. They didn't want to scare the dying man by showing up suddenly, smudged and charred with burned clothing.

But they did need to check on his father now that Severne's tally marks were gone as if they'd never been.

Neither of them knew what the disappearance of the marks might mean for Levi Severne.

John still hadn't told her he loved her, but he also hadn't let her go for most of the night. There was no mention of him going to see his father alone. He held her hand. She followed. She was glad to be with him after the fear and the flames.

"Without Grim, we'll have to do this the old-fashioned way," Severne said.

He led her to a garage a block away from the smoking ruin of the opera house.

In the back corner of a reserved section of the garage, a row of half a dozen vintage sports cars gleamed. An attendant met them at the gate and produced the key Severne requested. He led Kat toward the row of cars, and she somehow wasn't surprised when the car he chose was low and lean in a perfect mimicry of its owner. It was a foreign black roadster with minimalist, perfect lines and only a little chrome.

Its motor thrummed to life with a smooth roar once Severne turned the key, after he'd helped her sink down into a leather-upholstered passenger seat as soft as butter.

"French?" Kat asked.

"Of course," Severne replied.

He drove the car as if he hadn't been born when horse and buggy ruled the roads. Kat relaxed back in her seat and enjoyed the ride. He changed gears in the same way he handled everything, with grace and a purpose of motion gifted to him by a long life and so much practice that he was an expert. She discovered her cheeks were hot as her thoughts strayed to other ways that John Severne had shown her his expertise.

Too soon they came to a subdivision of older homes. The houses themselves were simple, but the grounds surrounding them were obviously the reason for the estates, much more extensive and elaborate than the houses themselves. The land around the houses provided space for gardens and privacy.

Severne pulled to the curb in front of a picturesque Craftsman.

He came around to open her door. Even from the street, Kat could see the bushes she'd seen before, heavy with clusters of hydrangea blossoms.

She paused.

Her mother had been here, and someone had taken her photograph in Levi Severne's garden.

"He's forgotten his former life. He doesn't know me. I have to introduce myself each time I visit," Severne warned as he took her arm.

But when Levi Severne met them at the door of his home, he greeted his son with his name.

The men hugged as if they were reunited for the first time in decades. Although she was frightened by the implications of her mother's photograph, Kat blinked back tears. She followed John and his father back into the house as he helped the elderly and frail man to his chair. The exertion had taxed Levi's strength. A nurse came from the rear of the house and helped him. He coughed until his handkerchief came away spotted with ashy blood.

"I'd like to go outside to talk," the old man requested. "I want to be with my flowers in the sun."

Severne looked at the nurse, and she nodded.

The sun had risen on a bright and cloudless day. The nurse hovered while they prepared her charge to go outside. She touched Katherine's arm before she could follow Severne and his father as they slowly made their way to the back door.

"Terminally ill patients often regain lucidity just before they pass…" Her warning trailed off, and Kat nodded to confirm that she understood.

It was possible John didn't have much time with his father. She would leave the questions about her mother unasked. But she did respond with movement when John looked around to see where she'd gone. He needed her near him. She understood. She wanted to be near him, too.

The garden was lush. Pale blue hydrangea clusters were showy against the verdant bushes. Their beauty hadn't been evident in the old, faded photograph she'd found. Kat allowed some privacy as Severne and his father murmured together. She guessed which bush her mother had been photographed in front of, and she went to it. She brushed its blossoms with her fingers until cool dew kissed her hands.

"The contract is fulfilled? I woke last night as if from a foggy dream. I remembered everything I'd forgotten." He coughed again, and Severne placed a hand on his quaking shoulder.

But when Levi saw Kat near the bushes, he lowered the stained handkerchief. She had turned from the hydrangea after picking a small cluster. The soft blooms were delicate. Petals fell like blue snow from her fingers.

"She came to me for help. She knew I was no friend to the Order of Samuel. You aren't her, but you have her eyes. Her hair. I remember Anne D'Arcy. I had to refuse. The Council wanted her lover. He was on their most-wanted list. A dangerous revolutionary. I couldn't help her," Levi said. He talked almost to himself, his words were so quiet. It was the confession of a dying man. "One of the Order's monks followed her here. He was documenting her betrayal for his master. He took her photograph near the hydrangeas. She hurried away before I could reconsider."

"Reynard killed her," Kat said. She allowed the hydrangea cluster to fall to the ground with its petals.

"I wanted to help her. But I promised my wife I would save our son. Though it seems now that he was the one who saved me," Levi said.

Severne continued to hold his father's shoulder with a supporting hand. The elderly man had slipped deeper into his garden chair. His head tilted to the side as if he didn't have the strength to keep it upright.

"No. It's the D'Arcy family that has saved us, Father. I didn't fulfill the contract. But my tally marks are gone.

The Council is at war with Lucifer's Army. I think our part in it is done." He showed his father his arm where only clear skin remained. He explained to Levi Severne about the daemon boy and the fire, about the trunk full of ash the workers had found.

By the time he'd finished the whole story, Levi had slumped even more in his chair.

"I forgive you," Katherine whispered as the old daemon hunter's eyes closed for the last time. "And my mother would forgive you, too."

Levi held his son's hand while he peacefully slipped away.

The contract had been broken by the daemon war just in time.

Chapter 32

She didn't refuse when Severne invited her to stay on board *The Blues Queen*. Cruises were canceled until they could procure more permanent lodging, but Katherine didn't mind the temporary arrangement. The night they'd spent on the riverboat had been her first indication that Severne cared for her as more than a means to an end.

The accommodations were in plush staterooms that had originally been fitted for Victorian ladies and gentleman gamblers, as sunny and colorful as l'Opéra Severne had been shadowed and dark. But still with an element of the dramatic.

She was grateful there wasn't a hint of bas-relief cherry carvings on the walls.

It was bittersweet to imagine Victoria with Michael in one of the staterooms. She was so glad her sister had known a great love after a lifetime of running. She knew exactly what it was like to be brought suddenly to a stop by strength of emotion that made the risk of opening your heart worth taking.

Sybil had come through with closets and drawers full of necessities. Severne assured her the clothes and toiletries were gifts from him to replace what she'd lost in his opera house and not daemon gifts she should fear.

Neither of them knew if she would have a typical gestation or if hers would be as fast as Victoria's had been. The Brimstone burn of Severne's blood wasn't entirely gone, and Kat's body temperature had risen slightly in response to the Brimstone in her baby's blood.

Yet Levi Severne had passed quietly without the torture of damnation seeming to claim his soul.

Different, not damned.

Forever changed by the Brimstone, but not condemned to burn.

The riverboat moved away from the quay as night claimed the city. John urged her to leave the lights off so that the fairy lights on all the columns and rails were their only illumination. *The Blues Queen* was as haunted as l'Opéra Severne had been in her own way. Kat could almost hear the music and laughter that had permeated the decks of the historic boat in the last one hundred years, but it was probably only the whoosh of the paddle wheels slowly churning the water, propelling them toward the cantilever bridge.

The bridge was also aglow and, as they approached, its light suffused the balcony alcove with artificial light on the moonless night.

We have to save ourselves.

John had been right. They'd had to face their own fears and needs to beat Reynard. She'd had to stop running, and he'd had to open himself to love and loss. And even though the Order of Samuel seemed to have been defeated, they would need to save themselves, day after day, night after night, for the rest of their lives. They'd had dark childhoods. They'd survived pain and abuse.

But they had saved themselves...and each other.

She watched her lover approach the alcove where he'd had the skeleton crew rearrange the tables and chairs to make room for a large upholstered lounge before he'd dismissed them to the bridge. The antique chaise didn't seem out of place on the plush balcony at all. It was an outdoor room separated from the deck by potted palms and columns, and when she'd sunk down on the velvet upholstery, she'd experienced a nostalgic warmth for the kisses that could have very easily led to other things if they hadn't had an audience on that night weeks ago.

Tonight, John had showered when he'd come home from the construction site. His black hair was damp, and it gleamed in the twinkle of lights around them. His shirt clung to his skin and his sleeves were rolled at the elbow, but he wore white poplin and shiny black fitted trousers similar to the ones he'd worn the night they'd danced on the riverboat.

She appreciated what he had done in claiming the alcove in a more intimate way for their "date" tonight. She'd played along, dressing in a moss-green dress meant for dancing, and wore nothing but soft wisps of lace underneath.

He still had a glint in his eyes and heated skin.

He still had the experience of decades that lent him grace and savvy style.

He still had a lean, hard edge to his jaw that only she seemed able to soften.

He softened now as he saw her watching him approach. His mouth curved—only slightly, but it curved. The full swell of his lower lip drew her eye and caused her mouth to go dry in anticipation.

On the table that had been left nearby, a bottle of non-alcoholic champagne chilled in a silver bucket of ice. He went to it first, and she forced herself to recline on the chaise and appreciate the movement of his muscles beneath the almost translucent material of his fitted shirt as he lifted the bottle and removed its cork. The practiced grace of his hands further dried her mouth, and she had to lick her lips.

He'd shown her his expertise in so many ways since l'Opéra Severne had burned.

He poured tall crystal flutes half-full of bubbling gold and brought one to her while the riverboat slowed to a stop near the picturesque bridge.

"I told them we'd like to recreate the midnight cruise on the river. This time just for two," Severne said.

The cello, the cruise, the hot nights they'd spent in each other's arms—all told her more than words what he felt for her. She could wait for the words. She would wait. Even if it took him forever finally to lower the last of his steely defenses.

He remained standing after he'd handed her the glass, and she sipped the icy drink while he sipped his. He looked up at the bridge, and the lights on its rails illuminated his eyes. Not enough to make them green, but she no longer needed the color to know how she affected him.

"I do miss the piano," Kat said.

The paddle wheels had slowed to a stop while they'd paused near the bridge, but now they resumed. The rhythm of the paddles churning the water caused a pleasant vibration in the deck and in the air that echoed the one she still felt beneath her skin when John was close to her.

He dropped one knee on the chaise beside her hip, then

leaned over to take her glass and place it on the edge of a potted palm.

"Wait for it," he said. And seconds later the sound of a piano floated out to the alcove. The tinny notes of jazz weren't live. He'd set the vintage gramophone to drop a record and play. The quality of the sound was rich and sweet and aged in the best ways. Much like the man who leaned in to taste the champagne on her mouth.

He gently sucked her lower lip between his and teased over it with his tongue from corner to corner. She drew a breath and held it while he lingered over the flavors on her tongue. When he eased back, she released air in a long, shaky sigh. John Severne was a lot to savor. She still wasn't used to having the time and freedom to experience his attention to detail and the discipline that allowed him to prolong his release while he indulged her every sensation.

He was a connoisseur of all things now that he no longer had damnation burning at his heels.

"You thought of everything," Kat breathed.

He joined her on the chaise, sinking close beside her so that one leg pressed provocatively between hers. The chiffon rode up on her thighs. The sultry night air had nothing to do with the gooseflesh that rose on her skin. Not when his warm fingers urged her skirt higher until he could cup the bare swell of her bottom in the palm of his hand.

"You have no idea how often I thought of everything about you. Your sigh. Your big chocolate eyes. The taste of sugary cream on your tongue," John said. "The feel of your heat around my fingers."

He illustrated the direction of his thoughts by easing a finger into the edge of her lace and running it around her hip. She moaned and he dipped to kiss her open mouth, using his leg to part her thighs so he could gain access to the heat he'd already caused to rise to uncomfortable levels of need.

His tongue teased against hers, eliciting more sighs that turned to soft cries when his fingers found her ache and teased it higher and tighter until she begged for his deeper touch.

"But I won't stop here this time. This is only the beginning of our night," he promised.

He entered her with a questing finger, and she met his penetration with a thrust of her hips that made him catch his breath. He held it while he gave her the rhythm she wordlessly asked for, and she tasted sweat on his upper lip as the heat of the night joined with the heat they generated together.

She wondered if he'd always have a hint of Brimstone in his blood. Her affinity still sang for him. He filled her senses as he filled her with his fingers. Her sweet ache built and built. He broke from her mouth to suckle one hard-nippled breast that showed through filmy chiffon and lace. As always, he knew when, just when, to do whatever he did and exactly how she needed him to do it.

Kat cried out as her body shuddered its release.

But he kept his promise.

He didn't withdraw to leave her, replete but alone. He rose only to slip off his shirt and his pants. They were outside, under the stars, but their distance from shore and the soft glow of fairy light along with the palms gave them all the privacy they needed. She watched him with lazily hooded eyes as he stood illuminated only by glow.

His body was still as hard as it had ever been. He would never be soft. He was all lean muscle and sacrifice, but now he accepted the softness of her touch whenever she gave it. And he didn't mind showing her what she did to him with her touch.

His erection was swollen and ready for her when he came back to join her. She sat up to take him in her mouth before he could lie back down. He jerked in reaction to her suction, and she accepted the inadvertent thrust of his hips with a groan. The ache he'd temporarily eased tightened again between her thighs. He recognized her pleasure in his, and he increased it by taking what she offered with a careful rhythm of hip movements.

But only long enough to make her crave the heat and hardness in her mouth to join with her, to completely banish the need to be filled that her body cried for.

The affinity and her desire for Severne were entirely responsible for the vibrations rocking her now. The paddle-wheels churned, but they had faded from her perception. He pulled from her mouth and pressed her back on the chaise. With gentle hands rough from callouses, he slipped the chiffon from her. His move revealed the barely-there lace of her underwear. He teased over its edges where it outlined the lush swell of her breasts, and then down to where it clung to damp chestnut curls.

But he'd maintained control as long as she desired him to.

He knew it. He read her reactions with an immortal's eyes.

He'd been nearly a daemon for too long not to know exactly what she wanted.

He snapped the lace from her hips. She didn't mind the brief bite of material as it pulled free. She opened her legs, and he drew in a sudden breath. She still surprised him occasionally with her desire never to hide again. With her need to be bold.

John sank down on the chaise between her open thighs.

She welcomed him as he unsnapped the front of her bra and fully freed her breasts. They moved with his thrust when he worked his hips to join himself with her. He looked down at her with eyes that glittered in the fairy-lit night. She couldn't see the color of his irises. It didn't matter.

She trusted their connection completely.

He took everything she offered then. Her trust. Her body. Her future. He plunged deep and long and hard until her body tensed in another orgasm that shook her until she cried his name to the sky above them. Only then did he allow his own release. He filled her with heat. His heat. And she eagerly wrapped him close with her arms and legs and her no-longer-hiding heart.

"I have a letter from my sister. Grim continues to guard them, but they've had no trouble. The Order of Samuel seems to have fallen apart without Reynard. Or maybe the Council has turned them into soldiers to join the daemon war," Kat said.

Severne had been busy with something on deck and had just returned. His skin was developing a natural glow from his time in the sun. With his torture chamber burned and no Grim to consider, he often ran at midday or worked out on the deck. He no longer kept himself jailed away.

"She says Michael is already crawling. Months ahead of a fully human baby's time." Kat ran one finger across the letter in her hand.

She placed her other palm against her abdomen. It was still flat, although a pregnancy test had confirmed Sybil's diagnosis.

"No matter the baby's speed of development, there's one thing he or she cannot do without," Severne said.

He came to her and placed warm hands on her shoulders. He was no longer closed off from her, but he still hadn't declared his love or his intentions. She could only read his feelings in his touch and see them in his mossy eyes.

He urged her to her feet.

"Come up on deck. I have something for you," he said.

He held her hand as they climbed upstairs. She didn't need the help. She was still as lithe and agile as the years of playing had helped her to be. What would it be like to play her cello with a large pregnant belly? She would never know. Her cello was gone.

"I enlisted the help of Tess in the choice. I hope you like it," Severne said.

They came up on deck, and he led her to the alcove where they'd danced and kissed for an audience, only to find it had been more for their own desires.

Her beloved cello had burned. But on a stand near a chair in the alcove was a shiny maple instrument accompanied by a bow.

Not new. One like her old instrument.

Yet as she hurried forward, she noticed it was far superior. An instrument that was a piece of polished art, crafted by a famous Italian master.

"You've missed your music. I wanted to give it back to you," Severne explained.

The baby fluttered when she picked up the bow. He settled as she played. Severne waited until she came to the end of a classic French lullaby.

"I don't deserve you. Or this. I don't deserve the chance to be a father after all I've done," Severne said. "But even though I'm afraid you'll be taken from me to mete out the punishment I deserve, I have to claim this blessing…you and the baby. I love you, Katherine D'Arcy. I want you to become my wife. A damned husband is not what you deserve, but I offer you my heart."

Kat eased the precious gift of her new cello onto its

stand. Then she rose to go to Severne's side. She pressed into the hard muscular body that had been his defense for so long. She easily detected the strong rhythm of the heart he offered against her breast.

"You aren't damned, Severne. You were imprisoned by your grandfather's evil choices. But you made your own decisions. Now you're free. And you helped me to free myself, as well. To stop running. To stop hiding. To take a stand for love and family," Kat said. "I love your strength, but it isn't the strength of your muscles. It's the strength of your heart and soul that held me and didn't let me go. Your soul was never the Council's to take," she said.

"No matter how hard I made my body, you penetrated to my heart. I was supposed to use you to fulfill my grandfather's contract, but the contract was nothing but ash to me long before it burned," Severne said.

"I'll marry you. And we'll reclaim the Severne name. We'll make of it something beautiful and courageous, as you have done. We'll leave the greed and corruption of your grandfather behind," Kat promised.

Her affinity had become something stronger and brighter because of John Severne. She felt the glow of it now, binding them together like the music she played even when she played no instrument at all.

Epilogue

The baby slept in his cradle. Kat completed the comforting ritual of rosining her bow while she listened to his soft breathing. Sun sparkled off the Mississippi, but the dancing light reflected on the nursery walls didn't seem to bother her son.

He'd experienced enough shadows while still in her womb.

She left the white patchwork curtains drawn back to let in the light. Some of the sparkle came from light reflected off the crystal beads Sybil had incorporated into the curtains' design. The ball gown she'd taken back to save Kat's life had been remade and regifted, this time with only forgiveness asked in return.

With practiced motions, Kat stroked the brown rosin cake up and down the horsehair of her bow. Again and again. Her playing was different now. She had settled into it as easily as breathing once Reynard was gone. She no longer had to hide from the madness with music. She was free. The cello was a part of that freedom now. Not a shield to hide behind, but a means of expression. Her voice to the world.

"He's a fine namesake. I'm quite pleased," a strange voice said from the door.

Kat's reflexes were not so out of practice that she didn't immediately jump up to place herself between the sleeping baby and the daemon at her door.

He had wings.

No. He *wore* wings. They were bronzed and folded down his back, suspended on a matching bronze harness he wore across a broad, bare chest. On the front of the harness was an iron brooch she recognized. Its stylized *L* flashed in the sunlight.

He came forward, straight and tall, but his face was craggy and lined. Not with wrinkles. He'd been handsome once. She could see it in his square jaw and the cut of his cheekbones. But he had battle scars from what must have been terrible wounds across his skin. Everywhere skin showed, he was marked. But he smiled when her eyes widened, and he brushed her horror away.

"Old pain is past pain. And every mark I suffered for my people is worn with pride. We faltered, but we didn't fall. The ancient ones had enough of falling to last an immortal lifetime," he said.

"I named him Ezekiel. After a daemon my mother had loved. Samuel Ezekiel Severne," Kat said.

"She was an angel. Her singing called to me even though I knew we couldn't be together. It almost called me to my death. But Reynard failed because she stood against him. For me. She gave her life for mine," Ezekiel said.

Her mother had loved this intimidating creature. And his love for her mother must have been the reason Lucifer's

Army was on the river boat that night. They hadn't been sent to harm her. They'd been there to protect her from the Council's daemons. They'd withdrawn when they saw she was unharmed and in good hands with Severne. The idea warmed her, and Katherine *had* named the baby after him, but she still stood between the daemon king and her child.

For a king was what he had to be.

"Lucifer's wings were shorn and bronzed to hang above the Council as a macabre prize and a symbolic crown," Kat murmured to herself. "John told me about them. He saw them when he was child."

Ezekiel wore Lucifer's wings. Only the ancient daemons had wings. The ones that had fallen from paradise to rule in hell. The Council had cut them away from Lucifer before they had bled him completely of his Brimstone and left him to die. Her sister's lover, Michael, had reclaimed his in death. He'd been a ghost with mighty wings when she'd known him as an icy shadow.

"I will never harm him. He is my grandson in every way but blood. I've only come to offer him a gift," Ezekiel said.

At his words, a snuffling growl sounded from the doorway, and a black-muzzled nose poked its way into the room, followed by a dog the size of a German shepherd. Only its movements revealed its true nature as a puppy. It was clumsy and quick, tumbling over its big paws. It was also occasionally transparent, winking out of their world and into another in turns.

This was how Grim must have looked when he first came to Severne all those decades ago.

Tears burned behind her eyes. She hadn't realized how badly she'd missed the monstrous hellhound until now.

"Will you permit this gift, Katherine D'Arcy?" Ezekiel asked.

Sammy gurgled and rolled over in his sleep. The hellhound came and stood by the cradle just as a much more adult Grim would have done. Paws planted. Legs stiff. Muzzle down.

"Yes, we will," Severne said from the bedroom just off the nursery. "If Kat approves."

Daemons couldn't be trusted.

"What will you ask for in return?" Kat asked cautiously.

Ezekiel, Lord of Hell, Prince of Darkness, or whatever his title, looked askance. One eyebrow lifted in surprise.

"So many daemons were trapped in l'Opéra Severne's walls. It was a cursed and cruel purgatory. You freed Lucifer's Army. The battle we waged to overthrow the Council is responsible for my scars. They were defeated. That wouldn't have been possible without your help," Ezekiel said.

"That's why my contract turned to ash," Severne said. "It never would have burned in ordinary flames."

"And why the tally marks disappeared," Kat said.

He'd come to stand by her side. Baby Sam had woken, but he only kicked his legs in the air and gurgled at the vigilant shadow of puppy nose on his bed. He was either unaware or unconcerned that the Lord of Hell considered him beloved.

"For us in hell, the battle raged for centuries. For you, it was an instant conflagration," Ezekiel said. "The pup is a thank-you. No more. No less. We owe you that. I feel a personal interest, but this is no daemon bargain you have to fear. This is a gift from a grandfather," he said.

"A daemon king," Kat surmised.

Ezekiel inclined his head.

Kat looked at him through narrowed eyes. Not damned. Only different. But they were fallen. There was mystery in that, and danger. Daemons were beautiful and tragic. Much like l'Opéra Severne. She could feel Ezekiel's Brimstone burn. She was glad when he ordered the pup to stay before turning away.

"Samuel was born with an affinity for daemons. He was taught to fear us and fight us, but the affinity led him to love us instead. It also led to his death, but not before he passed his ability to your grandmother," the daemon king said.

"The gift he gave us wasn't the ability to find daemons," Kat whispered.

"It was the ability to love us," Ezekiel said.

"And overlook the Brimstone blood," Severne said.

"Or crave it." Ezekiel laughed darkly. "And once you're daemon-marked, you're never forgotten. Your family will always have a hint of Brimstone. A remnant. Consider it a gi—a mark of favor," he said.

Katherine had experienced both pleasure and pain from daemon marks, but she wasn't afraid. Even without Brimstone, her blood was bolder than that.

The baby had fallen back to sleep with his new hellhound by his side. Kat imagined Michael slept with Grim in much the same way. Her sister's lover was gone. Unlike the other daemons that had been trapped in the walls, Michael must have used the last of his immortal energy to manifest as the icy shadow. She still shivered when she recalled its nearly fatal freeze. She still wondered at the great love he'd had for his child.

Kat would always wonder how much of the daemon had been left in the winged threat that had almost killed her several times. She now suspected that he had stalked her through the catacombs. She knew that if she hadn't invoked Victoria's name, the shadow would have frozen her to the marrow in her bones. But it had tried to watch over Victoria and her baby. Michael had been gone, but his will to love had lived on. She would remember his angelic face on l'Opéra Severne's wall. He had been an ancient one. He had loved her sister. His son lived on.

Both of their sons would be touched by the gift Samuel had given their family. Only time would tell how love and curses mixed.

Severne took Katherine by the hand and led her onto the balcony and into the sun. When he kissed her, she tasted wood smoke and his unique masculine flavor. She also caught a hint of dramatic dust and powder, rosin and aged timbers.

Across town, the opera house was being rebuilt. Severne was helping in its construction. The opera master dirtied his hands every day with mortar and bricks, and there wasn't a single workman who could boast a stronger back or the ability to work longer hours. He'd been honest with her the evening he'd told her he wanted to build a perfect place for her to play with his own two hands.

It had been a sexy promise. Though they'd both fought the emotion behind it, she'd never forgotten the way he'd kissed the callouses on her fingers when he'd made it. And the fulfillment of his promise was even sexier.

There was no sign of where the catacombs had been. Only solid ground. The foundation had already been put into place where the new l'Opéra Severne would rise. It would be built from the blueprints of the old building, but both she and Severne had insisted on no cherrywood. The walls would be plastered and wallpapered with vintage Victorian paper. Flowers. Hydrangeas and calla lilies.

Kat wanted no faces on the walls.

Severne had been the master of the opera house for so long, she imagined the old haunted building would always be a part of him. Since she'd loved it in spite of its forbidding atmosphere, she didn't mind. But just as the

day they'd first spent in Baton Rouge away from l'Opéra
Severne, she was glad to see Severne's dark hair shine in
the sun.

He raised his lips from her and looked down into her
eyes for a long time. She could still see all the long years
of stark loneliness he'd endured in the depths of his gaze.
But then he sank back down into her kiss, and their lips
reignited the Brimstone burn. Heat flared between them.

No cello necessary.

He'd spent his long life burdened by hell's most wanted,
but they'd found what each of them wanted most when they
allowed the music to bring them together.

Some tragic pairs were meant to be together after all.

* * * * *

ive a 12 month subscription
to a friend today!

Call Customer Services
0844 844 1358*

or visit
llsandboon.co.uk/subscriptions